MW00777324

Felix Nesi

People from Oetimu

Translated from the Indonesian by Lara Norgaard

archipelago books

Copyright © Felix Nesi, 2019
English language translation © Lara Norgaard, 2025
First Archipelago Books Edition, 2025

All rights reserved. No part of this book may be reproduced or transmitted
in any form without the prior written permission of the publisher.
Library of Congress Cataloging-in-Publication Data available upon request.

Archipelago Books
232 3rd Street #A111
Brooklyn, NY 11215
WWW.ARCHIPELAGOBOOKS.ORG

ISBN: 978-1-953861-98-6

Distributed by Penguin Random House
WWW.PENGUINRANDOMHOUSE.COM

Cover art: Aming Prayitno

This work is made possible by the New York State Council on the Arts with the support of
the Office of the Governor and the New York State Legislature. Funding for the publication
of this book was provided by a grant from the Carl Lesnor Family Foundation.

This publication was made possible with support from the Hawthornden Foundation, the
National Endowment for the Arts, and the New York City Department of Cultural Affairs.

Printed in Canada

People from Oetimu

CONTENTS

———

I

Oetimu, 1998

One hour before the murderers raided Martin Kabiti's house on the night of the World Cup finals, Sergeant Ipi drove by on his motorbike. It was an RX King model, its muffler modified so that wherever he went, the bike's deafening roar would split the wooden walls of poor people's houses, incite a chorus of dog barks, and cause bats to scatter from nearby treetops. When he stopped to pick up Martin Kabiti, the bike's headlights gleamed in the chilly film of mist held between the banana leaves. A few scrappy dogs started chasing the two men as they sped off – one nearly snagged Sergeant Ipi's leg – but the driver kept revving the engine as though he were trying to goad them on. Sergeant Ipi was happy. He had set up everything for a party in the little police station where he lived, complete with a spread of spiced dog meat and roast pork, deer jerky, and a lot of booze – including some taxed, labeled bottles he brought back from the city and sopi kepala, locally brewed.

"We're watching the finals at my place. Come, celebrate with me." That's what Sergeant Ipi said to Martin Kabiti two days earlier.

Martin Kabiti wasn't the only neighbor to receive an invitation. Sergeant Ipi assigned two teens the task of spreading the word. Every man in town was welcome: elders and other respected residents, of course, but also high school students still struggling to grow beards, mototaxi drivers, and the local deadbeats who Sergeant Ipi frequently beat up. But Martin Kabiti's invitation was special, and the policeman took it upon himself to personally escort his esteemed guest to the party.

It had been a long time since Martin Kabiti had been on the battle-field. Clueless about the calamity headed his way, he'd thrown on the heavy striped jacket he won hunting down rebels on Mount Matebian, slipped Carvil sandals over his black socks, grabbed his keys, and rushed out of the house. His wife let him leave without any premonition of what was about to happen, and his kids were sound asleep, lulled by chirping crickets and the tunes of other nighttime animals on the edge of the forest. From his seat behind Sergeant Ipi, Martin Kabiti watched as boys in jackets and old men draped in betê hurried on foot towards the police station. Another motorbike rumbled behind them, carrying two

Javanese soldiers from the border who'd sped up when they heard the roar of Sergeant Ipi's bike. Martin Kabiti had been the one to invite the soldiers. He always advised them to blend in, and the party that night was the perfect opportunity, since they'd have a chance to mix with the locals and have a good time together. The motorbikes continued onwards side by side, and people on foot greeted the men respectfully as they passed.

Soccer fever had recently hit the town. Each night, everyone would get together in front of a TV and cheer on the little figures scrambling for the ball on the green field. They clipped the schedule of upcoming matches from local newspapers, sticking copies on the walls of living rooms, bedrooms, and sheds in the fields, marking in pencil which country had just lost and which was likely next to be defeated. They were all fans of one country in particular, the only team that could logically win: Brazil. Not only did the players make soccer look like dancing, but Brazil had an undefeated champion who went by Ronaldo Luís Nazário de Lima. Ronaldo was revered in Oetimu. People named their dogs and other household pets after the soccer star, and whenever it was Brazil's turn to play in a game, only women and children stayed home. Everyone else – men of all ages, from teens to the elderly – went out to root for their idol.

There were three TVs in town: one in the police station, one in Mas Zainal's house, and one in Baba Ong's living room. Baba Ong owned

Prosperity General Store – he was downright stingy and definitely wouldn't let people sit in his house if they weren't planning on buying something. He hung long, heavy curtains to shield his living room from the prying eyes of little kids trying to peek through the window to watch the TV. Mas Zainal was bucktoothed, which made him seem friendly, like he was always smiling. But he was a scrap metal collector, so watching a game at his house involved sitting among sharp, rusted objects, old batteries, and amidst a wide range of smells – mouthwatering aromas of food wafting in from the kitchen only to mix with the nauseating stench of motor oil. The police station was the most pleasant option by far. It had a floor spacious enough to stretch out on, smooth walls comfortable to lean against when you felt like standing, and – assuming you were one of the more important people in the room – a cushy sofa to recline on. But Sergeant Ipi only let respected guests into the station: Martin Kabiti, elders, schoolteachers, and the like. The rest of the town had no choice but to squeeze themselves into Mas Zainal's shop every time they wanted to watch TV, surrounded by old motorcycle parts and strong odors. All of this is to say that when Sergeant Ipi invited the whole town to the police station for the finals, everyone was overcome with excitement. And once they heard about all the meats and drinks that the young policeman planned on serving, the men flocked to the station. Even Mas Zainal turned off his TV to watch the game with the rest of the town.

By the time the two motorbikes arrived, a crowd of men was already gathered in the front yard, smoking and chewing betel nut while they waited. The cement building behind them was too small to be called a house but too big to be considered a typical police station. It had two rooms, one in the back that Sergeant Ipi used as his bedroom, and a large living room for work. That's where he typed up reports, watched TV, received guests, ate his meals, and beat up kids he caught skipping school or hanging off the sides of trucks.

After parking, Sergeant Ipi pulled a key from under the mat and opened the door. Martin Kabiti walked in first and took a seat in Sergeant Ipi's rolling desk chair, confident that he was the most respected guest in attendance. With all that thick padding, his chair was the most comfortable spot in the room. The two soldiers came in next and sat behind Martin Kabiti on a sofa big enough to fit another three people, though no one in Oetimu felt like they were important enough to sit beside two Javanese soldiers. Sergeant Ipi selected a spot on the long wooden bench, resigning himself to a sore ass. The town elders, a few school principals, and a couple of local thugs joined him. The table had been moved to a corner of the room so that Mas Zainal and other less important townspeople could sit on the floor. So many men had shown up that the spectators spilled into the yard. Heads bobbed at the window and eyes peered through the open door.

Before turning on the TV, Sergeant Ipi rolled out a spread of food and drinks. Teens helped carry trays and crates of bottles out from the back room, setting out booze on top of the table, on the floor, and on the TV stand; they hurried back and forth so many times that it seemed the host had bought an infinite supply of refreshments. Meanwhile, Sergeant Ipi picked up a bottle of sopi kepala, popped the corn husk stopper, and announced why he'd decided to throw a party that night. Silvy, the girl who had recently arrived in Oetimu, the one who'd caught the eye of every man in town, had won his heart and agreed to become his wife.

"Please enjoy this humble feast and celebrate with me," Sergeant Ipi concluded. "We're getting married in two weeks."

The jubilant atmosphere inspired by dried and roasted meats, booze, and the prospect of watching an idol in action dissipated when the young men heard those words. For months, they'd competed for Silvy's heart, but then the girl suddenly fell into Sergeant Ipi's open arms. What a despicable man, they thought to themselves. Just like that he stole the girl of their dreams, as if pushing them around and beating them up every day weren't enough.

Torn between jealousy and heartbreak, the men began to drink. Someone turned on the TV, where two commentators in yellow blazers gesticulated wildly, announcing every three minutes that the game was about to start – until another stream of advertisements cut them off, delaying the kickoff yet again. Martin Kabiti, the elders, soldiers, and teachers, as well as the thugs sitting on the bench all calmly sipped their drinks, leaning back and closing their eyes every once in a while. But the young men in the room drank as though they were about to die of thirst. They threw back full glasses of whisky, switched to sopi kepala, grabbed a few beers, and chased everything with wine. Soon enough, they were all drunk and rowdy, laughing at things that weren't funny and raising their voices in competition with the commentators on screen.

When the game finally started, everyone settled down a bit. It didn't take long for the room to fall completely silent; no cheers or whoops could be heard over the TV, which was broadcasting a match not yet living up to expectations. Ronaldo Luís Nazário de Lima seemed to have lost his edge. His mouth hung open, front teeth jutting out, making him look like a stupid rat. The men stared as Ronaldo the Rat jogged sluggishly from one end of the field to the other, as though he'd just swallowed a bunch of poisonous kotpese. Ronaldo hadn't pulled any of his usual astonishing moves. Ronaldo wasn't smiling with the mischievous grin that came across his face when he outwitted the other team. Watching Ronaldo play wasn't any fun at all. The men were fixated on the screen, nervous that their beloved Brazil was about to lose to France. They hated the French, a team that played soccer without smiling. And whenever the players did smile, their faces reminded Oetimu's residents of the Dutch who colonized their town.

In the twenty-seventh minute, their fears became reality. Zinedine Zidane, the French player with a bald spot, big as a horse, launched the ball straight into Brazil's net. That's when the room got noisy again. Everyone started asking each other what made Ronaldo play like a drugged rodent – had he forgotten to pray? Had the French put a curse on him? Or was he just hungry?

While the men in the police station debated what was going with Ronaldo, Atino and the other murderers arrived in town. They came from the north in the back of a pickup truck, which they parked on the edge of town before continuing on foot down convoluted paths towards Martin Kabiti's house. They'd been to Oetimu many times before, disguised as road surveyors or lost farmers so they could figure out which houses were guarded by dogs and which valleys by ghosts. That night, they launched an arrow at Martin Kabiti's dog before it could make a sound, kicked in the door, and woke up his wife and kids. They looted the house, ripped up letters and land titles, and sat their hostages down at knifepoint. An eye for an eye, that was Atino's logic, and he wanted Martin Kabiti alive to watch his family suffer. The assailant was from East Timor and had been captured during the war. He suffered in prison – not just from torture at the hands of Indonesian soldiers, but also from a raging desire for revenge. He decided to pay Martin Kabiti's family a visit to settle a debt, and he'd waited patiently for the day to come when all the men in town were away, leaving their wives and children alone. Atino was confident that his target would be at the police station for the next few hours and eventually come home drunk.

One of the men slapped Martin Kabiti's wife across the face with the flat edge of the long knife. She made desperate, futile attempts to fight back, fully aware that no one was around to help her; the whole town was out watching the game. Another slap, then an order to shut up, since one of the kids had started crying. Her eldest, a daughter whose breasts had just started showing, hid in the crook of her arm; her youngest son peed himself after being dragged out of bed.

Atino and his crew weren't in a hurry, confident that they had plenty of time to carry out their plan. But little did they know, Ronaldo was playing a finals game that was only fun for the French and their fans. When Zinedine Zidane scored a second goal at the end of the first half, Martin Kabiti stood up and kicked his chair. He accused Ronaldo of being paid to lose and blamed it on the Americans.

"He was bribed! The US did it. Fucking dogs, the lot of them. Pukimai. This isn't soccer, it's a scam."

He kept cursing, pointing at the TV, spittle flying through his mustache, and then laid out how greedy Americans were the masterminds behind every problem on earth. No one in the room mustered the courage to disagree, since Martin Kabiti started waving his fists as though he wanted to challenge the United States and each of its allies to a fight.

"Someone take me home before I smash this pukimai TV to pieces. Made in America, no fucking doubt!"

Seeing that his friend was about to throw the heavy rolling chair at his television, Sergeant Ipi wordlessly stood up, walked outside, and turned on his motorbike. Martin Kabiti skulked after him, pushing through the drunk, crestfallen guests without excusing himself. The men started muttering as they watched him leave. A few agreed with what he'd said and joined in, cussing out the Americans. Anyone who disagreed waited until Martin Kabiti was gone before voicing their opinions, and the rest just clutched their bottles and wallowed. In less than an hour they'd been pummeled by two calamitous events: Brazil's loss and the news that the girl of their dreams was engaged to another man.

They'd all fallen for Silvy the moment she arrived in Oetimu. The young men in town fantasized about the same thing: how lovely it would be to start a little family with Silvy as the mother of their children. So, even though the girl was still in high school, they all competed for her heart. Mototaxi drivers gave her free rides, thugs promised protection, and widowers offered her a comfortable life.

Whenever Silvy walked to Oetimu State High School, which was across the street from Prosperity General Store, or when she headed to the river carrying a basket of clothes, a gaggle of men would always circle in her general vicinity as though they'd been walking in the same direction by coincidence. Once they were nearby, they'd pray for some chance event that would turn her face towards theirs – which would lead to an introduction and then catalyze another chance event, like a mutual confession of love. But every time the men in Oetimu had an opportunity to introduce themselves to the girl, they discovered their mouths failed to form words and their cheeks felt heavy. When they heard that Silvy had been taken by a different man, they all leaned back against the walls of the police station and cursed their fate.

The older men watching the finals weren't so shocked by Sergeant Ipi's announcement. Some were even happy to hear the news. They kept sipping at their drinks, picking at their food, and chewing thoughtfully. If any of them felt on edge, it had nothing to do with Silvy's engagement; they were just worried that Brazil was about to lose the game. These men were old enough to remember that Sergeant Ipi had grown up under the tutelage of Am Siki, a man they held in high regard. Sure, the kid turned out ruder than they'd hoped, and maybe he didn't care about the people of Oetimu, but still, they felt that he was one of their own. And he'd live a life shielded from harm and showered with happiness, his engagement to Silvy was a sure sign of that. They suspected it since the day he was born: Sergeant Ipi would always be protected, with his mother and ancestors watching over him.

II

Lisbon, 1974

Júlio Craveiro dos Santos got the phone call on the day of his only daughter's sixteenth birthday. It was official: he received a post in Timor to help Mario Lemos Pires oversee the decolonization process.

"I've told you before and I'll tell you again," his wife Lena said, "God is always at work."

Six months earlier, soldiers in Portugal rose up against the reigning military regime and Júlio decided to stand by Marcelo Caetano. But after the former prime minister was detained in military custody and sent to Madeira Island, Júlio started to get nervous about what was next for him. The authoritarian Estado Novo was in pieces. If he wasn't thrown into jail as a collaborator, he'd definitely lose his job. Those soldiers who like to call themselves revolutionaries would be sent to his office, where they'd shoot him a skeptical glance before swiftly replacing him with some other bureaucrat who also happened to call himself a revolutionary. If he wasn't fired – an eventuality that made no sense at all – he'd have no choice but to work for a new hotheaded state, one that would always see him as the enemy. In other words, no matter how Júlio spun the wheel of life, he was out of options. Every path forward was a dead end.

All of this changed when the new government rolled out its decolonization plans. Júlio prayed with all his might, called up acquaintances, and asked to be sent to one of the African colonies. It would put some distance between him and his political problems, and he'd get to keep his job. After working as hard as possible, he might even return to Lisbon with a small promotion. Officers typically rise up the ranks after coming home from the colonies, don't they?

He fucked his wife with enthusiasm that night, like a teen who finally had the chance to sleep with the girl he fantasized about for years. His wife, who'd just prayed a novena to the Virgin Mary for her husband's safety, zealously matched Júlio's passion, kissing and biting and scratching him. It was only once Júlio fell back on the bed, worn out, that she looked up at the ceiling and realized the consequences of her answered prayers. Before she knew it, tears started rolling down her cheeks. She tried hard not to make a sound, but a little sob escaped from her throat as a wave of terrible thoughts rushed through her head. She knew plenty of officers and civil servants who ended up living with local girls in the colonies, or who'd wound up killed in rebel uprisings.

"It'll be five years at most," Júlio said when he heard his wife crying.

His wife took a deep breath, dried her eyes, and turned to kiss Júlio's lips. His cheeks. His eyelids.

"If everything goes well, only two or three. We just have to moderate elections," he continued.

They heard the roar of a train in the distance and the bustle of the streets. Lately, people in the city were drinking until dawn, boisterously debating politics as they headed home. That never happened when the PIDE patrolled the streets.

"Why can't the Africans take care of themselves?" his wife asked after a long silence.

"Timor. Not Africa. It's a small island near Australia," Júlio corrected her.

"They all sound the same."

Júlio laughed.

"It's the safest colony. There's no war. You should be grateful that they've sent me there and not to Africa."

His wife nuzzled his shoulder. He gave her a kiss, turned off the light, and let his hand rest on her body as he drifted off.

"If it's so safe, why shouldn't we come with you?"

She asked the question three times, as if she wasn't just asking her husband, but also trying to convince herself of the possibility.

"Why do we have to stay here all alone?"

Júlio opened his eyes and switched the light back on. A few moments passed, and then he repeated his wife's question: Why do you have to stay here all alone?

"You could teach at a school. Or hold classes from home, whatever you want."

Their daughter, Laura, liked the idea of living in a far-off colony, a small and exotic country where she'd be able to keep going to school without the tumult of regime change. And so, one month later, Júlio and his family set foot on Timor. After landing in Baucau they drove to Dili in a jeep with a military escort, peering from the windows as they passed decrepit towns that had more cows and water buffalo than human residents. People with foreheads wrinkled from worry roamed around in the hot, dusty air. The houses of Portuguese officers were extravagant, the markets filthy. They drove by walls covered with murals depicting revolution, tagged with the slogans of different political factions.

Political parties were banned in Timor under the colonial policy of the Estado Novo, and the PIDE was tasked with crushing any and all independence movements. After the Portuguese dictatorship fell, the colonial officers roaming the streets stayed exactly the same, but they no longer had a mandate to repress political activity. The Timorese people had been deprived of freedom for so long that when they were finally able to speak, they wouldn't let anything stand in their way. New political parties competed with intensity; leaders sought votes by any means necessary, democratic as well as underhanded, and every group had fanatical supporters and a militia willing to die for a cause. Soon enough, it wasn't out of the ordinary to hear that someone suffered violent consequences for pledging their support to the wrong group.

The feverish political atmosphere was palpable even in the offices of the Portuguese colonial state. Júlio's coworkers couldn't help themselves and started siding with one faction or another. Some quit their jobs to join a party, others stayed in the office only to meet with political leaders in secret, but Júlio was determined to stay out of partisan debates. After the Carnation Revolution almost destroyed his livelihood, he became committed to neutrality. He arrived at the office on time, completed the tasks assigned to him, and went straight home at the end of each day. His daughter bought an orange-sided thrush and was trying to teach it to sing; his wife was tending to a new garden behind the house, complete with a little gazebo where the family could read and sip wine. Being with family made his life in Timor feel like a vacation – one that kept him plenty busy. While so many of his colleagues were swept up in the politics of the moment, he managed to avoid it all.

Until he met Captain Gustavo.

The streets were quiet when Júlio heard a knock on his front door. It was the captain, an acquaintance from the Department of Political Affairs. The two men had met a few times and spoken at some length, but it was still strange that the captain would show up at his house. They last saw each other around two months earlier, when they discussed Indonesian interference in Timorese affairs. At the end of the conversation, Captain Gustavo slipped in a question: Do you happen to live in that house on Fernando Street with the three sandalwood trees out front? Júlio said yes but added that he wasn't sure that his was the only home with sandalwoods. My father was the man who planted those trees, the captain replied. There used to be four, he continued, but one of them died from a caterpillar infestation. That confirmed it: Júlio's was the house. There was a fourth trunk in the front yard, so at one point there must have been another tree. The captain, always puffing at a cigar, had leathery skin and a face that always looked weathered, as though he just stepped off the battlefield. When he came over that night, no cigar in hand but with the same expression of profound exhaustion, Júlio wondered whether the captain was about to lay claim to his father's three remaining sandalwoods.

"A long time ago, my father lived here," Captain Gustavo said from the doorstep.

Júlio invited him inside and uncorked a bottle of wine. Over the course of the next few hours, his guest talked about his family.

His father was very close with the Portuguese Prime Minister Manuel Gomes da Costa – that's what Captain Gustavo said when he resumed his story – and so, when Marshal Óscar Carmon seized power during the coup d'état in 1926, his father was discarded, exiled to Timor. Two years later, the captain was born to a nurse who'd cared for his father. Before young Captain Gustavo could talk, his dad had already left, returning to Portugal, abandoning him and his mother in Timor. He was only fourteen when Japan invaded. He was lucky to have survived. It was a horrible war. His mother died, and not long after, the captain decided to become a soldier; it was in his blood. He was on the battlefield when the Portuguese crushed the rebellions in Manufahi and other regions of Timor, and by all measures he should've ended up with a higher rank. But what can you do, Júlio? The system's corrupt.

Júlio responded with a throwaway remark and said he was tired. His wife and daughter were already asleep, their doors locked since they didn't know who the strange visitor was or what he wanted. Captain Gustavo knew that Júlio's comment was a signal for him to leave, but instead of getting up to go home, the captain asked, Would it be possible for me to stay the night here?

"I'll never forget the favor," he continued, though Júlio didn't fully understand what the captain meant. "Please, let me remember my father tonight, here, where he used to live."

Júlio agreed. He was tipsy, which made him sympathetic to such a sentimental request.

We all miss our parents, Júlio replied. "The guest room's over there," he added. "Make yourself at home."

Captain Gustavo thanked him, adding an apology for the imposition. Júlio said it was nothing, that he felt honored to be able to give a bit of peace to a man who missed his father.

After the captain went into the guest room, Júlio sat back down on the couch, waiting to make sure that his guest had everything he needed and had fallen asleep. During their conversation, he'd talked about his own parents, too. His father was also a soldier who'd died in Angola; his mother had gone back to her hometown in the south of Portugal. The whole thing made him feel lucky that he worked behind a desk and kept his family safe. Just as he was ready to go to bed himself, he heard footsteps approaching the house.

A moment later, there was a knock at the door. Tok tok tok. Júlio pressed himself against the wall to peer outside; eight men were on his doorstep, five of them holding Mauser pistols.

"We're here for Captain Gustavo," shouted one of the men, who seemed like the leader.

Júlio turned and saw that the captain had come out from the guest room, half-awake. He gestured for Júlio to open the door, and when Júlio did, two of the men rushed in and wordlessly stood on either side of the captain, ready to usher him out.

"Sorry, malae, but you're coming with us, too," the leader said.

Seeing that Júlio was ready to backtrack with a string of excuses, the man stopped him calmly: "Lieutenant Colonel Gouveia is at the office, he wants to see you. It won't take long."

Upon hearing the name of the chief of police, Júlio's wife unlocked her bedroom door. The man was upstanding, respected, and knew her husband personally. Everything was going to be just fine.

As it turns out, everything was not just fine. The UDT had launched a coup, taking over the city and all of its government buildings, the police station included. Júlio and Captain Gustavo were taken into the station, but not to meet with the esteemed chief of police. Instead, they were locked in a cell and treated like prisoners; armed men called them communists and demanded information about the FRETILIN's plans and other things Júlio knew nothing about. He brandished his Portuguese citizenship, which only made the men angrier, unleashing new rounds of blows. Captain Gustavo suffered his own share of beatings – enough, at least, to make the two men bond over their shared fate.

When her husband didn't come home the next day, Lena rushed to speak with Portuguese officials and demanded to know what was going on. But the moment she mentioned that her husband had disappeared with Captain Gustavo, and that the two had been together because the captain had stayed the night at their home, the officials were quick to blame her husband, claiming that the two of them must have been in cahoots with insurgents.

"We'll try our best. But if your husband was collaborating with the FRETILIN, there's nothing we can do for you."

Lena tried to convince them that her husband wasn't involved in politics, that the captain had only visited them one time. The officials told her to stay home. They'd work on it.

The next night, Captain Gustavo told Júlio to stand at the ready. At 2AM, he started moaning, begging to be taken to the toilets. Deep and drawn out, his cries seemed to plunge down into his stomach – noises sure to inspire pity. The two thugs keeping watch came over to check on the captain, but when they got close, he snapped the neck of the first one and punched the other square in his Adam's apple. The men were paramilitaries, not real soldiers trained in combat. Once the guards were immobilized, Captain Gustavo and Júlio scaled the prison wall and dashed through back alleyways, heads lowered. Finally, they reached the home of a woman named Sarah.

"Everyone retreated to Aileu," she told the captain.

Júlio wanted to see his family, but Captain Gustavo said it would only put them in danger.

"Your house is definitely being watched."

Júlio wanted to blame the captain for getting him involved in an uprising, but it was too late. His body was so sore from beatings that, without even realizing it, he'd started harboring deep resentment towards the UDT. He used to feel superior to Timorese locals, enlightened and civilized because of his level-headedness, but all it took for him to pick a side was forty-eight hours of being cursed out, smacked around, and repeatedly grabbed by the hair and slammed against the table until his forehead swelled.

"Why isn't Lemos Pires doing anything about this?"

"You're both as good as rebels now – enemies of the state," said Sarah. "You need to hide here for the time being. Francisco will come help soon."

Júlio took her advice. Meanwhile, Mario Lemos Pires moved the administrative capital to Farol, where he tried to get a handle on the situation and help Portuguese citizens in Timor. When Lena's complaint reached his desk, he sent men to the police station to get a status report on Júlio's case, only to hear news of Júlio and Captain Gustavo's escape. One of our men died – those two wrung his neck! That's what the men at the station said. And the guard who'd survived, ashamed and angry, claimed that Júlio and the captain hadn't acted alone.

"No doubt it was the FRETILIN that helped them out. I couldn't see very clearly, but a trained squad definitely infiltrated the prison. Those two men we were guarding, they must have been higher ups too, because the men who broke them out of their cell knew what they were doing. If you have any intention of helping them, you better watch your back."

When he heard the story, Lemos Pires swore he'd arrest Júlio himself if the man ever dared to set foot in government offices – and if he didn't, God help anyone who tried to protect him.

Júlio had been hiding out in Sarah's house for a week, playing chess and listening to Captain Gustavo's heroic stories, when the FRETILIN invaded Dili to launch an attack. UDT leaders and their supporters were arrested, including the chief of police. Imprisoned members of the FRETILIN were released, and Júlio met the party leaders, who welcomed him warmly.

"You and the captain joined the people's struggle and suffered in the name of the FRETILIN, in the name of the Maubere. You're the first heroes of our revolution."

Cautiously, Júlio was finally able to visit his family, but he never showed his face in Portuguese state offices again.

"Lemos Pires is furious," Lena told him. "You'll be arrested and taken to court if you go back."

So Júlio sent a message to the governor requesting a private meeting to plead his case. But he never heard back; a few days later, he found out that the governor, unable to maintain control in Timor, had moved off the coast to Atauro Island. Júlio felt abandoned by his nation.

The FRETILIN, in contrast, was more than happy to support Júlio and praise him for everything he'd done. Party leaders cited his exemplary behavior in public announcements and speeches: "Just look at this foreigner. He joined our struggle voluntarily, he was imprisoned by the UDT, and he even suffered torture in the name of our people. If this malae is willing to join arms with the Maubere, how can any of you stand idly by? That kind of apartidarismo is exactly what led our land to be colonized for hundreds of years!"

Time passed. Júlio slowly started to feel like he was a citizen of a new country, one that reciprocated his love. Why go back to Portugal? All that waited for him in Lisbon was a prison cell, while here, he was appreciated. So, he started working with the FRETILIN; he helped the party clarify the direction of their struggle, ostracize anyone who seemed disloyal, and prepare for independence. People were still killing each other, but Júlio and the rest of the party stayed optimistic that if they worked as hard as possible, the situation would stabilize. Then, the country would be safe, and Júlio's wife and daughter could go on with the rest of their lives in peace.

He was awake when the attacks began. Júlio wasn't able to get to sleep for hours. Time and time again, he paced across the floor of his small bedroom, walked to the kitchen and sat down, lost in thought, before going back to his room. The sound of the door opening and closing woke Lena up, too. Indonesian troops had crossed the border. There were casualties, a lot of them, including five foreign journalists, two of whom held British citizenship. All of the Australians in Dili rushed to the airport. Timorese people started running, too, fleeing into the mountains.

After Indonesian forces attacked and occupied Atabae, FRETILIN declared independence on the Eastern half of Timor, announcing a new independent nation: the Democratic Republic of East Timor. The first flag was sewn, a constitution drafted. The Portuguese flag, which had been hoisted for hundreds of years, was pulled down. Leaders read the declaration of independence in front of Portuguese state buildings, and as the new flag rose, people sang out *Patria! Patria!* to the sound of cannons being fired in honor of fallen comrades. The news of independence was announced by radio and dispatched around the world.

Even so, the declaration of independence didn't garner much international attention at all. The UDT and APODETI aligned with Indonesia and argued that Portuguese Timor should be absorbed into the Republic of Indonesia. Sovereignty was complicated – Mario Lemos Pires himself announced he would only acknowledge a new government based on results from a general election, but it was naïve to think that any fair vote could be cast while his transitional government cowered on a tiny island. Júlio, meanwhile, was part of the small team that developed the fifty-five articles of East Timor's new constitution. War didn't scare him, he told Captain Gustavo.

But I can't stop thinking about what might happen to Lena and Laura, he added.

"If Indonesian troops actually reach Dili," the captain replied, "just tell your wife and daughter to say that they're Portuguese citizens." This advice was coming from the trusted right-hand man of Rogério Lobato, and Júlio took careful note.

He heard the attack at 3AM, when the city was dark. Dili was hit from the sea and from the sky, by soldiers jumping from fighter jets that thundered above. Bombs sounded and the bra-ta-ta of machine gun fire broke the city's silence. Laura woke up and ran to her parent's room, shaking. Júlio could hear his wife chanting the Magnificat in the dark.

No one left the house. The commotion would occasionally die down and pick up again hours later. FRETILIN troops and their supporters fought back, but Indonesia seized control of the capital before the day was over. Every home in the city was searched; Júlio made no effort to resist when he was ordered to step outside. He'd hidden all of the weapons he'd been stockpiling behind the dresser, and when he faced the soldiers, he stated that he was a Portuguese citizen. But the men only spoke Indonesian and didn't understand a word he said. Together with a dozen or so other captives, Júlio and his family were taken to the eastern zone of the city near the docks and corralled into the big, empty building that used to host the Companhia de Intendência in the sixties. Indonesian troops holding long-barreled guns stood on every corner. A few of them walked around, dragging the corpses that scattered the streets into piles. No one had bothered to pull down the body of a dead parachuter, his limbs tangled in streetlight cables above their heads. When they got to the building, Júlio and his family were ordered to stay the night.

"It's too dangerous outside," the commander said, by way of an interpreter. "We'll make sure you're safe here."

Júlio recognized a few other FRETILIN party members in the group, but no one acknowledged one another. Everyone had worried looks on their faces and spoke only to family members. As he fell asleep on the cold floor, the sounds of Lena praying mixed with his daughter's voice repeating after her. He tried to convince them that they weren't in danger: we're Portuguese citizens, Indonesia doesn't want any trouble with us. They fell asleep and, eventually, even Júlio drifted off.

The family woke up to soldiers yelling in Indonesian early that morning. Júlio could only make out the words *communist* and FRETILIN. The young, tall, Timorese man with curly hair who was serving as the soldiers' interpreter soon arrived. After a few words from the commander, he started ordering people in the crowd to stand, forming a separate group. Júlio watched as the commander's finger landed on each FRETILIN member, along with the young UNETIM supporters, and a few others who he didn't recognize. When he was told to stand up and join them, he knew something bad was going to happen and tried to explain that he was a Portuguese citizen, but the commander cut him off, ordering a soldier to aim his AK-47 squarely at Júlio's neck.

The commander had separated out around fifty people, including Júlio and his family. The rest were told to stay put while the new group was herded outside and marched towards the port. Júlio walked next to his wife and daughter. The morning sun felt warm against the back of his neck, and swallows circled the docks. Every few moments, he felt his wife's palm pressing against his own.

Two soldiers stood by the gate that opened out onto the port. They stopped all the young girls, Laura included. She stood there, watching her parents as they were shuffled towards the ocean. When they reached the harbor, the large group was split into smaller clusters, each of which was told to stand single file along the edge of the pier. Then, the shooting started. A group was lined up, mowed down, and then the next set formed a row. The corpses were kicked into the ocean and floated around the docks. Three women broke into a sprint in an attempt to escape, but each received a bullet in the back and fell to the ground. Laura saw her parents take their turn, hands clasped. She couldn't make out their faces, but she felt sure that they were looking at one another. Her chest heaved when their bodies collapsed on the dock. Her neck felt stiff and her vision blurry, but she was too petrified to cry.

After the killings, a truck carried Laura and the other girls to the Hotel Tropical in Lecidere, far to the eastern edge of Dili. And that's when it began. She was raped, interrogated, tortured, asked over and over again if she had any connection to UNETIM, if she had tried to massacre the Timorese people, why she became a communist, and other questions she didn't understand. In response, she told them she had no idea what they were talking about, but that answer only caused them to whip her with fishing wire, call her a communist whore, and burn her skin with lit cigarettes. After a while, she stopped trying to communicate with her captors. She stopped saying anything at all, because every word that came out of her mouth felt futile.

There were many other prisoners in the hotel. Men were brutally tortured, then forced to grope her breasts. The other women received the same treatment as she did. Too exhausted to cry, they would look at one another with recognition. After a few months, Laura was transferred to what used to be the Sang Hai Too shop building in Colmera, where her treatment was no different; repeatedly, she was questioned and tortured. Sometimes a man would come into the cell to rape her, sometimes she was thrown in the back of a jeep and taken to the barracks, and the men would fuck her there.

Laura was soon gaunt, disheveled. She could barely force herself to swallow the terrible food, her face was a patchwork of scars from being hit, and her skin blistered from frequent burns. It was dangerous to have all those wounds, since prisoners had no choice but to sleep on a dirty, fetid floor, in rooms where swarms of flies hovered above broken toilets. The women were kept in a narrow cell and rarely saw daylight. Scabies started to seize her skinny body. As she lost weight, her belly began to swell. Something was growing inside her, getting bigger by the day. When she walked, her legs look too emaciated to hold the weight of her stomach. Her health deteriorated each day.

One night, a Timorese man pulled her from the cell. She thought she was going to be raped, but the man took her outside instead and ordered her to get into a car. Soldiers stood nearby, unperturbed, as though they knew exactly where he was planning on taking her. Maybe he was going to drop her off at the commanders' barracks. But instead, they drove west, leaving the city and passing two military checkpoints, until the man pulled over on a stretch of road that cut across an open field.

"I'm supposed to kill you," he said in Portuguese, "but I've seen too much death. Get out, go get yourself killed instead. Now, before I change my mind."

Laura wordlessly stepped out of the car and started shuffling across the field. Confident the man would try to shoot her from behind, she tried to speed up her pace, but her huge stomach and weak body slowed her down. She fell twice before making it to the thick forest that lined the far end of the clearing. Standing under the first trees, she glanced back to see that the car hadn't budged. Without giving it another thought, she shoved her way through the bushes and into darkness. Tree branches and thorns on shrub verbenas snagged her wounds, but she kept walking.

Eventually, she reached the banks of a small river running west. She slipped on the slick mud lining the stream and fell, then leaned down to drink some water before getting to her feet. She began making her way along the riverbank, leaving behind the solider and the city.

She walked a long way that night even though there was no moon. The forest surrounded her like dark walls and the reflection of stars bounced off the river, marking a path forward. Insects chirped in tune with the gurgle of water and the sound of her labored breathing. Hours passed. She eventually slumped against the base of a lontar tree and fell asleep.

Animals started rustling when the sun rose, and Laura woke up. She started walking again, following the stream, her mind blank. When she was hungry, she picked leaves from the ground and ate them; when she was thirsty, she crouched down to drink from the river. Things continued like that for weeks. The girl walked until she got tired, slept by the riverbank, and ate whatever she found along the way, though she was rarely hungry. The more she walked the skinnier she got and the bigger her stomach grew. A trail of flies flew behind her, since her open wounds were infected. Her skin and clothes were smeared with dead leaves and dirt since she slept on the ground. The pajamas that she'd worn in prison had originally been white and patterned with little dolls; now, they were tattered and dark gray. Her hair was matted and smelled. She looked alarming.

And she kept heading west. Occasionally, she passed by the edge of a small town, where people would keep their distance and try not to look her way. It wasn't the first time they'd seen crazy people wandering in the woods, and it wasn't so out of the ordinary to stumble across suanggi or evil spirits in the forest. She passed by dozens of towns until one afternoon, in the heat of the day, she chose not to sleep by the river and instead walked straight into a nearby settlement.

It happened to be an afternoon in the height of tofa season, when families took their cows and other livestock down to the river and farmers ate lunch in bungalows out in the fields. Everyone still in town shut their front doors when they saw the woman wandering down the street, but quickly they ran out back, trying to catch a glimpse of the strange figure. Kids sprinted into the fields and called out to their moms and dads. Someone finally took initiative and sounded the bamboo kentong that hung by the town lopo. It was the first time anyone had used the Javanese instrument since it was first installed according to instructions from the Ministry of Information, since no one really understood what the point of it was in the first place.

"Mom, Dad! A curse, a curse!" The little kids yelled. "A who-knows-what just came into town, a creature that lurks, that's sure to be cursed!"

The men and women who'd been in the fields lounging after lunch or bringing livestock to the river hurried back into town. The commotion was infectious; mere seconds passed before townspeople wielding machetes, klewangs, spears, and chants started following the strange woman. But she simply kept walking forward with her stumbling gait and empty gaze, which was almost completely shielded by her disheveled, matted hair. Surrounded by flies, she smelled like the dead.

The armed men kept their distance as they walked behind her, fortifying their courage with the few fragments of prayers to their ancestors they'd managed to memorize. Women and children hesitantly trailed behind the men, curious and afraid. Since the stranger lurched forward without so much as a glance to her surroundings, more and more town residents joined the crowd. Some men were still unsure of themselves and would rebuke the others for getting too close, wary of the possibility that the creature might radiate witchcraft. When the throngs reached a storefront – one of the few thatched buildings in town that proudly displayed its slogan, "Stay Steadfast and Prosper" – the appalling woman collapsed to the ground. The moment her bottom hit the rough, broken pavement, she started to cry intense, loud sobs; she reached both arms to the sky and then punched her bloated stomach. It was the first time Laura had cried since her mother and father were killed, and it had been a very long time since she'd made any sound at all. Nothing could hold back her thundering wail.

The men slowly lowered their weapons, and the rest of the town residents stood still from a safe distance – or rather, close enough to keep watching but also far enough to run away if something went wrong. The crowd took pity on her while she cried, but the way she raised her arms to the heavens also made everyone wonder if she was trying to summon lightning bolts that would crash down and destroy them all.

Am Naijuf was the town's chief, a man who was already considered old back when the Japanese invaded the town. No one knew his true age. He was short, every hair on his head was white, and the soles of his feet were wide and tough from the countless years he'd spent walking. He ordered a couple of kids in the crowd to mount their horses and go get the dukun, Ain Sufa, who lived on the far edge of town. The old leader stood calmly, chewing betel nut like a seasoned cattle trader waiting for buyers to appraise his livestock.

Soon enough, the two children galloped back.

"He's not home," they said, out of breath. "Ain Nel just went into labor out in the fields near Feftua Hill. Ain Sufa went to help."

The chief spat on the ground, his saliva red from the betel nut. The sound of the woman sobbing cut through the quiet crowd.

"Get Am Siki," he said.

The two boys got back on the horse and raced off. The chief pulled out some loose tobacco and a lontar leaf to roll a cigarette. After his fourth puff, the kids appeared once again, this time followed by an older man on horseback. He was wearing a white t-shirt two sizes too big, the shabby, worn-out kind that Father Verrharen used to hand out as missionary in the town. The colors in the woven sarong tied around Am Siki's waist were dull, just like those in the aluk hanging from his neck. He had wrinkly skin and his hair, long and straight, was neatly tied back.

He got off his horse and approached the chief. A few other elders joined the pair and shared some betel nut while the girl sobbed.

"It's been like this for a while now," the chief commented, placing some slaked lime on his tongue. "Whenever anyone approaches her, man or woman, she gets mad and screams louder."

The other elders nodded, waiting to see what Am Siki had to say. He spat into his palm and slipped his hand inside his aluk, for what nobody knew, and murmured a prayer. He glanced up at the sky and then pushed through the crowd of armed men to approach the girl. Everyone stood at the ready while he walked over, the elders with their prayers, men with their weapons, and women and children ready to run.

Am Siki moved very slowly as he got close. Suddenly, the woman raised her head, and when her eyes met his, Am Siki knew that the girl had lost her soul. He reached his hand out gingerly, as though approaching a wild horse. The girl stopped crying and stared at the elder with a sharp look in her eyes. In those few seconds, the whole town tensed up. Everyone had goosebumps and no one knew what would happen next. Was the woman about to attack Am Siki? Would she spit venom from her eyes?

III

No one was unfamiliar with the name Am Siki, not even in the most remote corners of the archipelago. He was the only person on earth to kill more than ten Japanese soldiers, burn a forced labor camp to the ground, and live on to tell the tale. It was unheard of to escape the samurai sword under Japanese occupation. If a soldier wanted to kill you, that was that; if he chose to let you live, you'd probably end up dead regardless, since you'd be whipped and forced to work without food or raped night and day. Famous for his impressive feats, Am Siki was respected across the country. His distinguished name spread from one town to another until he became known across surrounding islands as a hero, a knight who slayed the Japanese to defend his bangsa, his nation, from the colonizer's ironclad fist.

But Am Siki shrugged off the praise.

"I never killed anyone to save Bangsa," that's what he'd say, confusing the word with the name of another laborer who vanished when he set fire to the camp. "He and I weren't that close, actually. Nothing I did was in the service of anyone, all I wanted to do was save my horse."

People laughed, but Am Siki was being serious.

This is his story.

In 1941, Am Neno – Am Siki's father – fell from a palm tree and died. Am Siki never cried about the tragedy even though his father's death had a profound effect on him. His family believed that in ancient times, his ancestors came from the lontar palm, which meant that many of his relatives died falling from the trees. His father passed away in the shade of a palm, as did his grandfather, and so on. To tumble to the earth from a lontar tree was a noble way for Am Neno to reunite with his forefathers.

Aina Fai, Am Siki's mother, had also died many years earlier, bleeding nonstop while giving birth to another son. Once his father was gone, the boy was all alone.

Am Siki is the kind of character you hear about all the time in folktales: the strong, brave, hard-working orphan. He could slice flower panicles and tap twelve lontar palms in the same amount of time it took to roll two cigarettes; he could gallop on horseback through the dead of night when it was too dark to see a single obstacle. Never once had bad luck come his way, and his ancestors always watched over him.

After his father's passing, Am Siki's life revolved around horses and lontar palms. He painstakingly collected sap and then processed it into sopi, and he also gathered the leaves, which he used as a material for weaving. In the dry season, he went into the forest to collect beeswax, sandalwood, and sometimes a bit of gold, which he then carried to Portuguese-controlled Oekusi, where he could trade his goods for salt, tobacco, linens, and new machetes.

He had to hide his deals with the Portuguese from Dutch soldiers and the local aristocracy. The king had announced a decree: all goods harvested from the forest were to be traded exclusively with the Dutch. Everyone followed the rule except for Am Siki and his family. They kept trading with the Portuguese because of their deep-seated hatred for the Dutch colonizers, a hatred that been passed down from generation to generation.

And here's where the hate so fundamental to Am Siki's story first began:

Long ago, Ama Neno Manas Manikin, one of the family ancestors, ruled over the land. His nose was hooked like a parrot beak, and he was respected by all creatures. The forest canopy protected him from rainfall, the wind only blew when he gave it permission to do so, and if he rode his horse on a hot afternoon, clouds would gather above his head to shield him from the sun. Ama Neno Manas Manikin ruled over the lands of more than fifty tribes, stretching from the northern coast all the way to southern beaches. Together, they lived in peace, trading with merchant ships from China, India, Java, Makassar, Portugal, and Holland.

As time passed, conflicts broke out between the Portuguese and the Dutch. Both of the nations wanted sandalwood, and lots of it, so they took to the island with soldiers and guns, persuading the island's rulers to give either side support. Many agreed to form an alliance and ended up caught in the crossfire. Ama Neno Manas Manikin and the hundreds of others who refused to join the conflict cautioned their neighbors to stay out of the war – especially a war over things that were never meant to be owned. What grows from the land belongs to everyone. Why fight if you're free to take what you need? But these two nations kept attacking one another and tightening control over their territories.

Once the Portuguese secured their command over the east, the Dutch swept through the western half of the island and seized all the sandalwood they could from local people. But the island wasn't very densely populated, and tribes were scattered across beaches and valleys, mountain peaks and riverbanks. More than one leader held the title of usi in every tribe. The borders that separated the territory of one group from the next weren't clearly marked, and most were known only to the rulers themselves. None of the tribes had written language, so their laws weren't recorded on paper; instead, each person was taught norms when they were young, rules that began with how to tell day from night, and anyone who wasn't a foreigner remembered them well. In other words, these people had systems of governance that were very different from anything Europeans could understand, so different that it made the Dutch go cross-eyed just thinking about how these social worlds could possibly function. On top of that, imagine how no one on the island could understand a word of Dutch – then you might begin to fathom what the Europeans had ahead of them.

Since they had no desire to spend all that time and effort learning about things they didn't understand, the Dutch simply determined that the people on the island were primitive and set up a new governing system that resembled the one they had in Europe. After burning mountain towns to rubble, they forced everyone to live in the flatlands for ease of access and established an economy built on forced labor. Anyone who was willing to collaborate with the new system was given the title of usi and endowed with royal authority, which allowed these men to usurp the positions of traditional leaders. The new usi were provided with palatial homes built from concrete, complete with thrones and pools to bathe in; they stopped working and riding horses, directing all of their attention to taxes. Wherever they went, they were carried on a royal litter, and even though clouds never appeared overhead to protect the new rulers from the sun, there was always a servant by their side carrying an umbrella. Not only were they free to choose a wife, but the new usi were also able to keep concubines and women to serve them. They could even marry their own cousins if they felt like it.

As if all this wasn't enough, the Dutch pitched one usi against another and gave them weapons so they could wage wars. Rotenese people were brought to the island and ordered to kill anyone who resisted Dutch rule. Those who refused to be forcibly displaced or who led insurrections were taken prisoner and forced into exile.

That's what happened to Ama Neno Manas Manikin. He and those who were loyal to him never stopped fighting and managed to kill a number of Dutch soldiers, Rotenese mercenaries, and even the troops commanded by the new usi. But with a cruel trick (one that ought not be repeated, since it's known to spark civil wars), the Dutch captured Ama Neno Manas Manikin and threw him onto a ship. Whether he was drowned at sea or exiled to some far-off island, no one knows.

This story was told over and over again for years to come, in the rainy season and the dry season, and even though Ama Neno Manas Manikin's descendants didn't have the strength to overthrow their colonizers, they certainly weren't about to do business with them. That's how it was for Am Siki, too. In his eyes, the Dutch were cowardly thieves, so the only option was to trade with the Portuguese in Oekusi. His father had brought him there many times throughout his childhood, and now that he was alone, he made the journey there himself.

The road to the east was steep and winding, passing through forests and grasslands, spanning the territories of three different kingdoms. Am Siki always set out in the dark of early morning before the roosters cried. He brought along two horses, one stallion and one mare. He rode the stallion while the mare carried sandalwood, beeswax, gold, sopi kepala, and other goods made from lontar palm. He also brought a lot of dendeng, his only sustenance through the many complicated detours that he had to take in order to avoid towns, main roads, Dutch military patrols, and the outposts of usi soldiers. If he were to stumble across Dutch troops, he'd get slapped around and his goods would be stolen, but if he were to run into a local solider, he'd be beaten half to death and then forced to work as a servant scrubbing the bathtubs of concubines.

Am Siki walked for four months. He passed through valleys, forests, and grasslands, faced all kinds of ghosts and wild beasts, until finally he arrived in Oekusi. However, when calamity can't be avoided, luck rests in the hands of the ancestors. The moment Am Siki walked into town, a Japanese soldier arrested him: Japan now controlled the island, having defeated all of the white colonizers and the usi that supported them. Am Siki's goods were taken from him and the stallion he rode was shot dead. He was sent to the labor camp in Sanaplo along with his mare and a few other prisoners.

It took months to get to Sanaplo, and throughout the journey he was whipped, forced to walk with his wrists bound, and given barely anything to eat. When they arrived, he was ordered to work clearing the path for a road that would run towards the southern coast. This time there were only lashes and no food at all. Prisoners only received rations when a new laborer was brought to the camp along with a scant supply of corn. In the meantime, everyone went hungry, and if a man was half-dead from starvation, the Japanese were sure to finish the job with a whip. While Am Siki worked, his mare was tied up near the guard post where the soldiers could take turns raping her, using her however they pleased.

That was the breaking point for Am Siki, watching them do that to his horse.

One night, as he was chopping down a lontar palm that blocked the path of the road, fruit fell from the tree and hit him on the head. His knees buckled and his eyes rolled back. In and out of consciousness, he swore he saw the palm kneel down to examine his face. After Am Siki's initial shock passed, the tree read out two lines of verse in Uab Metô: "Sugarcane grows towards the heavens, the banana flower pierces your chest. If you rise tall, you are useless, if you return to the hearth, you will rot to your core."

After repeating the words three times while waving its leaves dramatically, the palm spat on Am Siki's arms and each of his eyelids.

Startled from the sensation of moisture against his skin, Am Siki opened his eyes. The palm stood sturdy and upright before him, and suddenly, he felt stronger than a horse. The foreman came over with the whip, and after just a few cracks against his skin, Am Siki got up and split the man's skull with a chunk of volcanic rock. He went on a rampage that night, killing every Japanese soldier in sight and setting the camp on fire. Bodies of the occupiers were scattered across the ground and flames licked the remains of buildings while prisoners sprinted in every direction.

When the camp had been reduced to ashes, Am Siki found his mare and headed north, but not towards his hometown, since the Japanese would try to hunt him down. Instead, he embarked on an itinerant life, wandering from valleys to mountains, mountains to grassland. He ate yams, grasshoppers, deer, and wild honey. He never entered any towns; when he spotted a nearby settlement, he headed in the other direction in search of somewhere safe he could stay the night.

One afternoon, passing by a cluster of homes, he noticed that it wasn't the Japanese flag that hung from a pole but instead a different flag sewn from red and white cloth. He mustered the courage to go into town and ask where on earth he was, and if the Nippon had ever occupied the area.

As it turned out, a lot of the men in town were forced laborers from Sanaplo who'd run away after Am Siki had destroyed the camp. The havoc he'd wreaked on the Japanese became a popular story passed along from one person the next, with a bit of flare added after each new telling, to the point that soon he was known as the magic man who'd liberated Timor from the cruelty of the Japanese colonizers. Am Siki was ushered to the town's big lopo where a huge party was thrown in his honor. People danced and drank for seven days and seven nights. According to what the local residents told him, the Japanese weren't even on the island anymore.

"And the Dutch?" Am Siki asked.

"Same thing. The Dutch are gone, and we're not called Dutch Timor anymore."

"Then what's that weird flag over there? Is it your kingdom's banner?"

"That's the Indonesian flag," someone in the crowd answered. "Now we're part of Eastern Indonesia."

Am Siki wanted to know what the Indonesian soldiers looked like. Were they white like the Dutch or short like the Japanese? Did they like to make people fight each other and did they enjoy raping horses? Could they speak Uab Metô? The last question was the only one he decided to ask the others.

"Of course not," the people replied. "But now we have a new language called Indonesian. If you want to learn it, they come teach it here in the lopo once a month."

Crestfallen, Am Siki felt a sharp pain in his chest. Foreigners kept coming one after the other, but none of them had any interest in learning his language. Every time it was the Timorese who were forced to decipher the meaning behind unfamiliar sounds that emerged from foreigners' lips: Portuguese, Dutch, Japanese, and now Indonesian.

"What's this town called?" he asked.

"Oetimu," someone answered.

"Which kingdom are you a part of?"

"We used to be in Timu Un. Now, we're part of the Makmur Sentosa District."

Am Siki asked what *makmur sentosa* meant, but people looked at him as though they had no idea.

"Do lontar palms grow around here?" he changed the topic.

"Are you from a family of palm tappers?" someone asked in return. "You're free to leave town if you want to, but there are thousands of lontar palms nearby, more than enough if you want to cultivate them."

After the long party was over, Am Siki approached the chief and asked for permission to stay. The chief felt very honored, and people pitched in to build a modest house for their venerated new resident, complete with an outhouse and a small 'saenhanâ for distilling lontar sap. As Independence Day approached, rumors spread that Am Siki, the disappeared savior of the Indonesian nation, was living in Oetimu. State officials visited the town to meet the famous man and invited him to visit to the big city on August 17 so that he could be awarded a medal. He was, after all, a hero.

"I've told you before, I'm no hero, and I had no intention of saving Bangsa. Besides, what's a medal? If it's food, just give it to my horse. That way, if I die, her descendants will live on."

The officials were confused, but the chief jumped in to explain what was going on: Am Siki was speaking in metaphors.

"Save the medal for his children," the chief clarified. "That way, when he dies, his descendants will receive the honor."

The Indonesian bureaucrats nodded for a few moments, noting down the information, and never returned to Oetimu again.

Lontar palms grew in the forest and the grasslands, standing tall amidst buri palms and rocky hills. Squirrels stole their fruit and mice and scorpions burrowed into their trunks to hide. No one claimed the trees as their property; anything that grew on the land of ancestors belonged to the ancestors, which meant that all mankind had the right to cultivate and harvest its resources. Am Siki cleared fronds from the trunks of twelve lontar palms. In the season when the trees began flowering in fat, juicy clusters, he would climb to the top and slice the panicles to gather sap. Those twelve trees gave him more than fifty bamboo tubes of sap each day, some of which he distilled into sopi, some of which he used to make sugar. He had so much supply that he didn't know what to do with it all, so he started giving some of the extra to kids in Oetimu. The children happily drank the sugar juice and pretended they were drunk, imitating the men in town who liked to chase after girls after having a bit too much sopi. In the season when there weren't any flowers to harvest, Am Siki gathered palm leaves to make woven mats and rolling papers for smoking tobacco. He used the leftover fronds to braid toys for the kids.

Am Siki soon became the favorite of every child in Oetimu, regardless of the season. But he was the most beloved when the rain started falling.

Long before any foreigners set foot on Timor, children would gather around a storyteller in the rainy season. Every child was sure to be there, since it was a well-known fact that if you missed the stories, you'd get stung by a scorpion. The pitter-patter of raindrops enticed insects to crawl out from the walls and punish children who didn't want to listen to stories. In the lopo, the children would hear tales about how the ancestors had changed form to become human, or why no one was allowed to eat quail, or which disasters might befall the town if children were to fight with one another. Once pastors started arriving in Oetimu, they also listened to stories from the Bible. And these stories weren't just entertaining for children; they also gave husbands and wives plenty of alone time. In the midst of chilly rains, while their kids were huddled around the storyteller, parents were able to make more babies.

Am Nu'an, Oetimu's storyteller, was going blind and eventually stepped into a hole he thought was a pond and died. Ever since, people started asking Am Siki to take on the role. It seemed like a good fit: as a national hero, he had more than enough life experiences to recount and didn't have a wife to make love to on rainy days. And they were right. Children were mesmerized by Am Siki. Not only did their new storyteller talk about ancient times and the tribes that used to live on their island, but he also narrated episodes from his own exceptional life: stories detailing how he managed to emerge victorious from altercations with evil spirits and wild beasts in the backlands, or describing how he fell captive to the Nippon, and other tremendous tales. He was a consistently excellent storyteller, the kind who knew how to combine colorful verbs with evocative gestures, which made the kids lose track of time. Even though he occasionally repeated an anecdote from the perspective of a different character, his audience would listen with amazement, as though they had no idea how the story would end.

And yet, Am Siki's skill at telling riveting tales concerned some adults in Oetimu. He certainly knew how to describe events in detail and with images that were so easy to picture, but he did so with topics that weren't appropriate for young children. Some stories simply described how the lontar fruit had transformed into earth's first woman, but others detailed how Japanese soldiers raped his horse, complete with an aside about the length and girth of each soldier's genitalia, whether it was only as big as a pinky or as fat as a child's thumb. This kind of information would sometimes turn into an interactive game; Am Siki might ask, for example, for the kids to stick out their hands so he could point out whose index finger matched the size of Tsuchihashi's penis, or whose thumb was roughly as thick as Sadashichi's. There were days where he'd do nothing more than describe the animals in the forest, but at other times he'd imitate the powerful thrusting of soldiers behind his mare's buttocks. As their worries mounted, a few of the parents refused to let their children go to the lopo.

"You're staying home today and taking a nap. Am Siki's stories aren't educational."

But children who sleep when it's raining get stung by scorpions, and children who don't sleep are notoriously bothersome, since all they do is beg and beg their parents to tell them stories. All of this means that parents had no opportunity to make new babies and finally agreed that the kids could keep going to Am Siki. But every time the kids came home, parents would grill them about the details of their storyteller's anecdotes and correct them with more appropriate versions.

"What did Am Siki tell you about today?"

"A lot of things. Thieves from the west, neonbal-bali and wild dogs, and the Japanese."

"Did he talk about a horse that was raped?"

The child would nod.

"Don't believe any of that," the parents would say. "The Japanese don't rape horses. They're too short."

IV

When he got off of his horse and saw the woman howling in front of Prosperity General Store, surrounded by apprehensive onlookers and strong men with glinting eyes ready to strike, Am Siki felt pity. The girl's legs were so skinny and desiccated it seemed impossible that they could support her distended stomach. Her loose hair was matted against her face and the nape of her neck; her clothes tattered and shapeless; her skin covered with sores and debris; a rancid smell emanating from her body. The only thing that indicated she was a woman was the tenor of her resounding cries.

He approached the figure and held out his hand. The girl fell silent and met his eyes straight on. Am Siki tried to soothe the girl with a steady gaze, silently communicating that everything was going to be alright, and almost imperceptibly, her expression relaxed, her body slumped, and tears collected in her eyes. But this time her sobs were deeper and full of feeling; her shoulders shook and her mouth hung open. When she collapsed, Am Siki came over to put his arm around the woman, supporting her so that she wouldn't fall over. She cried harder in Am Siki's embrace. The women watching also started crying, while the children sulked, disappointed that they didn't get to witness a supernatural battle.

"Huh, so there's not going to be a fight after all," someone muttered.

"How could there be? The witch gave up after just one look at Am Siki," someone else interjected.

With that, the town's respect for Am Siki grew even greater.

A few women tried to join in and help, but the moment they stepped within a meter of the pair, the girl started lashing out, struggling to get away. Am Siki gestured to the women to keep their distance and went back to soothing the girl.

After some time passed, everyone could see that the woman only wanted to be around Am Siki and that their presence was only making his job harder. The crowd gradually dispersed. Am Siki signaled to Am Naijuf and the other elders that he was prepared to take care of the girl by himself, and finally, everyone left.

Only then did Am Siki lift the girl's thin body onto his horse and ride home. There was only one place to sleep in his small house – a badly constructed bamboo cot that creaked with the slightest movement – and that's where Am Siki let the girl rest. He moved his things to the 'saenhanâ and then boiled cassava with sufmuti root, koknabâ shoots, eagle talons, and a few other ingredients.

It was dark by the time the girl woke up. She picked up the castor oil lamp hanging from a post in the middle of the room, walked outside, and for a moment looked up at the nighttime sky filled with stars. She went into the 'saenhanâ, where Am Siki was asleep on some sacks next to the fire.

Gingerly, she creeped towards the large clay pot sitting on top of a low flame and lifted the coconut shell lid to peer inside. Spotting cassava floating in broth, she fished a piece out with her free hand. It was so hot that she jerked back and dropped the coconut shell, which clattered to the ground and woke Am Siki up. He kept still for a few moments before rubbing his eyes, pretending that he hadn't noticed the girl acting so foolishly. Then he picked up a ladle hanging from a rack on the wall and spooned a large serving of cassava onto a bamboo plate.

Laura, who had only foraged leaves and lapped river water for months, eyed the food greedily. She pounced on the plate as though someone was about to fight her for the plate and started inhaling her portion. Once in a while, she panted from the heat of the steaming tuber, smacking her tongue against the roof of her mouth like a pig. Scraps of chewed up food gathered in the corners of her lips. Am Siki waited silently. A chilly breeze blew in from the east, and the sound of the girl chewing mixed with the chirps of crickets and other nighttime animals.

After consuming twelve large portions, the girl burped and leaned against a nearby post, staring with an empty gaze at the flame from the oil lamp flickering in the wind. Am Siki had gotten used to the smell of the girl, but flies started circling her yet again.

A few minutes passed and then she stood up, picked up the lamp, and went outside. She pulled down her pants and defecated on the ground next to the 'saenhanâ, cleaned herself up with some leaves, and then went back to Am Siki's cot to rest. While she slept, her stomach heavy with cassava and medicinal herbs, Am Siki smeared ointments on her skin.

And that's what happened every day: after waking up from a long night of sleep, the young woman went to the 'saenhanâ and ate. Sometimes, she relieved herself outside before falling back asleep, at which point Am Siki applied salves to her wounds, which had started scabbing over. With every meal, always prepared using medicinal herbs, she slowly regained her heath. On day fourteen, there was a bit of meat on her bones and puss had stopped leaking from her sores. Flies still pursued her every step and the town dogs had taken to hanging around Am Siki's house, following the scent of the girl's feces, which grew more potent by the day.

On day twenty-five, the girl's body had filled out, her legs were sturdy enough to support the rest of her body, her scabs started to peel, and the army of flies had tired of following her. She also started using the toilet. On day thirty-four, she spoke for the first time. When she realized that the old man could understand what she said, she hugged him. In his youth, Am Siki had traded with the Portakes – that's what he called the Portuguese – so he was able to understand the language pretty well.

"The Dutch are not good traders," he told the girl. "They always attack and take things for themselves. The Japanese, they don't trade at all. They build roads, murder, and rape."

Am Siki was more or less aware of how the world worked. He learned long ago that foreigners would always come to his land and claim it as their own, killing anyone that stood in their way. But he didn't know about the atrocities that the girl had experienced: the way the Indonesian army slaughtered people in Timor of the Rising Sun. Sure, the military had come to Oetimu a while back with orders that every communist resident be killed, but that hadn't been much of a tragedy. Only forty-seven people were murdered on the steps of Oetimu's modest chapel.

"And that was a long time ago, senhora. Many seasons have passed, and they haven't killed anyone else."

I'm not the kind of person you should address as senhora – the girl replied. "I'm not even twenty years old. I should be young, carefree, but war robbed me of that. War took everything from me, down to the eggs in my womb."

"Mocinha," Am Siki said. "Portuguese girls are lovely. They have full lips and noses that turn red like tomatoes ripening on the vine. Hey moça, listen here, what burdens your heart? Uisneno, our creator, is all-knowing. Be strong, moça, be strong. You have ancestors, don't you? It's not like your ancestors would just abandon the flowers that grow from their roots. I too have ancestors, and they've never once left my side. They come from the lontar palm and always help me. Once, when I was a laborer at Sanaplo…"

And so, in his rusty Portuguese, Am Siki recounted the story of how his ancestors helped him survive those dark years when he was imprisoned by the Japanese. He talked about the forced labor he endured and the crazed whoring out of his horse that happened before his very eyes.

The girl cried – not because of Am Siki's story, which she found crass and absurd, but because of his sincerity. While she was being tortured and as she struggled in the forest, Laura repeatedly asked herself if a single honest person still walked this earth. Then, she thought about her father, her mother, everyone else who'd been detained at the Hotel Tropical, at Sang Tai Hoo, and at countless other places on the island. Her tears fell to the rhythm of Am Siki's words.

The old man concluded his story proudly, convinced he told it exceptionally well since his listener had lost herself in his words and experienced such heightened emotions. The girl wiped her face, forcing herself to smile. Her lips tentatively found the smile that had been absent for so many months.

"And that's what happened, moça. I have lots of other stories, too. If you want, I can tell you another."

"Not right now," the girl said, and laughed.

"Alright. I think we'll have plenty of time."

Eu chamo-me Laura, avó. My name is Laura, Grandpa.

Am Siki smiled wide. There he was, being called grandfather, even though he still had a full mouth of teeth and had never been married.

A few days after Laura laughed, the girl announced that she needed a bath. The smell was only one small motivation – dirt and sweat also coated her skin as her scabs healed. The pair made a trip on horseback to the river. It was the beginning of the dry season. The earth was starting to crack, and monkeys came down from the hills to wander through corn stalks that had just started tasseling. The sun was bright and hot in the clear sky, and green leaves rustled in the breeze.

The horse walked slowly. Whenever they passed by a farmer, Laura would bury her face in Am Siki's back. The people they passed also shrunk away, stepping to the edge of the road so that the woman's witchcraft couldn't touch them, but not so far away that it would insult Am Siki. They venerated the old man for being the only person brave enough to care for the lost demon who wandered into their town.

Laura finally took a bath in the river. She scrubbed her body with a smooth stone and Sunlight Soap, then washed her hair with wild lemon. By the time she finished soaking, half of the killifish in the river were dead from the grime washing off her body.

While he waited, Am Siki looked after the lontar palms that stood on the southern bank of the river. He emptied the tubes that had filled with sap and sliced the tips off the panicles so that more could keep flowing. He appeared on the riverbank every once in a while, checking that Laura understood how to use the stone and lemon. After dropping off the tubes of sap, he paid a visit to the chief to ask for a bolt of fabric.

"The girl is taking a bath, but I don't have anything for her to wear."

"Are you going to marry her?" the chief asked.

"She's my granddaughter," Am Siki corrected him. "Someone who likes listening to my stories."

Am Siki headed back to the river with a bolt of woven tais in tow.

To his surprise, the woman waiting for him by the river was lovely, with full lips and a nose that looked like a plump tomato. Her back was speckled with scars, but her skin was flushed and clear. She wrapped herself in the fabric that Am Siki brought and, as they headed home, the news spread that the grotesque pregnant witch who wailed in front of Prosperity General Store had transformed into a lovely-looking woman – a girl with Portuguese features, wavy hair, and bright eyes. The news made its way to far-off towns, and new variations were added with each telling. Some people claimed that an angel had come to earth to test the people of Oetimu: she'd been disguised as a witch, but resumed her original form because Am Siki welcomed her. Every time someone heard the story, they embellished it anew, swearing that they would always attend church on Sundays and make offerings to their ancestors.

Eventually, people went to Am Siki's house to witness the miracle for themselves. They kissed the girl's nose and prayed for the health of her unborn child. Some brought fabric, some carried rice, others offered fruit, chicken, pork, and so on. When visitors were old enough, they'd try chatting with Laura to see how their Portuguese was holding up after so many years. Children ran around the yard while mothers cooked rice porridge. They even grumbled about Am Siki, complaining that he'd put a pregnant woman on the back of a horse without a saddle, riding through hills and fields rife with lustful monkeys, only to leave her alone in a river filled with ghosts.

"What if something happened to the baby?" they asked him.

"And where would you recommend that she take a bath?" Am Siki asked in return.

So, the town residents built a small bathroom for the girl using river tamarind for posts and lontar palm leaves for a roof. They took a new clay pot from the town lopo and carried it to the small bathhouse.

Am Siki's house was bustling ever since Laura came back from the river. Children ran to fill the clay pot with fresh water each day while women prepared delicious meals or taught the Portuguese girl a few skills – cooking, spinning thread, and weaving – so that she'd never be idle, and her future child wouldn't end up lazy.

With such care from the entire town, Laura seemed truly happy. She listened to stories with enthusiasm and exclaimed joyfully whenever she learned something new. She looked healthier, brighter even, with each passing day. The scars from her sores slowly faded and she was prettier and prettier as she prepared to give birth.

Noting how Laura had started laughing with delight like a love-struck young girl, Am Siki assumed that the girl's heartbreak had started to heal. But after she gave birth to a flawless, healthy baby boy, Laura refused to eat or drink. Am Siki realized that the girl had only stayed alive to survive her pregnancy.

"I gave birth safely, Grandpa," she said and kissed Am Siki on the nose. "Now let me go to my mom and dad."

After Laura said those words, there was no talking her out of the hunger strike. Her breastmilk dried up, and the baby was sent to Tanta Domi to be nursed.

Four days later, before she chose a name for her son, the girl died. The town buried her just as they would anyone else, with Catholic prayers and a few traditional rituals. The night after she was put in the ground, dogs barked nonstop and the wind howled, filling Oetimu with noise. Trees crashed to the ground and monkeys ran down from the hills. The girl wasn't going anywhere, people said to themselves. She would stay on in Oetimu to protect her son.

If the decision had been entirely up to Am Siki, the child would be called Portakes Oetimu, since, as he put it: the boy is a Portakes, born in Oetimu. But on the day of the baby's baptism, the pastor added the name Siprianus, since the child's birthday coincided with the celebration of Saint Cyprian, the bishop of Carthage who was martyred after Emperor Valerian chopped off his head.

And so the boy was christened Siprianus Portakes Oetimu. Years later, people called him Ipi. Sergeant Ipi.

V

Located in the southern corner of the Makmur Sentosa District, Oetimu was the hub connecting the large capital city with old rural towns scattered across the lowlands and hills – the few traditional settlements that had managed to survive destruction at the hands of the Dutch. The town was neither too busy nor too quiet, not too big, not too small. The pothole-ridden district highway ended at the southern edge of town near the border with the eastern province, where soldiers were always stationed. Roads connecting Oetimu to rural towns were basically footpaths that could only be traversed at certain times of year. In the rainy season, these dirt roads became swamps, and it was said that the rivers without bridges rose so high that only the most honest of Timorese people were capable of crossing them – that is, people who always spoke and acted with integrity, even in the dead of night when their ancestors couldn't see them. In the dry season, wild animals slinked through nearby foliage, waiting for an unsuspecting snack to walk by. Traders, people selling medicine, and even pastors from the area always thought twenty-two times before making the journey. They weren't just afraid of the beasts; all of them were well-versed in trickery, which meant they wouldn't dare traverse overflowing rivers.

Since outsiders never had the stomach to venture down the dirt roads and into the forest, only people from remote areas made the trek to Oetimu. Each Sunday, they'd arrive in town to attend mass in the Santa Maria Chapel and buy necessities from Prosperity General Store. For many years now, the store was the beating heart of the town, the sole institution that kept Oetimu alive. It was an establishment that sold everything you could possibly imagine, from matches to rice, sewing needles to coffins. And Prosperity General Store didn't just sell things: it also acted as a trading post, where farmers could barter their tomatoes, hot peppers, candlenut, sandalwood, and especially cassava and corn. There were no rice paddies in Oetimu; people cultivated tubers and maize on the land that sloped down from the hills. But rice was nevertheless a staple in their diet, and the vast majority of town residents were ashamed to eat cassava and corn – and if people weren't embarrassed to eat local crops, they nevertheless felt sick to their stomachs whenever they did, since their guts were used to digesting rice. Every harvest season, officials from the Ministry of Information drove big trucks through the town, blasting official regulations through huge loudspeakers:

"Ladies and gentlemen, smart, healthy residents of Oetimu – harvest season is here! We're about to have a heaping crop of corn and cassava, but do you even know what that slop does to your body? It's what our ancestors ate – our ancestors, who were stupid and malnourished and colonized, all because they ate corn and cassava. There's new research in the West showing that these crops contain substances that make your brain weak! These are foods with no nutritional benefits, none whatsoever!

The meaning of this, residents of Oetimu, is that it is your responsibility to reject these primitive, ill-advised habits. Eat rice! Rice will make your children cultured and civilized, and they'll grow up to believe in One Almighty God, following the first precept of our nation's core values, our Pancasila."

The announcement rolled through town year after year, beginning roughly when the communists had been rounded up and killed. It was a message that people from Oetimu never forgot. And so, each year during the harvest, farmers hauled their corn and cassava to Prosperity General Store to trade for rice. Nearly four kilograms of shelled corn was worth a little less than a kilo of rice, and a full kilo of raw cassava could only be traded for two instant noodle packets. If you sweetened the deal with a heaping basket of peanuts, you'd get a single egg. People from remote towns crossed flooding rivers and faced wild beasts just to trade their goods at Prosperity General Store. Some walked dozens of kilometers with huge bunches of bananas on their backs, which were good for bartering when fried into tasty chips. Others hauled sandalwood wearing flimsy flipflops on their feet, only to return home barefoot, worried that the long journey might ruin the new shoes they'd just purchased in town. If they happened to stumble or trip on a sharp piece of coral, or if a snail shell pierced the soles of their feet, they'd pause on the side of the path, treat their bloody injuries, and think about how blessed they were that the new sandals were safe – after all, if they hadn't been barefoot, the shoes would've borne casualties instead of their skin.

The small building next to the store was another important destination for those visiting Oetimu. Leaning at a slight angle, the Santa Maria Chapel had a roof made from reeds, walls built with bebak, and a slatted mahogany door riddled with termite holes. The entryways and pews were always adorned with spiders since the building was only open one day a week, on Sundays, when Father Laurensius gave mass. Father Laurensius was the town's pastor. He relished eating soggy bread, boasted a round potbelly (as priests often do), and complained incessantly when his old car shuddered as his driver navigated the rutted district road.

"The Japanese built this road, and no one's fixed a thing since," he'd say.

His driver was a young man who grew up in an orphanage. The church had always treated him like a real human being – so he felt obliged to pay back that debt by lowering his eyes and agreeing with whatever came out of the pastor's mouth.

"We're lucky to have this car, Alfonsius," Father Laurensius continued. "You know, German cars are sturdy. Stronger than seven horses, even."

"Yes, Mister Father, yes."

In addition to leading mass, Father Laurensius also handed out free medicine to sick people who then had to wait a full week to get a second dose. He usually concluded his service with a brief prayer for those who died before making it to Sunday.

"And so, faithful people of Oetimu," Father Laurensius would say, "if you're sick, pray and endure in God's grace. Do not visit a healer or use chewed up leaves, stems, roots, or other useless plants to cure your body. And do not let healers smear your skin with spit and betel nut. All of these things are filled with bacteria, with germs, and carry sickness. It's clear, they will kill you, and faster still if spells are cast... Oh, that is the meaning of idolatry, and idolatry violates the will of God! God says:

you are my children, and mine alone! Listen to Him! What do you think will happen if you worship idols? Death will strike you down – is that not so? God is all-knowing, and sinners will be punished."

A bustling mototaxi station stood next to the chapel. After he came back from Java, Om Pati introduced this new line of work to Oetimu: you simply offer people a ride on your motorbike and then ask for money in return. Instead of working in the fields, teenagers put up their land titles as collateral and bought motorbikes on credit. But it turned out people in Oetimu would rather walk or ride horses than pay for a ride, so the teens usually didn't have much to do but hang around the mototaxi station drinking and playing chess. When a payment was due for their bikes, they'd steal a pig from their father's farm and sell it to Baba Ong. It wasn't uncommon for parents to report stolen livestock – a crime that Sergeant Ipi investigated himself – only to discover that the culprit was their own child. The town policeman was more than happy to punch, kick, and slap the kids around in order to teach them a lesson, not that it did any good; they'd just repeat their crimes the following month.

Sergeant Ipi was stationed at the police post on the northern edge of Oetimu. Whenever he drove to the town center on his motorbike, the mototaxi drivers would pray that the policeman was having a good day. If not, he'd look for any possible infraction of the law and beat them up mercilessly. He would inspect every inch of their vehicles, accuse them of placing bets on their chess games, or announce that the way they were looking at him was a "threat to an officer on duty." If he was having a good day, on the other hand, Sergeant Ipi would tell them all sorts of funny stories until the teens at the mototaxi stop were bent over laughing. Sometimes, he'd even stop Baba Ong's delivery truck and wrestle money out of the driver:

"Om Jon! Yeah, I'm talking to you, Jonny Bottle," that's the sort of thing he'd hell. "Give me five thousand so that our grandkids here can have a drink."

If Jon the Drunk tried to make an excuse about how his kids needed school supplies or how his wife was pregnant, Sergeant Ipi would pull the man down from the truck and smack him around.

"A bit of spare cash won't make you poor. Hand it over."

Sometimes he wouldn't stop there. He'd also hop into the bed of the pickup truck and check to see if there were any cowering schoolchildren hitching a ride to school. If he found some, he'd undo his belt, thrash them, and then order the children to do push-ups while lecturing them about the dangers of riding in a truck bed.

And so, whenever Sergeant Ipi appeared in town, someone inevitably ended up black and blue, whether a mototaxi driver, a deliveryman, or a kid on their way to school. No one was brave enough to challenge the policeman; he was a uniformed officer of the state and acted in the name of the Indonesian Republic for the good of all citizens. A challenge to Sergeant Ipi was a challenge to the nation. Either type of defiance would make you a communist, and communists end up dead, their corpses thrown into the soft soil of the teak forest.

That said, it's not as though every officer took such delight in beating people up. There were other soldiers stationed on the southern edge of town; they also wore uniforms and went into the center of Oetimu to buy cigarettes and razors at Prosperity General Store. These men were muscular and always seemed to be smiling, since they had slightly buck teeth (as was often the case with people from Java). If they passed by the mototaxi stop, they'd share a pack of cigarettes with the boys and ask if anyone knew of girls they could sleep with. Other than Neeta, that is, since she was a little crazy. She had a very big mouth and was famously good at sucking cock, but she also got a kick out of gossiping about how small Javanese soldiers' dicks were compared to those of the Timorese militia, which made the men uncomfortable. Since the mototaxi stop was right in front of Oetimu High School, the boys promised that the soldiers would be the first to know if there was ever a young girl who decided to become a prostitute.

Oetimu High School had been established eight years earlier. Originally, the chief donated a plot of his ancestral land on the east side of town for a refugee camp, but then he changed his mind and asked the district to build a high school there instead. Children in Oetimu liked school, but they had to walk all the way to the district capital. The local government agreed, and plans were drawn up – the school would accept students from refugee families as well as from Oetimu and the surrounding areas. The building was simple: a longhouse made from bebak with a reed roof, partitioned into three rooms – a classroom, a principal's office, and a teacher's lounge. There were a lot of students, but hardly any purchased the school uniform. Most couldn't even afford shoes or the little caps adorned with the school crest.

It was to this same school that Om Daniel took Silvy when she arrived in Oetimu. Om Daniel was a tax collector, which meant he wasn't very well liked, but on that day when he dropped Silvy off at school, people looked at him affably, hoping they might be introduced to the young girl by his side. Silvy had stolen Oetimu's heart. She was polite, she smelled wonderful, and her face was captivating. Every man in town dreamed of making her his wife, and she appeared in the wet dreams of all the young boys.

Sergeant Ipi had already heard whispers about the stunning girl who arrived in Oetimu. Supposedly, she hailed a mototaxi from the

Kefamenanu Bus Terminal and then paid for the ride with a large bill without asking for change. The man who drove her gave the full report: She thanked me with a voice as sweet as an angel in a nativity play, and her eyes were as clear as the headwaters of a river.

The news became the hottest topic in town, spreading even faster when Om Daniel brought the girl to the new high school. People usually talked about Brazil and Ronaldo, but all of a sudden, every conversation started and ended with Silvy.

Her peers claimed she was the smartest girl they'd ever met and that every comment she made in class was accurate. Others reported that she carried herself with the modesty of a true Timorese woman. A combination of clashing feelings grew in the chests of young men who struggled to articulate what they felt for the girl, torn as they were between the desire to cherish and honor her like a lady and a fierce need to fuck her with all their might.

And so, everyone in town talked about Silvy, even Baba Ong, who generally avoided the goings on in town and never gave a second thought to anything other than profit. He stopped Sergeant Ipi as the officer left his store one afternoon, ignoring the fact that Ipi was hungry and hurriedly trying to buy rice on credit.

"Marry her, Ipi. I've never seen a prettier girl."

"Who are you talking about?"

"You know, Daniel's niece. What's her name? Silvy? Yeah. That's the one to marry. She's a real beauty."

"You don't get out enough, Baba. You work at your store, count your money, order around the cleaning staff… Go on a vacation! You'll see that there are plenty of beautiful women out there," Sergeant Ipi replied flippantly, even though he'd never even seen the young girl in question.

"You don't get it. Look, this girl…" Baba Ong started praising Silvy with long sentences so overflowing with adjectives that Sergeant Ipi couldn't interject an excuse to leave. Finally, as the shopkeeper launched into his eighth tribute to the girl's exquisite features, he paused to take a breath and the policeman managed to slip in a quick goodbye and rush out of the store. Annoyed and hungry, he headed to the mototaxi stop to kick around the kids playing chess.

"But what did I do, officer?" one boy asked, pressing a hand to his bruised lip.

"You looked me straight in the eye when I parked my motorbike. What were you trying to say with that look, huh? Are you picking a fight? What, you're gunning to attack an officer of the state?" Sergeant Ipi kicked the boy in the stomach a few times before pushing him into the gutter. Satisfied, he fired up his bike and sped off.

No matter how buzzy the gossip was and no matter how enthusiastically Baba Ong described the girl, Sergeant Ipi was convinced that he didn't need a woman in his life. And here's why: he'd never been in love, never had a mother, and yet he was totally fine. Sure, at one point he made frequent trips to Kupang's red light district, burning through cash at karaoke bars and brothels, but those days were behind him. He didn't need a girl to feel pleasure. One hand with all five fingers was more than enough to get the job done.

He harbored no warm feelings towards his late mother. His own name – not to mention hers – was reason enough for him to feel bitter. What kind of woman saddles a child as good looking as himself with the name Siprianus? It's frankly hideous, no offense to the saint. His mother, as a Portuguese woman, had a wealth of names to choose from that people in town would have actually appreciated. He could've been a Ronaldo, or Rivaldo, or Bebeto… Cafu wasn't a bad option either, no one has a problem with the name Cafu. Sure, Ramos Horta or Xanana wouldn't do, of course, he didn't want to be seen as a terrorist. But his mother decided to die before leaving him with a decent name, and just like that, she abandoned him to be baptized Siprianus, and he was cursed to sit through biology class after biology class at school while the rest of the kids pointed at the anatomy drawings in their textbooks and called him Anus.

His grandfather wasn't any better. He was to blame for Sergeant Ipi's middle name, which was undeniably terrible. It was so bad that Ipi often chose not to write it on official documents, and if he was forced to, he'd just shorten it to "P." Por-ta-kes – what kind of name is that?

Hunger gnawed at his stomach when he got back to the station, so he started cooking right away. The cord to his electric rice cooker was broken and only worked when it was carefully propped up with a stack of paper. He'd already asked for a new rice cooker twice, but the head of his unit had been replaced with a new arrival from Java who'd never heard of Am Siki, and so his requests were always brushed away. His superior even asked why someone with a sergeant's rank was stationed alone in Oetimu, as though he commanded the entire town. He had no clue who Ipi's grandfather was, that's for sure.

While waiting for the rice, Sergeant Ipi filled out his reports. The number of crimes had gone down that week. One farmer reported a pig stolen; Ipi had already beaten the man's son to a pulp. A mototaxi driver hit a dog and kept driving, dragging the animal twenty-five feet. The dog died, the bike was practically totaled, and the driver himself was already injured, but Ipi still made a point to punch him around a bit, ensuring he wouldn't be fit to drive. A resident had made a statement about how some of his teak trees had been chopped down, but Martin Kabiti was the culprit and had already bribed Ipi to cover up the crime, so the police officer was just waiting for an opportunity to ruff up the man who'd made the report. There was no need for that particular entry to go into the books, not unless Ipi wanted to share the bribe with the other officers in his unit.

Ding! The rice cooker. Sergeant Ipi grabbed some lu'at and dendeng from the cabinet, scooped up a heaping spoonful of steaming rice, and started to devour his lunch while simultaneously blowing on each mouthful to cool it down. While he was still chewing, a teacher drove up to the station, parked his motorbike in the middle of the yard, and called out Sergeant Ipi's name with a panicked look on his face.

"Sergeant, Sergeant!"

"What is it, Darius?"

"Two of my students in class 2C, Tafin and Kletus, just got into a fight. They're threatening each other with machetes, no one can figure out why."

"Who the hell let them bring machetes to school?"

"It's community service day. Students are either fixing the school fence or working on the principal's pig pen, and they all had to bring tools. Now these two are fighting. We finally managed to corral them into the teachers' lounge, but I think you should get there as soon as possible."

Sergeant Ipi took another bite of food and nodded, gesturing for the teacher to leave. Darius thanked him, causally noted that the police station windows needed cleaning, and then headed back to the school.

Boys fought all the time when Ipi was young, but no one beat up the weak kids and no one used weapons. These days, on the other hand, you had schoolchildren threatening each other with machetes. One year earlier, during the growing season, Ameta, the son of a refugee, cut off Fanus's finger. Fanus's older brother was pissed and got a bunch of his friends together to plot their revenge. These kinds of conflicts tended to break out between the boys from Oetimu and the nearby refugee camp. Kids from the camp fired homemade pistols into the air and waved knives, shouting: "What do you want, Oetimu? We're not from these parts – we're from the east. And you know what happens in East Timor? Bullets whizz past your ears and graze the bridge of your nose. Death doesn't scare us." But then the local punks came with their own arrows and machetes and Molotov cocktails, yelling threats of their own: "If you all are so brave, why did you come running to our side of the island like scared little dogs? Come any closer and we'll hack your skinny bodies to bits."

Luckily, adults quelled the tension before a real fight broke out. Sergeant Ipi knocked around the kids from town, Martin Kabiti handled the refugees, and armed soldiers stood by in case anything got out of control. The warring factions ended up making peace and drank sopi together. Ever since that day, the town agreed that if young boys ever fought with weapons, police were best suited to handle the situation.

And so, Sergeant Ipi finished his lunch and then headed straight to Oetimu High School. He found the two kids and started teaching them a lesson: he dragged them to the middle of the lawn, took off his belt, and thrashed them. After seven lashes, the boys begged him to stop.

"Only thieves and sissies fight with knives," Sergeant Ipi said without pausing the punishment. "And those are two kinds of men I don't want in Oetimu."

He swung hard, over and over again, until he was tired and asked for a chair. The children who'd been observing the scene rushed to find him a seat and then gazed at their classmates with pity until the teacher from their Civics and Pancasila class shooed them back inside.

"You see what happens to boys who get into fights? You saw that, didn't you? Good, so go back to class and focus on studying."

After reclining back in his chair and mopping the sweat from his forehead, Sergeant Ipi looked down at the two kids sprawled on the ground in the afternoon heat and nudged them with the toe of his shoe. He asked why they'd threatened each other with machetes. As it turned out, the disagreement itself was even dumber than the way they decided to handle it – and once again, Sergeant Ipi was forced to hear about the infamous young girl.

Five days earlier, Tafin had a dream about Miss Silvy – his first wet dream. Ashamed, he confessed what had happened to Kletus. It was scary but felt amazing, he said. Kletus told Tafin that he was a nasty boy and had tarnished Silvy's reputation in his sleep. There are so many girls in Oetimu, Kletus declared, and plenty more on magazine covers. Why did you have to disgrace Silvy like that? Kletus kept insulting Tafin all day long, calling him a pervert and making all kinds of crass remarks, leaving his friend to feel like the most sinful boy on the island.

The next morning, when they were assigned to work together on the principal's pigpen, Tafin retaliated by calling Kletus a self-righteous sicko – not much of a surprise, he added, since Kletus's mother was having an affair with Ah Teang, Baba Ong's only son. He knew the two were messing around in the abandoned house near the Cilu grasslands. Kletus was hit hard by the comment even though the rumor was widely known. Crying, he punched Tafin in the face. Tafin retaliated with a kick in the gut, which sent Kletus flying backwards to the floor. That's when Kletus grabbed his machete. I only wanted to scare Tafin, Kletus explained, and that's why I picked up the weapon. But Tafin pretended he wasn't afraid. Instead, he also picked up his machete – and that's when the teacher arrived, right as the two boys were trying to intimidate each other.

Annoyed, Sergeant Ipi stood up and slapped the boys, first one and then the other. "You can have wet dreams about whoever you want!" Sergeant Ipi said. "Who cares if it's Miss Silvy, Ah Teang's wife, or even

Lady Diana – just don't fight with knives, you idiots, for God's sake. You boys are so weak that if either of you pissed in the dirt right here, I bet your stream wouldn't leave any mark at all."

Sergeant Ipi worked himself up and started hitting the boys again. When he eventually got tired and took a break, Tafin and Kletus had taken such a beating they couldn't stand. With the little strength they had left, they begged for mercy and swore never to make a scene about wet dreams ever again. Sergeant Ipi decided to pardon them. He lectured them using some of the edifying maxims he'd learned at police academy and then ordered the boys to go find sufmuti leaves to treat their injuries.

After Tafin and Kletus left, Ipi looked up at the sun thoughtfully. He needed to meet the girl for the safety of Oetimu. Today, two schoolboys almost killed each other over her. Who could say, tomorrow Oetimu might try to secede from Indonesia on account of that girl.

———

Atino – the man who plotted the raid on Martin Kabiti's house – had once fought in the name of the Indonesian nation. He was the first man from the Viqueque district to cross the border into Manatuto and join the Indonesian army. His godfather, a cattle farmer, had been stabbed to death by the FRETILIN because he was a card-carrying UDT member. As Atino planned his revenge, he thought Indonesia might be useful to him. Together with some other local young men, he was trained, armed, and sent off to annihilate the FRETILIN.

After Indonesia took control of Dili, the FRETILIN and some other citizens of Timor fled to the mountains in the east where they organized a unified resistance movement under the acronym CNRT. They employed every tactic they could to halt the Indonesian offensive, from diplomatic appeals to guerilla warfare. The resistance really did make things difficult for the Indonesian army, killing many soldiers. They knew the land and carried protective amulets, blessed by ancestors, which is why the Indonesian military needed to recruit Atino and other Timorese men like him to block their attacks.

And it wasn't just that these locals had the lay of the land. The Timorese recruits also possessed the most important capital a fighter can have on the battlefield: they weren't scared of death. They could lead raids in the forest and march on the front lines without fear of the venomous snakes or malaria-filled mosquitos sent their way by the guerilla fighters' spells. If someone in their ranks was bitten by a snake, they knew how to treat the wound; if resistance fighters hid themselves with an incantation, they had their own mantras that would expose the enemy. Locals in the infantry were what allowed the Indonesian army to survive out in the hills, combing through remote towns and open valleys, ready to shoot anyone who disturbed the public order.

One Thursday in December 1983, the troops returned to Dili to celebrate Christmas and Atino went berserk. He was shaving in the barracks when a fellow solider told him about the Viqueque incident. Under the leadership of local police, a group in Kraras rebelled against the Indonesian state and killed twelve soldiers. "Don't worry," the man said to Atino. "We shot every one of those traitors and leveled the town to the ground. Some women and children tried to resist so, yeah, we had to kill them too."

Antino was suddenly restless.

"Did anyone survive?"

"A few of the women. But every man in that town was a subversive," the soldier said.

"Do you remember anything about a man who taught religion there?"

"The one with a big kesambi tree in front of his house? Oh yeah. He was hiding some of the insurgents; we razed the place to the ground. Poor guy, that teacher."

The soldier's tone was sympathetic, but Atino reacted by slashing the man's face with the razorblade he'd been pinching between his thumb and forefinger. Blood spilled quickly that afternoon. Shrieking like a man possessed, Atino went on a rampage, swinging at anyone or anything that stood in his way. He smashed a black and white TV, broke a commissioned officer's jaw, and incapacitated six soldiers before four others managed to restrain him.

Fuming from the humiliation of finding his face bloodied in front of a crowd, the commissioned officer pressed his gun to Atino's temple. He would have pulled the trigger if an officer who outranked him hadn't ordered him to stop. He told Atino to sit down, brought him a glass of water, and spoke to him in a mild, soothing tone.

Atino sat. He accepted the water and drank it. He looked to his left and right with a dead look in his eyes, deaf to every word said to him. A few seconds passed before he spit the water straight into the officer's face, smashed the glass, and then stabbed the man who almost shot him straight in the groin. He resumed his frenzied attack: he broke three armed soldiers' arms, wrenched a door from its hinges, and hurled a grenade into the yard of the barracks. A soldier who happened to be walking into the army base shot Atino in the stomach, and the high-ranking officer rushed to wipe the saliva his face off and grabbed his gun, ready to split Atino's head in two. But then he too was stopped by a different officer, one with an even higher rank.

"Don't shoot him – just thrown him in jail. And make sure no one lets him out till the sun rises in the west."

Tied up and bleeding from his abdomen, Atino was tossed into a cell. From that day onwards, every soldier would stop by for a visit when they were having a bad day. They could bludgeon a prisoner to a pulp without violating the one clear order from their superiors: keep the man alive.

"They might be untrained, but they have our fighting spirit," one officer said, commenting on the local men in the infantry. "They love their country and bring their all to the battlefield. These men play an important role in service of our nation, which makes them our brothers, fellow children of the motherland, ready to sacrifice their lives for the unity of the Indonesian Republic."

Those words stopped the others from killing Atino even though low-ranking officers had been itching to shoot local recruits for a long time. The locals had the gall to act however they pleased just because they knew the terrain. Plus, they were seen as valued assets to their superiors. Javanese soldiers mocked the young recruits constantly, calling them monkeys.

"Hey, monkey, you got a cigarette?"

"What are you daydreaming about, monkey? What, you craving Javanese pussy?"

The locals calmly explained that referring to peers with a racist nickname was out of line, but the soldiers just sneered.

"Since when are we peers, monkey? If I remember correctly, I changed your diapers out in the jungle."

The only time they managed to restrain themselves was during prayers, as though they worried God might come down to earth at that very moment for Judgement Day.

Now that Atino had been thrown in jail, he became a consolation prize for every occasion. Whenever a soldier was mad at his superior, or whenever he missed his girlfriend who was far away on a distant island, he could just walk to the prison and kick the local around. And if a soldier was pleased because he received a positive evaluation from an officer or a pledge of loyalty from his sweetheart, he'd visit the prison for a celebratory beating.

Two weeks into the new year, Atino was transferred to Java. A few officers made the call out of fear that a riot was brewing among local recruits who were increasingly unsettled by the Javanese soldiers who harassed their compatriot morning, noon, and night.

On Java, Atino was moved from prison to prison, making his way westward towards Jakarta. He was never tried for his crimes, but he was also never executed. The higher-ups immediately recognized the kind of soldier he was, since they'd all been stationed in East Timor at one point or another and interacted with troops of local fighters, famous for their tenacity and loyalty. But wherever Atino went, a document traveled with him explaining that he was a traitor who knocked the teeth out of a commissioned officer's mouth. And that always meant he was greeted with a fresh beating.

In the final months of 1984, the officer who ordered that Atino be imprisoned until the sun rose in the west walked into a Jakarta prison. He had garnered even more prestige during his deployment in Timor and returned to Indonesia's capital with a higher rank, more subordinates, and many, many obligations. One of his duties was to eradicate any enemies of the state remaining in Jakarta and to stamp out all budding threats to public order.

"Every time I think about this operation I remember you, Atino," the officer said. "You're a fighter, I know it. I've reviewed your file, and you always followed orders. Meanwhile, there are plenty of criminals out there on the streets trying to upset the peace and stir unrest, threatening the unity of this country. So, I'm here to cut you a deal. Either you stay here and get treated like a dog or you can be free, so long as you help me blast the brains out of some traitors. The choice is yours."

It made sense to take the job when the alternative was an indefinite stay in a prison cell. Atino was released and driven to a large house in South Jakarta surrounded by a high fence. A few dogs roamed around the spacious yard and inside there was some workout equipment and twelve bedrooms. Whoever lived there had no reason to leave the compound. The other residents were all from islands in eastern Indonesia: three from Ambon, six from Flores, four from Sulawesi, and seven others from Timor. They all seemed to have some amount of military training, since they stood up straight and kept their belongings neat. Every day, a soldier came to the house, dropped off some supplies, and then explained the plan for an operation, listing the names of the individuals who were to be eliminated.

After being assigned to logistics for roughly a week, Atino was promoted and joined an operation. He left the house each evening, sometimes in the afternoon, and went to shoot people who disturbed public order. That is to say, he shot criminals committing armed robberies, gangsters covered in tattoos, unarmed students living in rooms crammed with books, and anyone else on the list of names.

Atino worked hard and quickly became a valuable asset. His jobs were clean, he followed orders. He had excellent aim, and sometimes, he didn't even need to use a gun, since he knew how to sneak up on someone from behind and kill them with his bare hands.

Soon enough, he made a name for himself among the assassins. But what no one knew is that while he murdered all of these nobodies, he was secretly plotting to kill people who were far more important. He'd done some digging and began writing up his own list of names – a list of the people who'd been responsible for the slaughter of his family in Kraras.

VI

Like most people in Oetimu, Om Daniel had a modest home. Its weathered walls, built using bebak, were peeling in a few places, worn down from age and termites. A few patches were still chalky white from Independence Day celebrations when the house had been painted with the colors of the Indonesian flag. The roof was made from reeds, the floor from cement – signs that the family was rather well-off. Inside there were four rooms: a living room for receiving guests, two bedrooms, and a dining room that doubled as a space for the family to spend time together. That last room also had a little gas stove in one corner, which was used when no one wanted to bother going out to the kitchen, usually because it was raining or because the family didn't feel like lighting a fire. The kitchen stood apart from the rest of the house, just about four leaps of a horse away, in a little unfinished building; some of the materials for the kitchen walls had been used to fix up the bathroom so from outside you could catch a glance of the bamboo chaise that Om Daniel's father used to rest on back when he was still alive. A lopo built with sturdy wooden pillars stood in front of the house, but antlion holes peppered the unpaved earth, indicating that the space was rarely used.

After knocking twice, Sergeant Ipi decided to knock once more and leave if no one answered. Maybe it was an inconvenient time, he thought. He rarely visited that particular house or spoke to Om Daniel, an upstanding citizen who didn't drink sopi except during ceremonies for his ancestors and who attended church each week without fail, all of which meant he had no business with the police. The man wasn't very well liked either; his job was to appear with unpaid bills in hand, and whenever anyone saw him out and about, they were reminded of all the taxes they still had to pay, which made them think about how difficult life was. No matter the choices you make, you'll always have to cough up cash for the government.

The sun hung over Oetimu, pounding down on Sergeant Ipi. He raised his arm to knock again, calling out two long hellos. Three puppies scampered out from behind the house, chasing after their mother and yapping for milk. Instinctively, Ipi put a hand on his pistol when the door swung open. The girl stood before him, still in her school uniform. For a second, he felt the earth stop spinning.

"Sorry, sorry, I was out back…" the girl said. As she spoke, the corners of her lips pulled back slightly, revealing two straight rows of white teeth. The expression on her face was so perfectly adjusted to her words that when she apologized, her mouth also appeared to be sorry, as did her lips, her eyes, and every part of her body.

The officer smiled slightly, then dropped his gaze without saying a word.

"Please, come in," she continued, shooing away the barking dogs: *psst*!

The pups spun around and dashed back behind the house when the girl opened the door wide. Sergeant Ipi cleared his throat in an attempt to regain composure. As he sat on the stoop to pull off his shoes, he took a few deep breaths. The sun was still scorching. The orchids blooming from a half-dead, dusty jackfruit tree looked like little nipples. He stepped inside.

"Please, take a seat. Oh, wait…" her invitation trailed off, and she started moving tall stacks of books from the wooden chair to join other volumes scatted around the floor. "Sorry it's so messy."

Sergeant Ipi sat in the chair. The girl also took a seat without any hint of awkwardness, as though she were from some other town where young women weren't embarrassed to sit with guests. Ipi suddenly recalled why he'd called on Om Daniel in the first place, but he forgot how he'd planned to deliver his message. He thought about it for a second, growing unsure. Why had he blamed this sweet girl for an idiotic fight between two high school boys?

But Silvy was waiting for him to say something.

"Is Om Daniel around?" That was the first thing that popped into Sergeant Ipi's head.

"Om Daniel and Tanta Mery took Ori to the city," she replied, her back straight and her words clear. "They met with the parish priest because Ori's in fourth grade now and ready for his first communion. But that would take too long here in Oetimu… the church only organizes it once every three years, right? So, Ori wanted to go to the city instead. That's all."

When she finished speaking, Sergeant Ipi didn't how to respond. Silence enveloped the room. Beads of sweat started to collect on Ipi's brow, but he couldn't think of how to add to the conversation. The clock was ticking.

"Uh…oh, I'm sorry, I forgot to ask," the girl said after a long pause. "Would you like something to drink?"

"Oh," Sergeant Ipi was overjoyed. He finally had an opportunity to participate. "No need," he replied.

And again, they were silent. Not a single question came to mind. Tick, tock. Tick, tock.

"Erm," again, the girl spoke. Again, Sergeant Ipi was happy. "We haven't introduced ourselves," she said and reached out for a handshake, just as a girl from the city would.

Sergeant Ipi took her hand.

"I know who you are. Silvy, right?"

She smiled.

"I know who you are, too, Sergeant Ipi."

"How did you know my name?" Ipi's nostrils flared slightly. Well, well, this girl knows who I am. Surely, she asked around about me – she must like me. Aha.

"That's how," she replied, pointing to the right side of his chest. He looked down and remembered that his name was printed across his shirt in big letters: SERGEANT IPI.

Oh.

He tried to hide his embarrassment.

Silvy laughed.

"Hey now," she said, "I was just joking around. Who hasn't heard of Sergeant Ipi?"

Ipi turned his face to the wall. This time, his nostrils really were flaring. Hmm...I was right, he said to himself. But he still couldn't think of anything to say to her. Tick. Tock.

"Erm," Silvy jumped in again, but then hesitated, as though she didn't know how to continue. Sergeant Ipi looked at her, waiting for her to speak. Those eyes. That nose. He started memorizing the contours of her face in his mind.

"Are you hungry?"

For a second, Ipi didn't know what to say. If he told her he wasn't hungry, that meant he'd need to leave soon, since the girl probably wanted to eat lunch. He didn't want to leave; he wanted to stay and listen to the sound of her voice. But it would be shameless to say that yes, he was hungry – after all, he'd just wolfed down a strip of deer jerky the length of a ruler.

But what was that smell?

"Well, actually…" Silvy spoke hesitantly, "actually… I was frying up some eggs, but it seems like…they might've…burned a bit…"

She spoke with an oddly resigned expression on her face, as though she'd just watched a horse gallop off a precipice and lacked the will-power to run and save it.

Sergeant Ipi looked at her with concern.

"Do you mind if I go take a look at them?"

"The eggs are burning, Miss Silvy, and you want my permission to go check on them, really?"

Silvy made a silly face and dashed into the back room. Sergeant Ipi chuckled, Silvy let out a loud laugh, and the awkwardness in the room melted. A second later, she called out from the other room to report on the condition of the eggs, which were glued to the base of the pan. Looks like a baby's head, fresh out the womb, she said. But

Sergeant Ipi had never seen anyone give birth. Like a fish that got run over by a truck, she added. He laughed: "Why did the fish cross the road?"

"Well, they look weird. It's hard to describe. Come over here, see for yourself."

"Can I?" Sergeant Ipi asked.

"Only if your intentions are good," Silvy replied.

The desire to see what a fish would look like after being squished by a truck seemed innocent enough. Sergeant Ipi pulled back the fabric that partitioned the two rooms and went over to Silvy, peering at the pan she held in her hand. The blob really was oddly shaped. The young police officer snorted and said that not even a dog would deign to eat an egg in that condition. Silvy walked to the back door and scraped off the pan, calling out the names of the pups, who dashed towards her to scramble over the scraps.

Then the pair agreed to fry another two eggs. Spotting a green papaya sitting near the little stove, Sergeant Ipi asked if Silvy liked the savory fruit.

Definitely, I love that it's chewy and just a bit bitter. But I don't know how to cook it, and I've never seen a recipe for it before.

"Leave that to me, Miss Silvy," the sergeant said. "I've been single for a very long time – I could turn stones into bread, if I needed to."

Silvy hid her smile. It was a victorious expression, one that was not a reaction to the joke Ipi had cracked, but to the information he had just confessed.

———

While Sergeant Ipi rinsed the papaya, Silvy started asking him a long string of questions as though they were two close friends who hadn't seen each other in years. She started light, inquiring about the youngest boy Ipi had ever beaten up in his career as a policeman, and then moved onto heavier topics, like family, which was a subject Sergeant Ipi never breached with anyone else. He always dodged questions about his childhood, but now he found himself telling Silvy all sorts of things.

After Tanta Domi, the wetnurse, weaned baby Ipi, Am Siki took the little boy in. The old man raised him according to strict ancient customs to which everyone else in town had long stopped adhering. At the age of six, Ipi was able to spur a horse to a full gallop while riding backwards. He had a horse of his own, a young mare that Am Siki had broken in at the foot of Mount Mutis. By the age of seven, little Ipi was able to scale the tallest lontar palm and tap its sap. At nine, Am Siki forced the boy's horse to drink a concoction that made it act wild, as though it were drunk. Out of its mind, the horse kicked this way and that before charging all the way back to the foot of the mountain. A week later, Am Siki gave Ipi a kitchen knife and ordered him to track his horse down.

"You're only welcome back in this house with that horse in tow."

Ipi wandered the forest for weeks, battling ghosts and wild beasts, rainstorms and bad dreams, until finally, he found the horse. Then Ipi spent several additional weeks trying to approach the creature and tame it before leading it back home.

"Was Am Siki still a merchant at that point?"

Ah, well.

In the early 1990s, Am Siki's mind started to dim. The old man spent most of his time sitting in a stupor under the shade of the tamarind tree where he usually tied up his horses. He started talking to himself, narrating whatever he was doing or reflecting on Ipi's upbringing.

"The boy started high school. The school is far away, but he has a horse. He hasn't been circumcised, and yet he's industrious, just like a bird. What? What did you say? Oh, no. No. Don't you start, I said no. He's very diligent, but he's not one of us. Remember, always remember," Am Siki said, pointing his finger at nothing, "He isn't a child of the lontar palms. He's Portuguese."

Sometimes, the old man would wake up before the roosters crowed, light an oil lamp, and talk about his dreams.

"I met an Elder. He used a walking stick even though he didn't have a limp and could stand up straight. His beard was long, and he nibbled at the ends of his mustache as he spoke. I know he was one of you – who? Am Maunu, Am Leko? Or Am Neno? It could've been. It really could have been Ama Neno Manas Manikin, the one driven out by the Dutch. This is what people say about you, Am Neno: He never used a walking stick because his feet always showed him the way, no matter if his beloved rain fell or if the clouds sat in the sky, hot as dogs. Oh, and your nose, was it like a parrot's beak? People always say: If you look to the green bird that's made a home in your chest, you'll see that he hasn't given in, neither to recognition nor oblivion. Hahaha. Yes, that's definitely you. You have that parrot's beak, same as me."

He rubbed his nose as he spoke.

"But you must have other descendants, right? One would hope. Hopefully you went to Banam or Belus or courted a girl from Rote, who took you wherever she went. And hopefully you left a trail of footsteps, a few broken branches, even, and hopefully she's tending to lontar palms who knows where, right at this moment, in the dark of night. Because soon I'm going home, oh, I'm going home. Please open the door for me." His voice then became weak, whiny, like a little boy's: "Please, I don't want to die in my sleep. I don't want to die somewhere in town. Let me die under the shade of a palm."

He grew lonely in his old age. Gone was the Am Siki who raised Ipi so strictly, gone were his suspenseful stories. He still went to the town lopo, but the kids listening to him fell asleep, bored. He repeated the moral of the story over and over again, which made him sound like Father Laurensius from the Santa Maria Chapel.

"Do not kill, even if your enemy is evil. Do not rape, even if your victim is a horse. Repeat after me children, so that you never forget."

All the kids said he'd gone senile. They had never dreamed about killing people or raping horses.

Sometimes he sat in front of the 'saenhanâ with tears streaming down his cheeks. But when Ipi asked him what was troubling his heart, Am Siki said that he was fine, that nothing could make him cry.

"My eyes even stayed dry when I found my father under a lontar palm, his body stiff, his soul no longer in his body. That's how Timorese men are. We don't cry!"

Ipi pointed at the old man's cheeks and asked how Am Siki could ignore the fact that tears were running down his face.

"Hah, my little man! The elderly always suffer from watery eyes in the morning. You spend all this time at school but you're still as dense as kotpese. Just wait till you get old, you'll see how it is."

Ipi knew all too well that no matter how hard the old man tried to hide it, Am Siki felt alone, abandoned by his ancestors.

"I don't want to die in my sleep, I don't want to die in town. Let me die with all of you, in the shade."

With every new season, the men who trim lontar panicles change out the foot straps attached to the trunks of the trees, since rain, heat, and insects weather the cords. In his old age, Am Siki only replaced the straps that went ten or eleven meters up, intentionally leaving the highest ones untouched with the hopes that they might snap, swiftly bringing him home to his ancestors. What he didn't know was that in the afternoon, while he rested under the tamarind tree, Ipi snuck out to replace all of the straps, keeping the old man safe. But Am Siki never suspected. What would the boy possibly do without him?

After little Ipi received his high school diploma, Am Siki met with Am Naijuf. The chief still walked upright, and his eyesight was sharp, even though his toes were crooked, the bottoms of his feet flat, and his hair was falling out.

"Is it possible for the boy to become a kase although he's not a true descendant of the palms?" This is what Am Siki asked the chief.

Am Naijuf told his grandson, who'd become a mototaxi driver, to go to the capital and arrange a meeting with government bureaucrats. Even though the officials themselves weren't the same, everyone knew that the state had unfinished business with Am Siki.

Two weeks later, a car with red plates rolled into Oetimu. Children chased alongside it, since the car was even nicer than Baba Ong's truck. They jumped up and down, tracing their names into the dust on the car's windows with their fingers. A middle-aged woman rolled down the glass and flicked a few coins and pieces of hard candy in their direction, hoping that she'd get the chance to take a picture of village kids gleefully scrambling for money and sweets. But the children didn't try to pick any of it up, since they assumed the woman was greeting her ancestors with a modest offering.

The car pulled to a stop in front of the chief's lopo. The woman and three men stepped out. They were neatly dressed, but their suits were made from woven tenun fabric, which onlookers found very funny. City people don't know how to wear sarongs, so they have to sew tenun into western clothing, they thought, but they nevertheless made an effort to greet their guests with respect and hold back their chuckles. The woman, who was wearing dark sunglasses, was plump and never dropped her wide smile as she surveyed the people who had gathered to greet them. The men, meanwhile, craned their necks as they walked in an effort to seem taller and more authoritative, as though they were watching over the town. That's how the four entered the lopo.

The chief and several other elders were waiting out front in new sarongs. Musicians were playing the juk and he'o, and a few young women had put on lipstick and face powder in a hurry, which made their faces look a little worse than usual. They also wore brand new outfits, complete with new earrings, bracelets, beaded wooden necklaces, silver crowns, and other accessories. As the musicians played, the girls danced and draped scarves over the shoulders of the officials and the chief recited a long poem to welcome the guests, even though the officials didn't understand what was happening in the slightest.

After the niceties were complete, the chief invited the bureaucrats into the spacious lopo. Am Siki was already sitting calmly inside, wearing his sacred aluk and the sarong he'd been given decades earlier, when the town celebrated him for seven days and seven nights, a garment he reserved for special occasions. Several elders sat next to Am Siki and poured sopi for the guests. The prettiest girls milled about with betel nut and snacks. Women who weren't as pretty stood outside the lopo, bearing witness to the small event from afar as babies breastfed on their withered brown nipples. Barefoot young boys dressed in festive clothes that were too big for them hung around the lopo, their noses dripping, a sour smell emanating from their bodies, and sweat streaks running down their dirty, dusty chests. The officials sat back in amazement as they watched the dances and greetings as though they were from a different hemisphere and had never seen anything like it before. One of them held a piece of laku tobe in his hand and said, my god, I've missed this! I ate this as a kid! I mean, not that often, obviously, since it's village food and makes you dumb.

At that point, everyone was seated and pleasantries about the food, the weather, and the tiring journey from the city had been exchanged. The chief then gave Am Siki a chance to speak. The old man called Ipi over, who'd been sitting with his friends in the outer part of the lopo. The boy made a jingling sound with every step, since he was dressed from head to toe in traditional clothing, like a young warrior walking to meet his future wife.

"This one, respected guests," Am Siki said in Uab Metô, "he's the only tooth left in my mouth. A long time ago, I didn't even want him. Look at my hair, braided like a horse's unkempt mane. But Uisneno, He the guiding flame, He who burns, pried the dust from his feet and threw it into my eyes. Even though this boy isn't my arrowhead, he's a machete, one who trims panicles. He's my canine tooth. Allow him to cut that which I must leave uncut, slash whatever I cannot. But he is also Oetimu: never, ever unsheathe a knife with the assumption that you won't get hurt."

The officials frowned, glancing at one another, and asked the chief what the old man was getting at.

"Am Siki," the chief said, "the lady here and these gentlemen are from the city. They don't understand poetry or such traditional sayings.

When you're speaking to mounds of dirt, you have to state what you mean clearly, like the rain that pours during the growing season, or the sun that shines during the dry season."

Am Siki glanced around, stunned, and asked how any group of honorable people could fail to understand poetry. Besides, he'd used simple metaphors and clear diction, the sort of thing even the dumbest person in Timor would easily comprehend.

Am Siki spoke again, but this time his words were curt:

"Take him, gentlemen. Make him a kase – someone important, like you. He doesn't have any ancestors here, so he can't die under the shade of a lontar palm. But his name is Oetimu, which means he must live in this town. I've used the most naked of words to tell you this, and my bones will remember what was said today long after I'm in the ground."

The residents of Oetimu shuddered when they heard the outrage in Am Siki's voice. The officials conferred amongst themselves for a minute, then turned to Ipi and asked him what he wanted to do with his life.

"I want to be like Am Siki. I want to kill bad people."

"Young man!" Am Siki interjected. "You must not kill, even if your enemy is evil. Remember? You must not rape, even if your victim is a horse. Now, repeat!"

Ipi said both sentences word for word, and all of the children outside the lopo followed suit, showing off their recitation skills to the important adults. The teachers looked at the children with surprise, asking themselves how the boys and girls managed to repeat those statements with such perfection when they were entirely incapable of memorizing the five guiding principles of the Indonesian Pancasila.

That same day, young Ipi was taken to the city. There, he was given an exam and asked to do some training exercises; three weeks later, he was shipped off to a police academy in Bali with dozens of other teens. When he finished his education, and while all of his classmates were being assigned to different cities across the archipelago, a police station was built especially for him along the northern edge of Oetimu, complete with everything he could possibly need, including a TV and a motorbike. With his sergeant's rank, Ipi stayed there, looking after Oetimu and other nearby towns. All he really wanted was for Am Siki to come live there with him, but the old man passed away a mere three weeks after the boy left for Bali. Am Siki fell out of a lontar palm fourteen meters from the ground and died smiling.

"Now, do you remember Am Siki's parting word to me?" Sergeant Ipi asked while spooning slices of green papaya out of hot oil and into a small bowl.

"Do not kill, even if your enemy is bad," Silvy quickly answered. "Do not rape, even if your victim is a horse."

"Nope," Sergeant Ipi said.

The girl shrugged.

"His last word was *repeat*!"

Silvy was speechless for a moment, then burst into laughter.

"So, every time I do something wrong, I remember the message he gave me," Sergeant Ipi said, "and I keep making the same mistakes. Repeat!"

That made Silvy laugh again.

"I had no idea policemen could be so funny," she said. "You guys are better known for your fists."

Sergeant Ipi laughed too, then set the bowl of fried papaya on the table with a cover over it. Silvy cracked eggs into a cup and beat them with a dash of salt. Ipi cleaned out the pan and set it back on the stovetop. After all the drops of water dissipated, Silvy added some oil.

"By the way, isn't the police station pretty big?" she asked. "Bigger than your average guard post. It's more like a house. Or a city police station. Yeah, like a station-house. Hm, or a big guard post. Or…"

She entertained herself trying to come up with the perfect description, and Sergeant Ipi chuckled.

"The point is, it's too big," she said, pouring the eggs into the hot oil. "Have you always lived there alone?"

"Seems that way," Ipi replied.

Silvy snorted. "Seems?"

Sergeant Ipi didn't answer right away. He flicked his lighter a few times and cleared his throat. Since she wasn't getting an answer, Silvy turned towards him. Their eyes met, and then Ipi lowered his gaze.

"Sometimes," he said, still looking at the floor, "I feel like Am Siki is there with me. He starts talking in the yard, usually in the morning before the roosters crow. I can hear him. Sometimes he speaks to his ancestors, sometimes to me."

Silvy studied Ipi's face, contemplating what he had just told her.

"And sometimes he talks to my mom," he took a deep breath. Silvy was still looking at him.

"What kind of woman delays her death, so she can give birth?"

Silvy touched the back of Sergeant Ipi's hand. The puppies nipped at each other and yawned by the back door. Outside, a chicken clucked. A breeze gently entered the room. A motorbike rumbled in the distance.

The eggs sat on the stove, ready to eat, while Silvy and Ipi kissed.

———

They did it just like that, without closing the door or taking off their clothes. Silvy sat on the edge of the table while Sergeant Ipi kissed her. She let out a gasp when he entered her, hard as a doorknob. Just as she began moving her hips, Sergeant Ipi grunted and pulled away. His penis twitched for a few moments before spitting up a thick liquid onto Silvy's school uniform.

She smiled, partially out of obligation. As she slid down from the table to clean off her clothes, Ipi kissed her greedily, grabbing her ass and pulling her body to the floor. Shocked, she wrapped her arms around his neck as he forcefully pulled her shirt open and squeezed her chest. He took off his pants and creeped up her body, kissing her nonstop and biting her before entering her for a second time. Silvy lowered her hand and corrected the position of his penis. He was still hard as a doorknob.

The sex started off gentle but soon became wild and drawn-out. Silvy gasped and scratched Sergeant Ipi's back while he thrusted his hips as fast as a needle in a sewing machine. She moaned, rolled her eyes back, tensed her muscles and trembled. Sergeant Ipi stiffened and started hissing, as though he'd eaten too many spicy peppers. Their bodies curved into one another. Silvy felt something pour into her vagina. She caught her breath and opened her eyes.

"Pull out?"

Ipi nodded and lifted his pelvis. Silvy peeked down. The liquid that coated the sergeant's penis dripped onto her soft pubic hair.

"Did it get inside?" she asked.

Sergeant Ipi nodded.

"I might be pregnant," she said in a voice so low it could barely be heard.

Ipi kissed her forehead. He kissed her eyelids.

"Don't worry, Silvy, don't worry. I'm not going anywhere."

Silvy looked into the man's eyes and saw that he was being honest. She kissed his chin. His neck. His broad chest, covered in sweat. But all she could think of was Father Yosef's neck. Father Yosef's chest, which was hairy. And also covered in sweat.

VII

The Honorable Archbishop Agung handed Father Yosef the letter that made it official: the young pastor would be transferred from the Saint Ferdinandus Parish in the heart of the capital to Saint Helena High School near the bay. Since the school was far from the city center, and since its students were the children of fishermen, dockworkers, prostitutes, and other working-class families, the move was a topic of gossip in the clergy. People said Father Yosef wasn't being transferred, he was being exiled – ousted from a parish with nice facilities and wealthy benefactors, sent off to a poor outpost on the coast.

"Maybe they found out he had backwards, village ways and felt it wasn't appropriate for him to serve a community in the city," that's the explanation a few pastors came up with.

The fact that Father Yosef had only been ordained a few years earlier added to the shock of the news and led some clergymen to think of different theories. It was very rare for the church to trust such a young pastor to lead a community on their own, be it a parish or a school. Usually, pastors worked as assistants for years after their ordination, attending to the head pastor's every need. They carried out all of the unimportant important tasks in the parish, like organizing the schedule for mass, distributing employee salaries, or babysitting the Catholic Youth Organization. If a driver needed a day off, the assistant pastor was expected to be a chauffeur. If the cook was out sick, the assistant pastor would make all the food. Every little decision a young pastor made had to be run by their superior. Even if the head pastor had an antiquated way of doing things, the young assistant needed his blessing for the most trivial decisions, like whether or not to neuter the parish dogs, or which color was best suited for new window curtains. So, a lot of pastors were shocked: even though Saint Helena was an underfunded high school with only a few hundred half-wit students and a mere nine teachers, Father Yosef was going to be head pastor. He wouldn't ever need to seek out the blessing of those older, senile members of the church with their outdated beliefs.

The Saint Ferdinandus Parish community planned a farewell celebration for Father Yosef the evening before his departure. They invited pastors from nearby parishes, schools, and seminaries to a banquet of meats and fish: some grilled, some poached, some fried, and some marinated with spices. One community member owned a liquor store, so he trucked in the drinks ranging from illegally brewed sopi to alcohol in expensive glass bottles. By 10 PM, everyone was singing badly and at the top of their lungs, accompanied by a middle-aged, chain-smoking, pot-bellied organ player dripping with sweat. "Congratulations, Yosef. Now that you're free from all those old-timers tracking your every move, you can reign over your own little kingdom," said a young pastor whose every idea was shot down by his superior.

A different pastor who liked to joke around couldn't stop himself from asking if Father Yosef wasn't at all disappointed that he'd be leaving fertile pastures for the parched earth of a poor parish.

"Fertile pastures?" Father Yosef asked.

"Yeah, you know what I mean," the main replied, laughing.

Stony-faced, Father Yosef said, "I don't. Wouldn't you agree that our job is to find lost souls, not the landscape we prefer most?"

"Forget about it, I was just making a joke," the young pastor snapped back.

Senior pastors overheard the exchange and chided the jokester, ordering him to be more serious when speaking to his superiors. The target of their criticism skulked into the other room to grab another beer, then rebuked one of his peers for drinking too much.

The faithful congregants, meanwhile, didn't have nearly as many jokes to make. They really liked the young pastor who was leaving their church. Sure, Father Yosef used all kinds of philosophical and theological terms they didn't understand when he preached, and sure, the stories he told were usually boring and clichéd, but he was friendly, dedicated to his work, and very good-looking. He had clear skin, shining eyes, and a distinguished nose. Word had it that he'd inherited the nose from his grandfather, an Australian soldier who fought in the Oesao War and decided to stay in Amarasi after his side lost. The goodbye party was a sad occasion for the dioceses; their beloved pastor was being transferred to an institution infamous for its poverty, backwardness, and the reputations of the students it served, who were smelly children of workers. The mere name of the school incited fear among their own kids – "Saint Helena" was frequently used as a threat when children misbehaved: Clean up your act or I'm enrolling you in that high school by the coast. And just like that, the kids would fall in line.

Saint Helena was established and managed by nuns at Convent of the Sacred Heart. The school used to have a good reputation and counted a number of successful people among its alumni, including two pastors, seven nuns, and one state legislator. But by the time of Father Yosef's appointment to the school, the institution had fallen into disrepair and neglect. By then, most sisters from Sacred Heart decided to focus their energies on working with young refugees. The war in East Timor had escalated, and more and more people were running to Atambua.

Even though the Indonesian army hadn't crushed the East Timorese resistance by any stretch of the imagination, soldiers celebrated boisterously after capturing Kay Rala Xanana Gusmão. The repressive government and its numerous acts of violence, meanwhile, only made people from the east love their homeland more, adding fuel to the independence struggle. In the years following Gusmão's arrest, more and more people joined the resistance movement. The Indonesian military labeled this a threat to public safety, and soldiers shot any dissident they could find squarely in the head or, if they kept their victims alive, tossed them into their truck beds, after which the detained were never to be seen again. Those who didn't want to die left their homes, fled into the forest, and crossed the border into the western half of the island. Sometimes they sought help from churches and convents. Once they were safe from war, they were tortured by empty stomachs, traumatic memories, chronic unemployment, and all other sorts of problems that refugees have to face.

The nuns at Sacred Heart were moved by what they witnessed. God had put them on earth to serve His followers, they were sure of that, so they used their convents and schools in Atambua and Dili to house and serve refugees.

With each passing day, more and more people from East Timor ran westward in search of help and fewer women were interested in taking on the veil and serving God. So, the congregation sent their best nuns eastward to deal with fallout from the conflict. As time passed, their schools on the western half of the island, from Kefamenanu and So'e through to Kupang, started to crumble. Financially speaking, the convents focused all of their fundraising efforts on the plight of refugees, handing the schools over to the authority of the diocese.

"For now, the plight of the refugees is our most urgent call to service. We'll go back to teaching after the crisis dies down," they determined.

The nuns at Sacred Heart had been in charge of nine elementary schools, five middle schools, and three high schools – and these were the largest educational institutions in West Timor. One was Saint Helena High School on the coast near Kupang. Archbishop Agung willingly took charge of the schools.

Father Yosef's first order of business as headmaster was to search for donors willing to fund improvements to the school. This wasn't a difficult task. All he did was craft a letter outlining the school's impoverished state, making sure it was heart-wrenching and filled with sob stories. He attached some photos of the school's crumbling walls, classrooms that didn't have enough desks, and children bravely trying to study in miserable conditions. Then, he mailed his letter to people and organizations that seemed to have lots of money.

Wealthy people are often charmed by poverty and are eager to play the hero. The recipients of Father Yosef's letter would say:

"Let's be grateful that we weren't born poor. We're so fortunate that God made us rich. Just look at all of these people who have nothing! They're unlucky, but if they just worked harder and prayed more, God would have definitively rewarded them. What miserable lives they must lead.

"But yes, let's donate just a small amount of what we have and save these poor creatures. If we're generous, then God will see how kind-hearted we are and reward our efforts."

Father Yosef started receiving donations less than a week after sending the letters. Some were from honest businessmen, some from dishonest ones; some from bureaucrats and politicians who were only a little corrupt, some from those who were very corrupt. With money pouring in, Father Yosef began fixing up the school.

First, he mended the leaks in the roof and filled in cracks in the walls. Anything built from bebak was torn down and replaced with cement. He transformed an empty plot near the school into a flower garden complete with a little fish pool and a small fountain. The original barbed wire fence was removed, a tall brick wall built in its stead. In front of the school's main entrance, Father Yosef erected a seven-meter-tall plaster statue of Saint Helena surrounded by a pond. Goldfish and a white swan swam in the water, which was lit by neon spotlights. A big sign adorned the display with English words that read: WELCOME TO SAINT HELENA SENIOR HIGH SCHOOL.

Next, Father Yosef built a security guard booth near the main gate. He hired four gangsters who usually hung around by the docks and told them to put on uniforms, hold batons, and watch the school entrance day and night. He also offered jobs to Om Lamber and Tanta Yuli, an elderly couple living alone in a nearby town, abandoned by children who left for big cities and never looked back. Om Lamber became the school's head gardener, ground manager, head of security, as well as their point person for delivering coffee, while Tanta Yuli was named the school cook, head janitor, head laundrywoman, and the person in charge of doing all the tasks that women are expected to do if they never went to school.

Father Yosef forced an elderly teacher into retirement and fired a couple of younger instructors who, despite showing enthusiasm for their subjects, were too fond of complaining. He offered them sufficient severance pay and then listed the job openings, hiring four new obedient teachers with bachelor's degrees, one man, three women. In addition to their teaching roles, he also sent the new hires to nearby Catholic boarding schools to observe how dormitories are managed. He erected two new buildings: one would be a dorm for boys, the other for girls. Our facilities meet international standards, he'd say, boasting to parents. We've got clean kitchens, bathrooms with running water, bedrooms, cafeterias, recreation areas with TVs and games, laundry rooms, and exercise facilities complete with swimming pools.

Next, the pastor offered help to seven women who'd been detained for trying to work overseas in Malaysia with fake papers. The broker who falsified their documents managed to escape during the police raid, slipping out the front door and walking through a crowd of hundreds of policemen who all swore they never saw him leave the building. He even succeeded in hypnotizing the officer who drove him to El Tari Airport, at which point he flew to Batam and vanished for good. Since the criminal behind the scheme was at large, the case couldn't go to court, and since the case couldn't go to court, the women arrested in the raid sat in jail until finally Father Yosef managed to get them out. The police released the women on one condition: they were not permitted to leave the city.

"They're dangerous criminals, these ones," an officer said. "We have reason to believe that they orchestrated their boss's escape."

Father Yosef assuaged the police officers, promising to personally supervise the women and make sure they never left Saint Helena's campus, not even to visit their families. He gave them jobs as cooks for the students living in the dorms, paying them an exceedingly meager salary, which he justified by saying that much of their labor was in the service of God, since God resides in each child eating their food. Even though you don't get paid very much, he said, the Almighty will reward your efforts many times over. The women thanked the pastor for saving their souls and bodies and then dedicated themselves wholeheartedly to work.

After the renovations were complete and the dorms built, Father Yosef spruced up the school uniforms, adding blazers, ties, handkerchiefs, and other little accessories. The results were really extraordinary. When the schoolchildren walked side by side, they looked less like students and more like a crowd of Yakuza surrounded by airplane stewardesses from a Japanese gangster movie, the boys strapping, the girls elegant and educated. Father Yosef also began enticing smarter kids to register at Saint Helena. He established an entrance exam that was more difficult than national standardized tests, and the students with high scores were offered scholarships. If anyone received full marks, the school would open a savings account in the child's name. This was reason enough for all of the clever boys and girls to switch schools, while kids who weren't as gifted didn't have the slightest chance of being accepted.

And with these changes, Saint Helena High School reopened. All students were required to live in the dorms, since there was a schedule for both academics and extracurriculars. After a long day of class, students went straight to the residence halls to face their grueling evening schedules, during which they carried out community service projects, practiced foreign languages, played sports and music, learned how to sew and cook, and went to tutoring hours for their academic subjects until the bell for evening prayers finally rang at 10 PM.

All activities took place on school grounds, and students only received permission to leave campus on weekends. Even those excursions were allowed just three out of every four weekends; at the end of each month, the school put on an arts and culture festival. Local guides and staff at the tourism office always encouraged visitors to attend the show, and it was said that if you didn't go to the arts showcase at Saint Helena High School, you never really visited eastern Indonesia. A few tourists wrote up reviews of the festival for newspapers with high praise for the school, calling it a civilized institution. That sounds nice enough, but if you read any of these reviews slowly, thinking critically about what they wrote, you'd quickly see that the compliments had more to do with the arrogance of the city people who penned them than about the school itself. In those backwards, eastern islands, there's a school that tries to be as we are – and even though those people are actually primitive and unrefined, at least they made an effort, so we (as properly sophisticated people) should support the institution. But these reviews ushered in more and more tourists, both from other Indonesian islands and from abroad, which meant that the school was always bustling with activity at the end of each month.

Saint Helena quickly became a popular topic of conversation. The design of the buildings and grounds were praised, and the international standard of its facilities often referenced. Newspapers and magazines published article after article about the institution, and its students were highly respected. Somewhere between two and ten children came to the school each day to try their luck at the selection process. Standards were exacting, and parents always told their kids to study hard and then harder still just to have a chance at a seat in Saint Helena. If their child succeeded, enrollment was a badge of honor for the parents. They'd strut around their neighborhood with their heads held high, suddenly several degrees more important than the rest of their community. Meanwhile, each month, somewhere between three and five children killed themselves because they didn't pass the test. Some hung themselves in the shower, some swallowed poisonous plants, others doused themselves with kerosine and struck a match, and others still jumped off the Liliba Bridge. Enrolling in Saint Helena High School became an obsession. If you asked a young child:

"Jon, what do you want to be when you grow up? A policeman, a pastor, or a tax collector?"

Without the slightest hesitation, little Jon would reply: "I want to be a student at Saint Helena High School."

Upon hearing this answer, adults would applaud the child's noble ambitions.

As the school grew increasingly famous, it accepted more and more qualified students, which meant that the children of fishermen, dockworkers, prostitutes, and workers had no choice but to drop out. The fees had become four times as expensive, and even if the children managed to get one of the merit scholarships, the requirement that everyone live in the dorms made the less wealthy students think not just twice, but twenty-two times about whether or not to enroll. Their families were poor, which meant they could barely justify attending school for half a day let alone full time. Loads of work waited for them at home. Boys were expected to look after livestock, fish, or collect leaves to sell as animal feed to the stockyards by the docks, which earned them pennies. Girls, meanwhile, had to look after their younger siblings while their parents worked, sell knick-knacks on the beach, dry salted fish in the sun, or occupy themselves with other small tasks that would help them make ends meet and avoid the only sure way to make money – prostitution. They all knew that their lives wouldn't stray far from the material conditions they were born into. Children of fishermen die at sea, the sons of workers replace their fathers, and the daughters of whores end up fucking their mothers' customers.

When these students dropped out of Saint Helena, most stopped going to school altogether. The ones still committed to their education transferred to the public high school fourteen kilometers further away. They had to commute by minibus taxi in which drivers and konjak reeking of sopi blasted music at a volume comparable to that of five fish grenades exploding at the same time. If the children had money, they could pay for the ride. If they didn't, girls would play along as drivers coaxed them into being fondled, while boys had to accept that, without any breasts to offer as collateral, they'd have to take a beating.

"Hey, tolo! If you don't have money, why don't you just walk to school, you piece of shit? What, you think this is your grandma's car, huh? You think I pay for gas with leaves or something? Mai pu puki ni."

As time passed, all of these children gave up. Some of the young girls turned to sex work, and most of the boys dedicated their days to gathering leaves for the stockyards. They all came to terms with reality: being educated means being wealthy. Minibus taxis only drive you to school if you pay them; teachers only hold class when students pay their dues.

But getting your hands on cold hard cash – there's the challenge. Sure, you can always gather leaves in the forest if you come from nothing, but only the cows by the docks will give you a second thought.

VIII

When Silvy Hakuak Namepan received record-high marks on the Saint Helena High School entrance exam, her father, Yunus Mafut Namepan, sobbed like a herdsman who'd lost his cattle. These weren't tears of joy: he was crying because he'd failed as a parent.

Years earlier, his wife slept with a businessman, got pregnant, and ran off to Kalimantan. Yunus lost it. His sense of self vanished, and the sole reason he went to work at all was to make enough money to buy booze. Eventually, on one scorching afternoon, he received a termination letter from the Tâmoe Kaesna Public Middle School, where he worked as a teacher. He read the letter and laughed. He had some savings, after all, so what was the point of having a job?

Soon enough, Yunus burned through those savings and decided to sell off his concrete-walled house in central Kupang and the large plot of land surrounding it, moving to the coast with his daughter. He rented a tiny bebak-walled house that was on the verge of collapse. It had a reed roof, which kept the space cool, but was infested with bugs. The house had no yard and only three rooms: one for eating and relaxing, and two bedrooms – one for Silvy, the other for Yunus and his cheap whores. Since the man was almost always drunk or sleeping with prostitutes, the money he got from selling the house didn't last long. When Silvy finished elementary school, Yunus was spotted trying to pickpocket a sunbather on Lasiana Beach. Police officers beat him to a pulp and threw him in jail. The woman he'd tried to rob was the wife of a highly respected politician, which meant that after his arrest, he was a popular target for both guards and inmates who supported the ruling party.

Mere hours after Yunus was caught, the politician's wife decided to visit her assailant's home. She heard rumors that he was a drunk and had a young daughter. She called up dozens of journalists to bear witness to her meeting with the child. The woman burst into tears after the first glimpse of the hungry little girl standing in the doorway of the slanted, dirty house. She embraced the child, then opened her purse and slowly pulled out a large wad of cash, making sure the journalists' cameras panned as she handed over the gift. Unable to simply abandon the girl, she hired a nanny to watch the child while her father was in jail.

The next day, the woman's acts of kindness became the biggest news story of the year. Her heartwarming generosity earned her the nickname Mother Teresa of Timor. "Victim of Pickpocketing, Mother Teresa of Timor Sympathizes with Fatherless Child." That's the kind of headline papers printed. Photos of Mother Teresa hugging the little girl went viral, as did the shots of her handing over stacks of money; the images were plastered across the front pages, shown on broadcast television, and described in detail over the radio. In the next election, Mother Teresa of Timor even had enough votes to win a seat in congress, joining her husband in elected office.

On his ninth day in jail, Yunus looked at a lightbulb and saw Jesus emerge from the glow, asking him:

"Yunus Mafut, son of Namepan, what are you searching for?"

For the first time, Yunus regretted all of the terrible things he'd done. He cried hard, like a pig about to be castrated. Guards rushed to his cell but quickly left after the prisoner kissed their boots one by one, begging them to beat him.

"Mea culpa, mea culpa, mea máxima culpa," he wailed.

A few police officers agreed that the pickpocket had gone crazy and organized his release – despite the fact that he didn't want to go, and that he begged to stay in prison just another week.

There isn't a man on earth who wouldn't fall to his knees if he saw Jesus. Even the cruel murderer from Tarsus became a militant evangelist after being thrown off his horse, and so too did Yunus adhere to God's path after leaving his cell. Never again did he touch a bottle of alcohol or a woman's naked body. He confessed every month without fail and was always the first to arrive at Sunday Mass. He regularly testified to his encounter with God and began to search for work.

But after Mother Teresa of Timor brought a horde of journalists to Yunus's house, he couldn't shake his criminal past. A headshot of Yunus was typically printed next to that of Mother Teresa. The caption always included some kind of description, stating that he was a thief who'd abandoned his daughter, or that he was a pickpocket who tried to steal from an honorable woman, or something of the sort. All of this meant that every school he approached refused to hire him, despite the fact that he held a degree in education and had set upon a new path in life ever since the son of God came down to earth and spoke to him.

"Jesus doesn't come out of lightbulbs, you dumb pickpocket. You're so hungry and stupid you probably dreamed the whole thing up."

Failure didn't break Yunus. He couldn't work as a teacher, but he managed to get a job from Om Nus, a newspaperman and used bookseller. Yunus had mentored Om Nus's kids back at Tâmoe Kaesna Public Middle School, and now, with a humble heart, Yunus asked for work. Om Nus agreed but kept a close eye on Yunus, worried that his new employee would run off with the cash box. With no intention of robbing the business, Yunus went about his work, delivering newspapers to their subscribers and peddling novels, crosswords, and various other books to people walking along the street or waiting for the bus. He worked hard, convinced that people would eventually forget about his crimes, and he could return to the classroom.

But no one forgot anything. Every three months, Mother Teresa of Timor stopped by his house to check on Silvy. And with every new visit, journalists flocked to the scene. Yunus's photo reappeared on the front pages, right next to Mother Teresa's. Anyone who read the news would take one look at him and say: You're that thief, aren't you?

Such a public reputation meant that Yunus would never get a better job. He applied for positions as an administrator, typist, HIV awareness educator, NGO employee, and so on, but was consistently turned away. Selling newspapers and used books barely gave him enough money for food. He wanted to blame Mother Teresa, but without the money she gave Silvy, his daughter would have to drop out of school. Trying to convince himself he wasn't the worst father in the world, Yunus gave Silvy newspapers and books as presents. He could get those for free if he helped clean Om Nus's store and lawn, or if he gave his boss's kids a ride to school.

But Yunus became more and more convinced that he really was the worst father in the world when his brother-in-law, Om Daniel, came to Kupang and asked that Silvy come live with him. Om Daniel lived in Oetimu, a town far to the east. He only had one child, and he owned enough livestock to provide for Silvy.

"We can't bear to see your face smeared across the front pages," Om Daniel said. "It's not that we want to take Silvy away from you. Think of this as support coming from family. Let the girl live with us. My wife will raise her, and you'll be free to look for a job and meet someone new, a life partner. Then, you can come take her back whenever you're ready."

Yunus wanted to raise his daughter, but his financial situation was growing more precarious by the day. He didn't have any savings, and Mother Teresa of Timor's support was dependent on the woman's whims. If she decided to stop visiting Silvy, his daughter would have to drop out of school. The little girl would probably have to sell sweet wine by the side of the road, or worse still, turn to . . . ah, Yunus didn't want to even think about what might happen.

"Talk to the girl, ask her yourself," Yunus said and turned his face away, hiding the fact that he was tearing up. "If she wants to go, you're free to take her."

Silvy was called into the room, but she laughed at the question, hugged her father, and said' wanted to be near her dad for the rest of her life. No matter what her future held, the one thing she was sure about is that she wouldn't abandon him.

Yunus was overjoyed, but his chest tightened with anxiety. His daughter would stay by his side through good times and bad, but what future could he possibly offer Silvy in return?

And so, when his daughter passed Saint Helena's enrollment exam with record-high marks, receiving not only a full scholarship but also a savings account in her name, Yunus sobbed like a herdsman who'd lost his cattle. He often saw articles about the new school in the newspapers he delivered. He'd read about how hard children worked to get in – and about the young boys and girls who took their own lives when they failed. That's when he realized his daughter was exceptionally smart and that he needed to do something to help her pursue her bright future. He swore he'd make enough money to send his daughter to university. This little girl, who stood by his side for better, for worse, had to get the best education, that's what he thought. She deserves to achieve all of her dreams.

When Yunus dropped his daughter off at Saint Helena, he gazed at the school buildings and felt confident that his daughter was in the right hands. She'd have more than enough time to study, regular meals, and an environment designed to support her education. Yunus started to think like a responsible parent – that is, he started thinking about the future, preparing for what Silvy might need after she graduated from her new school.

Yunus decided right then and there to look for work in Malaysia. He'd considered the possibility for some time, the thought churning in his head like a storm cloud, but he always shooed it away because he didn't want to leave Silvy alone. But now, his daughter had a comfortable room in a dormitory, plenty of books, and access to expensive facilities. He could reasonably go away for three years and work in a fast-food restaurant or on a palm oil plantation.

As a father, it was his responsibility to make money so that his sweet, clever daughter could attend university, he thought. Peddling books gave him enough to scrape by, but nothing close to the kind of money he needed to give his daughter a meaningful life.

"What do you want to do after you graduate?" he asked her time and time again. "Do you want to be an airplane stewardess? A doctor? Don't be afraid to dream. If money's the problem, I can help."

But Silvy insisted that all she wanted from her dad was for him to stay nearby.

"I'll get a scholarship for college. Don't worry, Dad, just stay home. Don't go to Malaysia, don't go anywhere. Please, just keep sending me books and newspapers."

Yunus turned away from her, looking out from the pendopo where they were sitting. Shelves stacked with papers and old books stood in each corner of the open-air space. If Om Nus had this many things to read, surely the school library had even more. Saint Helena probably kept their newspapers neatly bound and set in bundles in front of each hallway in the dorms. Their staff probably selected newspapers of quality, unlike the tabloids he was tasked to deliver, which were filled with vapid gossip columns about people like Mother Teresa of Timor and boasted ads for pills, hair growth treatments, and supplements that promised to enhance virility.

He was fully aware that Silvy didn't need his books anymore. He also knew that Silvy was capable of getting a scholarship at any university she wanted to attend. But what kind of parent didn't even try to scrape together some money for their child's future?

Two weeks after dropping Silvy off at school, Yunus sold the few possessions he had in the little rented house on the coast. He sent word to Silvy that she should stay in the dorms and wait for him to get back from Malaysia. His daughter cried when she heard the news, but her father promised that in three years, he'd come back home with lots of money – the kind of money that could send Silvy to college and allow Yunus to buy back the family home that he'd sold long ago. He sent a letter and a kiss to his daughter, then started gathering the relevant forms to apply for a permit as an overseas worker.

But filling out official documents in Indonesia is about as complicated as trying to study Latin with a bad teacher. Let's say you need to fill out one of three documents to become a migrant worker: document A in case X, document B in case Y, and document C in case Z. In order to get document A, you first need to fill out document A1 in case XI, document A2 in case VI, document A3 in case XII, and also obtain a formal letter confirming that you're a follower of an official religion recognized by the government. If you fail to submit that letter, you won't only have your application rejected, but you'll also be called into the police station for questioning, since you might very well be a PKI-communist-traitor-of-the-state. In order to fill out document A1 in case XI, you first need to complete document 1-A1 in case IX, document 2-A1 in case X, document 3-A1 in case I, document 4-A1 in case XIX, and get a signature from your local district official for document 5-A1. And to fill out that first document (that is, 1-A1 in case IX), you first need to file document a-1-A1 in case P, b-1-A1 in case Q, or x-1-A1 in case R, and so on. Just thinking about it makes your head spin. And after filling out the series of forms and soliciting numerous letters of reference, months of your life and most of your money will have been spent on photocopying sheets of paper and dizzily attempting to distinguish one case from another. Even then your case won't be approved, not unless you have bribe money or an inside guy. Unfortunately for Yunus, he didn't have either.

Since he didn't want to waste his time on endless paperwork, Yunus instead met with one of the brokers who falsify work papers and send you wherever they choose. Six days later, he went to the docks at Tenau, after which he was put on a series of unnamed boats and ships and smuggled into Malaysia.

Silvy never heard from her father again.

Silvy Hakuak Namepan rapidly became the new star student at Saint Helena High School. Everyone was taken aback by her intelligence. She was involved in almost every activity since she quickly picked up new skills: she was able to sing while playing the sasando, she wrote for the school newspaper, and she also modeled for the school's tourism magazine. Not only could she solve complex chemical equations, but she was also a talented poet. Her teachers were often left speechless when Silvy interrupted their lectures to propose a different point of view, citing accurate data with sound logic. No one could argue with her.

"When she starts going on like that, none of the other students can follow the lesson."

That's what the Indonesian Language teacher said, complaining about Silvy in one of the weekly teacher staff meetings. The clever instructor spoke in complex sentences that high schoolers couldn't possibly understand in an effort to conceal the fact that he was the one who didn't know the obscure vocabulary that Silvy often used.

"I was about to say the same thing," this time, it was the History teacher who jumped in. He was the young instructor who managed the boys' dormitories, and he also felt as though he'd suffered at the hands of the young woman. In class, he lectured about how the Indonesian army defeated Japan during World War II, and Silvy corrected him, listing the various factors that had really caused Japan to surrender, naming all the countries that had ganged up on or betrayed the Japanese and describing the economic conditions in the period.

Soon enough, Silvy had more authority in the classroom than her teachers did. During any lesson, students looked to the girl as though to ask, is that true? Rather than speaking to their teachers when they were confused, the students directed their questions to Silvy, and whenever she launched into an explanation in the middle of class, citing experts and titles of books, everyone would look at the adult standing at the front of the room with expressions that said: *Hello*, who even *is* the teacher here?

Staff lodged complaints about Silvy at every staff meeting, and eventually, Father Yosef sought advice from a professor in Ledalero. The expert didn't come to Saint Helena himself but instead sent four of his assistants. They walked into the school with several large suitcases filled with books and strange objects. They told Silvy to pray, then asked her a number of questions and requested that she perform various activities with props. They took notes as they interviewed her, and then they left.

Six days later, the professor himself came to Saint Helena. He only had one suitcase, and this time it only contained books. Silvy was called in again, and the professor asked that she complete exams and respond to numerous questions from ten in the morning to three in the afternoon. That evening, he sat down with Father Yosef in the cafeteria and told the pastor that he managed an excellent institution.

"Indeed, I do," Father Yosef replied. "I've poured my blood and sweat into this school."

Without waiting for the professor to ask any questions, Father Yosef jumped into an explanation of Saint Helena's abysmal conditions before his tenure as headmaster. This served as an introduction to the story of how he built the school from the ground up. It was the script he always used when speaking to guests and donors: first, detail how terrible the school used to be, then outline his improvements, making it easy to picture the exact achievements for which Father Yosef was directly responsible.

But the professor cut him off:

"This school, however, is not where that girl belongs."

"What do you mean?" Father Yosef asked.

The professor handed the pastor a stack of reports.

"Her intelligence is leaps and bounds ahead of what's typical for a child of her age," the professor explains. "I came here today because I couldn't believe it myself. But it's true. If she stays at Saint Helena, she'll probably drop out from boredom. Or she'll stay in class but cause trouble with your teachers."

Father Yosef asked the professor what he should do.

"It's always my opinion that students like Silvy graduate early and enroll in university," he replied. "She needs to work on a real research project, not sit at a desk while high school teachers talk at her."

The professor left, and Father Yosef considered the advice. In theory he agreed that Silvy should attend university – he'd read about children blessed by God with extraordinary intelligence, outshining their peers. Besides, such a move would allow him to brag about the girl's aptitude in front of other headmasters, his fellow pastors, and even the bishop and the governor: Saint Helena produced a student so smart that she finished high school in less than three years, he'd tell them.

But then he thought about it again: in those days, Indonesian college students were swept up in a movement called *reformasi*. Every day, young people took to the streets, demanding that President Suharto step down from power. They burned tires, attacked the police, and vandalized office buildings. The army had no choice but to crack down on the protests, and countless students were shot and killed. Father Yosef didn't want Silvy to go to university, not at a time like that. She was far too young to be thrown into such an environment.

And yet, how was he expected to keep a child like Silvy in a high school classroom? She'd just keep bothering the other students and undermining her teachers.

Then, during one of the staff meetings, the Arts and Crafts teacher came up with a genius idea:

"She likes books," the instructor piped in. "Every time she sits down to read, nothing in the world could distract her. I have a feeling she'd give up her spot in heaven if it meant leaving all her books behind."

"Let's have her do an independent study in the library. We could call it an internship," Father Yosef suggested.

"Father," the Indonesian Language teacher interrupted. "If she's already ahead of everyone else, won't the library books just bore her?"

"It's true . . . she grumbles and makes a fuss while she rummages through the stacks," the school librarian added.

Father Yosef turned the idea around in his head and suddenly remembered that the nuns used to have a reading room in the rectory stocked with theological texts and books on philosophy, literature, art, culture, and so on. Plus, he had a few dozen crates of books of his own from when he was at seminary. That should be more than enough to keep Silvy occupied, he thought.

And so, the staff came to a decision. A new reading room would open in the rectory, one with advanced books, and Silvy would be assigned to manage the space. She would be the first student at Saint Helena to pursue an independent study. She'd still be responsible for her quarterly exams and any other assignments that her teachers deemed necessary; they could speak with her directly about any tasks they expected of her. And if another student happened to show a similar amount of promise – that is, if the kid could get the same recommendation from the professor in Ledalero – Father Yosef would come up with some other, more permanent solution.

———◆———

Seven nuns originally lived in the building that stood against the Sawu Sea. After the school's renovations, it served as the rectory where Father Yosef lived. It was way too big. Each wall in the living room used to be lined with floor to ceiling shelves displaying glassware and vases, but the objects had long since been removed, and now the room stretched out like an empty volleyball court. Several u-shaped bedrooms faced the living room. Father Yosef used the largest one on the left as his bedroom; the window looked out onto the front garden, which had a fish pool and a small fountain. The pastor liked to toss breadcrumbs into the pool and watch the fish splash in the water as they rushed for the food. Three other rooms, all empty and unused, were on the other side of the living room. There were four additional rooms in the middle of the house, the last of which opened up to the central hallway. Each had an en-suite bathroom, a dresser, a desk, and a bed with a mattress and pillows. All the spare rooms meant that Tanta Yuli could simply hang mosquito nets, make up the bed, and add a few other finishing touches whenever a respected guest needed to stay at the school, such as the honorable grand bishop, or other pastors, or any other visitor with a high-ranking title. For less important visitors, like students' parents or a tourist hoping to attend the monthly arts festival, there was a different building on the grounds with rooms available to rent at the price of a four-star hotel.

Father Yosef placed a round, teak table in the corner of his living room, near the door that led to his bedroom. The table was encircled by seven chairs, also made from teak. It was at this table that Father Yosef hit or spanked students who acted out, and after the punishment, it was there that he'd describe their sins in detail, drawing contrast between their behavior and a mother's love or the goodness of God, which made the children fall to their knees and cry from pain and guilt. As a result, students at Saint Helena gave the spot a nickname, the Table of Lamentation. When other clergymen visited the school, Father Yosef like to have a few beers at that table and discuss a number of issues, like the interminable war to the east, or poverty, and then reminisce about their time studying at seminary. A lot of new ideas for the diocese were born around the table so it only seemed fitting that the pastors deemed every gathering around it a Conference of the Round Table.

The hallway that extended out from the living room was so wide that an army tank could easily roll down the corridor. It separated the spare bedrooms from another two rooms next to Father Yosef's, one of which used to be the reading room back when the nuns lived in the rectory. For some time, the reading room had functioned as nothing more than a storage space. A film of dust covered the books, but Om Lamber and Tanta Yuli helped Silvy clean the space up, mopping the floor, dusting all the volumes, and wiping down even the highest shelves, which rose all the way up to the ceiling.

Next to the reading room at the back of the rectory was the dining area. It held a long table lined with twelve chairs. On the wall to the left was a huge painting of Jesus eating penpasu alongside fifteen old men wearing Timorese sarongs – an image reminiscent of the last supper, minus the table. None of the old men had any teeth, and as a result, anyone who saw the painting couldn't help but ask why the artist would depict a scene of people sharing a meal and choose to make everyone toothless. Father Yosef couldn't give them an answer, since the painting was attributed to a French artist who faked his death and ran to Timor in an effort to escape the stifling European art world. He became known as Kaes Muit Aseket, since for all the years he lived on the island, he only came into town to draw or ask questions about pigments used to dye yarn until finally he was killed by people from the north who assumed that all white men were thieves.

A long, narrow side table stood against the right side of the room, holding thermoses, three tea kettles, glassware, jam, a toaster, and a few other appliances, while cups and plates were kept in a row of cabinets above the side table. Two big cupboards the height of an adult man stood next to the side table, and both were always stuffed with food. Rich families from Kupang liked to come to Saint Helena for Sunday mass; they were drawn to the calm atmosphere of the little chapel facing the sea, and they also liked to compete for who was most generous in their donations to God. If a family brought a tray of fruit and a bottle of sopi and also hired two dancers to perform one Sunday, the following week a different family would offer several trays of fruit, a roast chicken, and hire four dancers; the week after that, a new family would donate five trays of fruit, a platter of cakes, a bottle of imported wine, and a roast pig. This would continue until a holiday finally came around and every devout family was expected to offer a donation to the church. The spoils from weekly Mass were stuffed into those two cupboards, together with bottles of beer that one of the congregants dropped off every two weeks. In the back corner of the room past the cupboards, a door opened out into a spacious kitchen; that's where bigger appliances and kitchenware were kept, and it also had a bathroom and a small backdoor leading outside.

The wide hallway running through the rectory opened onto a veranda, which had a small table and two rattan chairs made on Alor Island. Father Yosef often spent his evenings by the table, sipping at a beer and looking out past the flickering oil lamp onto the vast Sawu Sea. Every time he sat there, facing the depths of the ocean and his feelings, he realized how small he was in the face of God. Then he'd get very drunk – whether from God's grace or the cold beer, no one can say.

The rectory was never locked, so anyone who needed something from one of the rooms could simply walk inside. Despite this, nothing had ever been stolen from the building, neither by bands of robbers nor a stray thief.

Once in a while, Father Yosef would call over a student who happened to be walking by and say:

"Go to my room. You know where it is, right? What? Well, you've been to the Table of Lamentation once or twice, haven't you? That's what I thought, and don't misbehave again, okay? Now, go to my room, open the door, and you'll see a lamp on your left. Got it? Yes, on the left. Turn on the light and look for a cookie jar on the table next to the window. Open the jar, okay? You'll see a lot of cash. Count out three hundred twenty-five thousand rupiah and bring it back to me. Got it? Don't forget to turn then light off when you leave."

If he was in a good mood, Father Yosef would add: "Oh, and then take another five hundred – no, a thousand rupiah. That's for you. Buy yourself a comic book or something. Just don't get one of those lude Fredy S. novels."

The kid would sprint to the rectory, excited that he'd have enough spending money to buy the latest Fredy S. novel in town the next weekend. He'd feel lucky, and luckier still when he'd open the door to the reading room and sneak a glance at the pretty girl leaning over a stack of books. If she looked up, he'd say: Oh, sorry, I thought this was Father Yosef's room. Then she'd smile, and he'd excuse himself as elegantly as possible before going back to the correct room with a grin on his face, overjoyed that he talked to such a lovely girl.

Ever since she'd been tasked with organizing books in the reading room, Silvy practically disappeared from the halls of Saint Helena.

She used to star in the monthly arts festival, but now she just took a quick look at the performances from the back of the room, a book tucked under her arm. The reading room stole Silvy's heart: to her, it was heaven on earth. She felt like she'd never have the time to read everything, so she dedicated every moment, no matter how brief, to making progress through the volumes.

Each morning after mass and breakfast, her friends hurried to class while Silvy dashed to the rectory. She'd been tasked with cleaning and organizing the thousands of books and newspaper clippings that filled the reading room. Those tasks occupied her until two in the afternoon, and then she used the rest of her time to read or translate books from foreign languages. She'd stay there for hours, often losing track of time and missing the cafeteria lunch hour. But Tanta Yuli was nice to her, so if she missed lunch, she was able to rummage around the rectory's kitchen for something to eat or walk to the old woman's house and have lunch there.

Once in a while she got tired of reading, tired of clipping newspaper articles, tired of doing anything at all. That's when she'd slip into one of the empty bedrooms and stretch out on a bare mattress. Or she'd make herself a cup of tea in the dining room, steal a little cake from the cupboard, and go out to the veranda. Relaxing on one of the rattan chairs, she'd sip tea and look out at the ocean, counting ships on the horizon or tracing her mother's face in her head – she'd worked hard to retain every memory, no matter how vague, of the contours of her mom's face and the scent of her body. Every now and again she felt like her memories were getting hazy, so she needed to bring them back. She didn't want to wake up one day and find that she couldn't picture her mom anymore. Her mom, who was smart, who smelled nice. Her mom, who her dad loved more than he adored his own daughter. Her dad, who disappeared without a trace.

She'd always wanted to be like her mother.

After vanishing from the halls of Saint Helena for four days, Father Yosef reemerged on school grounds, disheveled and unshaven. His face was weathered, as though he were coming home after liberating a nation. He threw himself onto his bed in the rectory and closed the door.

Ten hours later, Tanta Yuli knocked on the door to the reading room.

"Mister Father still hasn't gotten out of bed," she reported when Silvy opened the door. "He hasn't eaten a thing. He left his plate untouched."

Silvy glanced at the clock. It was just past four in the afternoon. She heard the faint sound of children playing on the field outside. A sea breeze drifted in through the hallway, ruffling the curtains.

The girl walked to Father Yosef's door and pressed her ear against the wood. She couldn't hear anything. Stepping away, she wanted to say that everything was probably fine, but Tanta Yuli looked as moody as a fisherman's wife waiting for her husband to return home after a storm.

"Try knocking," the old woman suggested.

Silvy knocked. Once. Twice.

She heard Father Yosef weakly tell her to open the door.

"Get Tanta Yuli," Yosef said when he saw Silvy. The girl stepped aside, and Tanta Yuli rushed into the room.

The bedroom was dim and stuffy. A small ray of bright light spilled through a crack between black curtains. Tanta Yuli went over and sat on the edge of the bed. From the other side of the threshold, Silvy could just barely see Father Yosef's pale face, coated in sweat. The old woman held her hand to the pastor's forehead, and the two whispered to one another for a few minutes. Then, Tanta Yuli left the room. Silvy's eyes begged her to explain what was going on.

"Mister Father is sick," she explained. "His forehead is burning up."

Silvy closed the door.

"He should eat some porridge," Silvy said.

Tanta Yuli headed to the kitchen with Silvy trailing behind. The girl lit the stove while the older woman cleaned a pot and rinsed rice. Tanta Yuli griped about how concerned she was for Father Yosef.

"Mister Father never complains, he never asks for help. No matter what difficulties he faces, he simply finds a way to manage on his own."

Silvy stayed quiet and kept her hands busy. She found herself preoccupied with a poem by Fanu Tki'un, a Timorese writer accused of being a communist, and later killed in Hue'buni. Silvy had found a copy of one of his poetry collections in the reading room, and Tanta Yuli had knocked on the door while she was immersed in his words. The poems were dark, composed during a period of scarcity when the only food the poet and his comrades had were tamarind seeds soaked in water. Fanu Tki'un fell in love with an older woman who gave him half of a rotten papaya. Silvy wanted to keep thinking about the poet, but the sound of Tanta Yuli's voice intermingling with rice grains being winnowed was enough to shake her out of her revery, and she decided to set her thoughts aside for a moment and listen to the old woman's frustrations.

"Can you imagine? How fortunate it is that we checked on him. Something terrible might have happened. I can't even bring myself to think about it."

She looked at Silvy, expecting a response. After realizing that the girl had nothing to add, she shook her head dramatically.

"I have two children of my own, Miss Silvy," this time, Tanta Yuli decided to express her concern using a more concrete example. "My eldest, Emilia, moved to Java for work. She takes care of the elderly in a nursing home. My second is a boy, his name is Toni. When he was little, he always said he wanted to be a pastor. Oh, Miss Silvy, when he first told me that, I cried almost every day. I swear, all I want is to keep him from suffering."

Silvy finally looked more engaged in the conversation, and Tanta Yuli was pleased to have a captive audience. Silvy, in turn, could tell that Tanta Yuli had taken note of her expression and started getting worried that the old woman would realize that the interest she'd plastered across her face was fake, so she dropped her gaze to the pot on the stove. It was spotless, rarely handled. Most people used the electric rice cooker. Silvy's mom used to have a pot just like that one, except it was a bit smaller and had a big dent on one side. When her parents got into arguments, her father would sometimes throw things, but it was only after her mother left them that her dad would hurl pots and pans and anything else her mother left behind against the floor and sob, leaving everything bent out of shape.

"I couldn't bear it," Tanta Yuli's voice caught Silvy off guard. "What if he'd been assigned to some godforsaken place? Like the interior of Sumatra – or Kalimantan? Or Java? Ah," she shook her head as though to forbid such a thing from happening.

"Don't worry, Tanta," Silvy finally spoke. "Kalimantan is pretty developed now. Same with Sumatra, not to mention Java."

"Eh, developed? What do you mean?" Tanta Yuli cut off the young girl's assurances. "Emilia told me all about Java in one of her letters. She said: Oh, Mama, don't believe what people say. Don't believe what you see on TV. It's all nonsense. The Javanese, they're more…" Tanta Yuli dropped her voice as though she knew she was about to say something untoward and struggled to find the appropriate words. "The Javanese, they're…they're not so lucky, compared to us."

Silvy's face betrayed her confusion. Tanta Yuli paused, glancing from side to side as though to make sure that no one was listening in on their conversation.

"You don't know, do you?" she said in a whisper. "Here's how it is. I'll be very frank, and this is just between us, okay? Here you go. I have no desire to insult anyone, but according to Emilia, the Javanese are way, way, way poorer than we are. Not just poor. Uncivilized. Some of them haven't learned to speak Indonesian. Others don't have houses, so they live under bridges. And they defecate in rivers, and they think that eating human flesh will give them knowledge. Can you imagine, Miss Silvy? Do you understand what I'm telling you?"

Tanta Yuli looked so appalled that Silvy giggled.

"Laugh all you want, Miss Silvy, but those are the facts," she said, her voice full of pity, as though she were communicating the worst news in the world and needed to take care that her interlocutor didn't fall into a deep depression. "I'm blessed to have a pastor as a son, because if not…"

Tanta Yuli stopped in the middle of her thought when the porridge started boiling over, the froth almost launching the lid onto the floor.

"Well, it's ready," she said. "How about you go to the dining room and make the pastor some hot tea? Use Mister Father's favorite mug, the white one with the little Jesus on it. And add half a teaspoon of sugar. I'll serve the porridge."

While Tanta Yuli reached for a ladle, Silvy went into the adjacent room to make tea. As she was stirring, she remembered the brilliant idea she'd had while reading the poetry collection. It had occurred to her that she could write an essay with her interpretation of Fanu Tki'un's poetry and submit the piece to newspapers – but then she realized that all of the observations she'd had about the poems themselves had vanished.

Tanta Yuli appeared at the threshold of the dining room balancing a tray that held a bowl of porridge. She took a look at the tea Silvy made, sampled it with a teaspoon, and announced that it was just right, and that Silvy should make tea for Mister Father more often. She took out the first aid kit, found a bottle of Aspirin, shook a few pills onto the tray and hurried to Father Yosef. Silvy trailed after her, helping with the door to the pastor's room. Tanta Yuli went inside and set the tray on a side table between stacks of books.

"Master," the woman said. Father Yosef writhed under the sheet. "There's porridge on the table here. Eat, before it gets cold."

He said nothing.

"There's also some medicine. Don't forget to take it."

She left the room and closed the door behind her without waiting for the pastor to reply.

"See?" she said under her breath. "Poor thing. No wife, no relatives. He doesn't have anyone to take care of him. It's so fortunate that you knocked when you did."

Silvy nodded, looking at the old woman.

"You'll be working here in the rectory today, right?"

Silvy said yes and asked what Tanta Yuli needed.

"Well, here's the thing," the woman said under her breath. "Listen closely, okay? I need you to check on Mister Father once in a while. He doesn't like to ask for help when he needs something. So, it's our responsibility to check on him. And if there's an emergency, you can come get me from my house."

Silvy nodded.

The old woman left, and Silvy went back to her reading room, closing the door behind her. She picked up the poetry collection she'd been immersed in before the interruption, rereading a few stanzas in an effort to recuperate the interpretation that had slipped her mind. But she still couldn't remember a thing. All she could think of was what Tanta Yuli told her: It's so difficult to be a pastor. To live alone. To give up the chance to have a family. Do pastors give up love, too? She wondered if she would've wanted to be a pastor, had she been born a boy. Then, she started questioning why girls weren't allowed to be leaders in the Church. God chose to ordain and educate men. Was being a woman such a curse in the eyes of the Church? As she contemplated the question, Silvy heard a groan from Father Yosef's room. She thought that the pastor might be calling out to her. She went into the hallway but heard a different name: "Maria...Maria..."

Unable to believe her ears, she creeped towards the pastor's room. "Maria...Maria..."

Was the pastor really crying out to Jesus's mother? Silvy placed her hand on the doorknob, pushing the door open. Light from the hallway poured into the room, illuminating Father Yosef's pallid, sweaty face. The pastor didn't open his eyes, though. He kept groaning.

Silvy stepped inside. The porridge and medicine hadn't been touched. She sat on the edge of the mattress and placed her wrist against Father Yosef's forehead. It was scorching.

"Maria... Mariaaa..." This time Father Yosef also thrashed against the sheets and sat up. The sheet covering his chest fell to his waist. He wasn't wearing any clothes, and beads of sweat stuck to his chest hair. Blood rushed to Silvy's face as, suddenly, she recognized Father Yosef's groans: they sounded like something that should be accompanied by a bed rhythmically creaking, a man's sweaty face.

"Maria...Maria..."

She'd heard moans like that come from her father's room. A sensation creeped up her body, and suddenly she found herself staring at the pastor's chest, her throat dry. She abruptly stood up and left the room. After closing the door behind her, she dashed to one of the empty bedrooms.

Silvy laid down on the bare mattress, breathing hard. She closed her eyes, trying to calm herself down. But a moment later she heard those moans again:

"Maria...Maria..."

Unable to stop herself, she slipped one hand into her pants and felt something wet. She rubbed herself. The hairs on the back of her neck were raised.

"Maria..."

She wanted to be someone else. Her spine weakened. She moved her free hand to her chest. Her underwear was damp, she kicked them off with her feet and they fell off the edge of the bed. She touched her nipples, her mouth fell open. She touched her clitoris. Her eyes closed tightly shut. She started to move one hand against her groin as she squeezed her breasts with the other. Soon enough, her body tensed up, and she started moving her hands faster. Faster still. Her chest rose from the bed, her spine curved. Right as her body started trembling, the door opened.

The man in the threshold watched Silvy's body buckle. The sound of the door creaking open surprised the girl, and her eyes opened to meet his. One second passed. Two. And then he slipped inside and closed the door. Before she could think of what to do, the man was nestling his head between her open legs. Silvy panicked when she felt his warm tongue, and she found herself pushing his head away. But one of his hands creeped up her body to grab her chest while he unbuttoned his pants. Silvy gasped. A few seconds later, the man crawled on top of her. He kissed her stomach. Her nipples. The base of her neck. Her earlobes. And slowly, something penetrated her. Silvy held back a yelp. She tried to say no, but instead, her hands landed limply on the man's chest.

Then the man thrust into her quickly, unrestrained. He was already twitching after a mere two minutes. Silvy noticed a strange liquid dribbling into her, then leaking out of her.

"Maria…" once again she heard that name.

IX

Of all the congregants saddened by Father Yosef's transfer to Saint Helena High School, Maria Goreti Naloek was by far the most distraught. She locked herself in her room for days, where she did nothing more than breathe and halfheartedly nibble on food. She never used the bathroom, that's how little she ate – just enough to stave off the pulsing headaches that plagued her.

Everyone in the congregation tried to guess why Father Yosef left. Was it an honor? A punishment? Or simply the archbishop's whim? The pastor was so young. He hadn't done anything to deserve a promotion. He managed to increase the number of parish dogs from three to nine, but that didn't warrant a new position. He also hadn't done anything to shame the Church, which was the other motive for transferring a pastor. Since they didn't have any clear answers, congregants invented explanations for the change. Those who despised the Church spread rumors that Father Yosef had been framed for a crime that the parish itself had plotted. They made sure to emphasize that the other clergymen were sons of bitches – hypocritical criminals hiding under their cassocks – and that no one should take a pastor's word at face value. Those who loved the Church, meanwhile, invented a story about how kind-hearted Father Yosef was, citing many small acts of goodwill that might explain his promotion to school headmaster. They made sure to emphasize how much the Church cared for people living outside of the city, how the diocese sent their best men to serve children living in poverty, and how wealthier congregants should support the Church's good works. People talked. But it was only Maria who knew what happened.

Maria met Yosef years before his ordination. Back then, he was a seminary student known as Brother Yosef who participated in university study group meetings. He wasn't involved in the student movement, nor did he understand their political causes, but if students wanted to outsmart the Indonesian military, they needed connections to the church. Suharto was indignant that students were resisting the government, so he ordered the army to take care of the young dissidents. Soldiers infiltrated university campuses to crush organizing efforts.

Some disguised themselves as meatball vendors, others made fake student IDs and showed up to class every few weeks. Students had to gather in secret, pretending to meet about things that had nothing to do with politics.

Ever since communists had been labeled enemies of the state, religion became an obligatory aspect of public life. So, Maria and her friends pretended to meet for prayer circle. They came up with a good name for their group: Ora et Labora Student Prayer Circle. They always brought rosaries and copies of the bible to their meetings. If an intelligence agent suspected their group and showed up to a meeting, they wouldn't discuss anything at all. Instead, they'd pray, read the bible, and praise the name of God. Once, a student who liked to mess around pretended he was possessed by the Holy Spirit and made fun of the undercover soldier in attendance. Later that day, he was hit by an unmarked car as he walked home from class. He was lucky to escape the incident with a broken leg, and from then on, the students realized how that kind of joke wasn't funny in the slightest. They created a more convincing weekly prayer schedule and searched for someone who could serve as their spiritual leader. Praying once a week wasn't the end of the world, especially not if they asked the Holy Spirit to come to earth and drop straight down on Suharto's head.

That's why one of the students reached out to Brother Yosef.

Yosef's polite demeanor and long nose often made him an object of romantic interest in the study circle, but Maria didn't pay much attention to him. He was the kind of man who liked to give people advice, and even though he was never judgmental, he spoke in sentences that left no room for other points of view – the kind that implied he spoke the truth and everyone else had no choice but to agree. He quoted bible passages from memory and tried to energize the students to commit to their faith:

"If you could switch on God's grace as though it were a light illuminating your path in life, then you have to try your best to do precisely that."

"Who among us has value in the eyes of God? God has an open heart. A heart that receives, that offers forgiveness. A heart filled with love."

"God will protect us. He makes sure we receive that which is best for us. The only thing we lack is faith and gratitude."

One day, Maria tried to refute his statements: "Brother Yosef – if God is the Generous One, why do his gifts always seem to end up in the hands of greedy people?"

Yosef looked at Maria with compassion and pity, as though she were a lost soul that needed to be saved.

"Maria, Maria," he said. "You're thinking about worldly desires. Look at the birds of the air, for they neither sow nor reap nor gather into barns; yet your heavenly Father feeds them. This is God's plan. Ever since He created the Earth, God…"

And then Yosef said many things about how ungrateful mankind was in the presence of God's grace. He completed his speech with a reading from the holy book and a prayer asking God to free the students from their worries. But the students in his prayers had lived under a repressive regime for a long time, a regime that haunted them day and night. Words about God rarely consoled them. The young activists always left prayer circle feeling sick to their stomachs, with thoughts of the crimes of a corrupt state propped up by the military.

They nevertheless listened respectfully to Brother Yosef, since he was becoming a pastor, a man anointed by God. Only Maria found it difficult to hide how frustrated she was with his words of solace and encouragement. Whenever he started rambling on, Maria would flip through her bible in an effort to entertain herself and shorten the seminary student's lengthy speeches.

"Brother, these birds of yours don't sow the fields, and yet they eat the crops, which makes life all the more difficult for farmers. Wouldn't that make the bird a thief?"

"It is our heavenly Father who feeds the bird."

"In other words, the bird is just a tiny crook protected by the Lord. What a dick."

The more Maria challenged Brother Yosef, the more she came to realize that the seminary student was as patient as a saint. She almost always swore and even raised her voice on occasion, but Yosef never got angry with her. He'd watch Maria as she spoke, listen to what she was trying to say, and then explain his own perspective in a new way in the hopes that with different phrasing, Maria would better understand what he meant. But she was rarely mollified by his explanations, which only sparked a fresh round of questions and curses.

That's how their friendship began. Maria enjoyed arguing with Brother Yosef and poking fun at the seminary student; Brother Yosef, meanwhile, liked listening to Maria's rants and explaining his beliefs. Maria was hard-pressed to find someone who could keep a cool head during a debate. The war in East Timor and the violent repression of the student movement meant that everyone had a short fuse. An unpopular statement or questionable convictions, not to mention a full-fledged debate, could easily cause a physical fight to break out. But with Yosef, Maria could openly express her opinion, and whether she did so politely or rudely, her conversation partner wouldn't get offended.

After many long talks, Maria and Yosef felt comfortable around one another. The pair made plans to get together outside of the campus prayer circle. They'd meet at the foodstalls in Oesapa that specialized in different kinds of pork, where they could eat and discuss everything from the weather to religious doctrine. Since they almost always disagreed, they never ran out of things to talk about. Sometimes, the owner of the foodstall fell asleep listening to the two argue about the ideal beverage to drink after eating ribs, or about the ethics of how the Vatican had amassed such immense wealth while people across the world went hungry. Even the waiters got bored of Maria and Yosef, so bored that every time the pair went to eat at the warung, the staff asked that they pay up front in case everyone in the establishment dozed off before the debate was over. Once, the owner's wife, a voluptuous, chatty woman from Manado, asked why the two weren't married.

"We're not dating."

"But the two of you are clearly partners," she said. "Don't you know what partnership looks like? Could be a chatty old maid with a short fuse who opens her home to young, obedient orphans. Or a well-educated man with a clear head who finds himself at peace by the side of a loud-mouthed woman who curses at him."

Brother Yosef answered with some philosophical ruminations on the concept of love; Maria simply laughed. That man, could he really be her partner?

Let's say that, someday, you decide you don't want to be a pastor and you don't get ordained, Maria said to Brother Yosef one day, would you marry me then?

Brother Yosef chuckled.

"I've never thought about it," he replied.

"I know I want to be a pastor. But I'm not sure what plan God has in mind for me. You seem a bit heartbroken, Maria. Is it that hard to meet someone you want to marry?"

Maria laughed.

"Do I seem like the kind of girl who gets lovesick, Yosef? I'm smart and pretty. I can marry whoever I please," she insisted. "But with you," she added, teasing him, "my family would be blessed. Maria and Yosef. Like two souls from Nazareth, we'd bring God down to earth," she concluded, giggling.

Brother Yosef laughed too, and his eyes dropped to the floor. He felt the need to avert his gaze, since his heart dropped to his stomach, making his blood pound and his cheeks burn.

Maria also looked away when she noticed that her joke made Yosef blush. She didn't realize that her own face was a bit red, but she did know that her heart was beating fast. And after that day, at every possible opportunity, she looked Yosef in the eye and asked him silly questions: What are you thinking about? What did you eat today? Why do you always look so cute?

Maria wasn't exaggerating when she told Yosef how cute he looked. The long nose he inherited from his grandfather looked like a cockatoo's beak, and the rest of his face, with its sweet, pleasant features, came from his mother's side. His mom was a beautiful woman from Amarasi who spent her life selling sweet wine on the streets of Kupang. Supposedly, it was her face who inspired poetry that women in small towns still sing when their lovers travel far away for work:

Guard your heart, my darling
When you arrive in the big city
Kupang girls are sweet, so sweet
Sweet as the wine they sell on the streets

Yosef's skin was pale and luminous, and whenever he had a few beers or got embarrassed, Maria would watch the blood rush from his heart, rise up his neck, and color his cheeks. His shy eyes shined behind his glasses, and his lips...

At one point, Maria asked if Yosef always wore glasses.

"Of course. If I don't, everything's blurry."

"Even when you play sports? Or when you're sleeping?"

"It depends," he said. "Why?"

"It's nothing. I was just wondering – would you take them off if we kissed?"

He blushed.

"Oh no! No, I'm just curious about your glasses!"

But her question seemed more like a prayer than an offhand remark.

And the two finally did kiss. One evening, on the beach. With seagulls flapping overhead.

Maria wrapped her arms around the boy's neck, digging her nails into his shoulders. Yosef held the girl tightly, as though to keep her from slipping away. That's what he said after they kissed: he didn't want to let her go. He'd rather let go of the seminary.

Maria looked at her feet.

"Let's get married. Like two souls from Nazareth, we'll bring God down to earth."

An expression of guilt passed across Maria's face.

"It's not just you, Maria," Yosef quickly added. "Don't worry. I've thought this through. I can serve God even if I'm not part of the clergy."

Seminaries rarely prepare their students to become skilled liars, and Maria could see the lie in Yosef's eyes. No matter what he told her, Maria knew that she was the reason he had doubts about the Church. She didn't want to someday meet the bearded man in the sky and face the question: Oh, you, you're that woman who stole one of my servants away from me, aren't you? And so, Maria decided to leave God's servant that evening for good, swearing she'd never see him again.

There existed another Timorese man with a desire to serve – not a desire to serve God, nor a desire to serve customers at a warung. He wanted to serve his nation and homeland. He wanted to be a soldier ready to die for his country.

This man's name was Linus, Linus Atoin Aloket. He grew up near Tanjung Bastian, a small town on Timor's northern coast. When he was eight, a group of soldiers hunting down East Timorese guerilla fighters passed through his town. They handed the boy a piece of chocolate and ordered him to scale a palm tree and get them some coconuts, since it was hot that day and they were thirsty. When Linus was less than four meters off the ground, he was attacked by a lizard lying in wait on the trunk of the palm. Caught off guard, he let go, fell, and hit his ear hard on the tough roots at the base of the tree.

The little boy passed out, but the soldiers helped him come to with a few light slaps across the face. Goading him on with a few brash remarks, they convinced Linus to kill the lizard. The boy wrung the lizard's neck and felt the poor creature die in his hands. From that moment onwards, Linus no longer dreamt of working at the Ministry of Information when he grew up, which had been his goal up until that point. Instead, he wanted to be a soldier. He wanted to fight enemies of the state. Enemies of the state were just like lizards on coconut palms:

if you don't get to them first, they'll only end up putting the lives of innocent people at risk.

After graduating from high school, Linus took the military service exam and failed. He took the test again the following year, and for two years after that, but only ended up failing each time. His father sold most of his cows and several plots of land so that he could bribe officials administering the exam, and still Linus never managed to get a decent score. The boy was tall and lanky, broad chested from his daily chores of carrying wood and herding cattle, but the lizard incident left him deaf in one ear. Deaf people can't be soldiers. When his dad was on the verge of going totally bankrupt, he told his son to forget his dream of joining the army and come up with more realistic goals.

Brokenhearted, Linus went on a two-week bender and then decided to enroll at a university in Kupang. He applied to the University of West Timor without any lofty ambitions. His new plan was simple: he'd get a degree in accounting.

When classes started, Linus discovered there were soldiers in universities, too. These soldiers were known as the Student Regiment, and they wore uniforms, held ranks, received military training, and were looked upon with respect by every campus security guard. Better yet, they were automatically registered in the reserves: should the state ever need them, they'd be called to jump into battle. Linus recovered a bit of hope from the forgotten scraps of his military dreams and signed up for the Student Regiment. But he went through the selection process only to be rejected yet another time – not only was he half-deaf, but he also wasn't very smart.

His stupidity hadn't been much of an issue in the previous exams, of course. The army was in need of brave recruits, not clever ones; it's not as though critical thinking is necessary when you're firing at targets on the front lines. So, you're a bit dense, what's the big deal? All that matters is that you're willing to shoot enemies of the state. The Student Regiment, on the other hand, actually cared about intelligence. The members of their ranks were regularly in contact with student protestors. If they were confronting kids who liked to read, the regiment needed their soldiers to come across as smart, too.

Linus broke down in tears when he found out that his dream was still out of reach. But despite it all, he was still determined to serve his country. The commander of the Student Regiment clapped him on the back and said, if you want to honor the Republic of Indonesia, being a soldier isn't the only way.

For most, such a statement would sound like the sort of thing people say to soften the blow of rejection, but for Linus, it was a noble idea, one he'd take with him to his grave. Each day when he woke up and before he went back to sleep, he'd think about how he might serve his country, how he could help exterminate enemies of the state.

Linus rented a room in off-campus housing where a lot of students from East Timor lived. Sincere and kindhearted, they befriended Linus and called him the Brother from Timor of the Setting Sun. At first, they just shared food and hand towels, but soon enough they were lending each other novels and drinking sopi from the same bottle. Eventually, the East Timorese students felt comfortable enough with Linus that they let him sit in on their clandestine meetings about the independence struggle. They invited him to participate in discussion groups and introduced him to leaders of the resistance movement passing through Kupang.

Linus wrote down names in secret. He took note of who was present at the meetings as well as the topics being discussed and then passed the information to the officers at the Military Regional Command. Thanks to his diligence, those insurgent students – those enemies of the state – started disappearing, one by one. As they dropped off, the Indonesian intelligence division in Kupang received a hearty thumbs up, and some of its members were promoted and offered posts on other islands. No one suspected that the Brother from Timor of the Setting Sun was behind the successful operation. A mere six months after Linus enrolled in university, not a single student in the city was willing to talk about human rights violations in East Timor, let alone utter the word "independence."

Linus was far more successful than salaried intelligence agents. Indonesian officials had attempted to sniff out rebel student groups for some time without any success. They'd scoop up a straggler now and again, but they never managed to detain anyone important. Somehow the students could immediately recognize the secret police, even when soldiers left their dog tags at home, grew out their hair, and carried fake student IDs.

"The more you try to blend in, the easier it is to spot you," said one student who'd been arrested at a protest. "You smell like blood. We can sniff you out kilometers away."

No one, however, came even close to guessing that Linus was the mole. Your typical informant was at least moderately clever, and Linus was famously stupid. There's no such thing as a smart soldier, of course, since they prefer burning books to reading – and yet, Linus was far too dumb to work for the government, or at least that was the logic among the activists. His face was a blank canvas while student groups debated who among their ranks had wreaked havoc on the movement.

The military, meanwhile, benefited immensely from their new informant. Linus grew increasingly well liked and quickly recognized as a valuable asset. Soldiers gave him cigarettes and took him to see prostitutes, sometimes in brothels, sometimes in nice hotels that had special deals for warriors of the Indonesian Republic.

"Life is short, and money can buy happiness if you know how to spend it," one soldier said to Linus.

Linus etched the quote into one of his bedroom walls. He wanted to make sure he'd never forget such a brilliant statement. He often said it aloud and tried to spend money on happiness each and every day of his ·short life. But while the soldiers around him received salaries, however modest, Linus didn't get paid for his intelligence work. He still lived off the allowance his parents sent him each month.

Happiness required extra cash, so Linus asked his parents for more money. In letters to his father, he described how the cost of student fees was rising and then invented necessities he had no choice but to pay for. The papers and the radio constantly ran news stories about how inflation was skyrocketing, so his father was understanding about his son's need for a more generous stipend. Besides, Linus was a responsible kid. The boy always sent detailed explanations about how he'd use the funds, and his dad was confident that his money was going towards worthwhile ends – oftentimes, towards the kinds of important educational expenses that his son could only explain using foreign words. The old man's tongue was stiff from chewing betel nut, which made all the English terms hard to pronounce, but nevertheless, he would do his best to announce his son's expenses whenever he went to the market, or at any town gathering. That way, he could bask in admiring glances and feel as though all the cattle and land he'd sold for his son's education hadn't been in vain.

"It's been tough to make ends meet," he told his brother-in-law, who had walked more than thirty kilometers to announce that Linus's father's son-in-law's grandfather had just passed away in Ponu.

"Why, what's going on?" his brother-in-law asked.

"The price of *study tours* for undergraduate students went up again this month."

Linus's father wasn't one to borrow money from family, and his brother-in-law was too shy to ask what *study tour* meant. The fact that he'd never gone to school was public knowledge, but nevertheless he worried that such a question would make him seem uneducated.

Linus's father went to the market and asked, is anyone interested in buying my plot of land near the coast?

"Why are you selling, Bapak?" someone asked. "Isn't that your ancestral land?"

At once glum and proud, Linus's father replied: "A letter from our university student arrived yesterday. The fees for his *praktikum non laboratory* doubled this month."

No one had any clue what that meant, and they didn't ask, since they didn't want to seem dumb. They did, however, start whispering about the price of Linus's education, which was riddled with English words and too much self-importance. The stranger and more difficult the foreign term, the higher the cost. Someone questioned under their breath why anyone would pay so much just to seem cultured.

"What's the use of all these foreign words? Can you eat them? Will they make rain fall during a drought?"

People in the crowd nodded in agreement.

"Ah, deep down, you're all just village people," Linus's father said, exasperated. "These strange words are going to make our son graduate from university. And if he graduates, he'll have a degree. And if he has a degree, he'll find work and get a monthly salary."

The crowd started nodding again, since this logic made more sense than the previous claim.

But the other man had a rebuttal. He said, "We spend this much money on a college degree, but then all the degree does is give us our money back. Does that not seem stupid to you?"

People in the crowd laughed, supporting the contrarian once again.

"Oh, you're trying to say we're stupid," Linus's father spat back. "If that's so, shouldn't we educate our children so that they don't end up ignorant like us?"

Murmurs of approval rippled through the crowd.

Then, one morning before breakfast, Linus's father brought his remaining livestock to the market. With a downcast look on his face, he asked an employee at the Ministry of Livestock and Agriculture if he knew anyone in the city who might be interested in buying all eight cows.

"Hey there, Mr. Unu Nakmolo. What's the deal with you selling so many cows all at once?"

"Student fees keep getting more expensive," the father replied. "I got a letter from my son last night; it was delivered on the Sinar Gemilang bus. The cost of student housing went up, and membership fees are due for the *Student Association of Chain-Smoking and Binge-Drinking*. At the end of the day, prices are rising like crazy these days, right? So, I have to sell," he puffed out his chest as though to say, of-course-you-know-what-I-mean.

But the cattle trader said that while he could understand rising housing costs, he'd never heard of that student group before.

Linus's father met the man's worried gaze, consoling himself with the thought that many people weren't nearly as educated as they seemed.

"You see," he explained, "*chain-smoking* is a monthly activity on a university campus. Same with *binge-drinking*. Membership fees cover some other activities, such as *study tour, praktikum non laboratory, hangover,* and so on. You went to college, didn't you? I'm sure you're familiar with what I mean. Oh, I see, I see, maybe these are new terms you're not acquainted with, since you graduated a long time ago."

Full of pity, the man translated the meaning of the itemized nonsense, reminding the father that the boy was supposedly studying financial management. Stunned, the concerned parent immediately hailed a mototaxi to the bus station and bought a ticket on the Sinar Gemilang bus. After eight hours of travel, he arrived at the University of West Timor. He spoke to a few administrators, and after confirming that his son had been running a scam, Linus's father swore of never spend another penny on foreign words. Instead, he sent his son the bare minimum for enrollment fees and housing. For food, he sent Linus rice, dried fish, jerky, and a bit of lard in a bamboo tube.

"You can get free pussy on campus. Just start dating a girl and convince her to mess around with you. Once you get bored, break up with her and look for someone else."

That's what a soldier told Linus when, despondent, the student recounted the tale of how his father had discovered his fraudulent money-making scheme. The man in uniform was just consoling the boy, but for Linus, those were words of wisdom he now needed to live by. So, he started searching for someone to date.

Linus, however, was unlucky in love. He was clean-shaven and smelled good, and he had a nice face, wavy hair, and a tall, athletic build. But not a single student wanted to date him. He could easily convince girls to go on walks with him but never managed to close the deal. In Timor, there's an old unwritten rule that when a man and a woman walk side by side, the woman has to walk on the left, so that she'd be protected if a lustful horse sprinted by – or, in those days, if a brazen military convoy raced down the road and grazed the couple. Linus, however, had been deaf in his left ear ever since the lizard incident of his youth, which meant that whenever he invited a girl to go on a walk, he couldn't hear a thing she said. In addition to that hurdle, Linus didn't have much to say – he was frankly very dumb and almost never opened a book. The girls at university were crazy for intellectual activists, even if this ilk tended to be grubby and disheveled, and were certain to be despised by their future in-laws.

But because Linus was a good-looking guy despite his flaws, girls found it fun to put him on display. They liked how it felt when he asked them to go for a walk along the beach, where they could pose for photos if a passerby offered to take pictures of them for spare change. The girls would later show off the photos to friends who didn't know Linus and invent stories about how they'd managed to snag such a handsome boy. But when they stood by the water's edge and Linus breached the topic of dating, the girls would look at him with thinly veiled disgust and quickly reject him.

"You're so sweet, kaka, but you're like a brother to me."

And Linus would leave, sullen and dejected.

"But what do they expect? You asked them to take a walk with you," a soldier said to Linus, who nodded.

"Better to just drug them," the solider added with a laugh.

Linus asked how.

The soldier showed him some cheap medicinal herbs that he could easily buy at a market. The right dose of the concoction would allegedly make a girl lose consciousness but also turn her on. All he needed to do was slip the drugs into her mouth.

Armed with his special potion, Linus took action. He bought ice cream and other snacks for every girl he took out for walks, each one of whom only thought of him as a brother. After a few swallows, they'd start to feel dazed, at which point he'd bring them back to his room to have some fun.

Lots of women were willing to go on walks with him, and each was more than happy to be treated to ice cream by such a good-looking man. Thanks to his concoctions, Linus managed to fuck somewhere between four and seven women each month. Afterwards, they all despised him for what he'd done, but no one had the courage to report Linus to the police. They knew they'd be humiliated by all the questions: If you didn't want it, why'd you go back to his room? How wet were you when it happened?

But one girl did go to the police. No one could make her feel more shame than she had felt already, and she was determined to press charges. I wasn't conscious when I was taken back to his room, she said calmly. I think I was drugged. No, I wasn't wet at all.

"Do you have a daughter, officer? Arrest that rapist."

The girl's testimony was strong enough to call the perpetrator down to the station. But once he got there, Linus just laughed.

"Two minutes after we started fucking, she got really into it. She even started moaning, 'oh, oh!' Just like that, officer."

The men snickered and didn't give the girl a chance to respond. Linus was released, and the police just assumed the girl was a student who slept around for extra cash, who submitted the report because she wasn't making enough money.

The experience only emboldened Linus to charge ahead with his plan. He groped body after body, entered vagina after vagina, some of which smelled like garlic, others like sandalwood. Some of his targets were virgins, while others had already sought out abortions because of trysts with other men.

Eighteen months passed, and Linus started to think that maybe something was wrong with his cock. Ever since his first rape, he'd stopped using condoms and always came inside his victims, just like that. But from the one hundred and thirty-eight college students he'd assaulted (he kept a list) he never heard of a single girl ending up pregnant.

Confused, Linus changed tactics. Every time he identified a new target, he made sure to ask the girl about the date of her last period. That way, he could count the days in her cycle and strike only when she was ovulating.

He tried it with Novi, first. He fucked her and waited. A month later, Novi gave him icy stares on campus, but her belly looked normal. No signs of pregnancy. He mustered the courage to ask her, Novi, are you pregnant? Did you get your period?

Novi looked Linus straight in the eye and spat at his feet.

"If I get knocked up, you're a dead man," she replied.

But Linus was persistent. He tried again with Rita, but she didn't get pregnant. Then with Imelda. No results. Reni. Nothing. Icha. Nothing. Jessica. Same result. Sinta. Desi. Nurul. Twenty-two other young women, and not a single one ended up carrying his child. After his forty-fourth try, he gave up.

God had cursed Linus. He was sterile.

X

Every time a new pastor is ordained, God stops working and comes down from heaven to anoint his new servant. People say that if you witness a ceremony, you can feel the presence of God.

She remembered her late father when the young pastors knelt in front of the altar. The archbishop and his seminary students wore billowing chasubles that rustled in the breeze and took turns placing their hands on the foreheads of the new clergymen. As the sound of the choir singing *Veni Creator* echoed through the room, she could see one student's eyes reflect her dad's face back at her. He was wearing glasses and crossed his thumbs tightly. She couldn't feel God, but she did sense the presence of her father. She glanced at her husband, who asked her with his eyes if everything was alright. She nodded, then looked down and kissed her son's forehead.

When she looked back up at the altar, her eyes met those of a new pastor, Father Yosef. Just ordained, he stood in a line facing the older pastors in order to receive his first blessing. She'd seen Yosef's face printed in the church newsletter as one of the seminary students to be ordained by the archbishop. She hadn't seen him in a very long time, not since the terrifying kiss they'd shared, and so she felt there wasn't anything wrong with bringing her child and husband to the ordination. They woke up early and got seats next to the choir, just a few rows from the altar. But she didn't expect that he'd look directly into her eyes.

Yosef ended up becoming a pastor; Maria had gotten married. But Yosef blushed, smiling. He was happy, and God loved him even though worldly desires still made his cheeks burn.

After Mass, Maria kissed the back of Yosef's hand and introduced him to her husband as "the pastor I told you about." Her husband chuckled and also kissed Yosef's hand.

"My name is Wildan, Father," he said and then held out the little boy Maria had kissed during the ceremony. "This is Riko. He's just about one year old." Speaking to Riko, he added, "say hello to the pastor. Hello! Kiss his hand. Yes, just like that. So smart!"

For years, Yosef asked that God grant Maria happiness, but on that day, he wondered if all his prayers were simply a way of nursing his tender heart. After all, now that he saw Maria truly content, he was pained by the fact that he hadn't been the one to give her joy.

The little family asked Father Yosef for his phone number, and every weekend they called to ask if he had time to come to their home for dinner. But with every call, the young pastor replied with, oh, I'm sorry.

"Oh, I'm sorry. I have to prepare for a first communion."

"Oh, I'm sorry. There's a wedding reception at a hotel that I promised to attend."

Wildan suggested that maybe it would be better for them to call on Father Yosef rather than the other way around. Pastors were said to be like Timorese kings – that's why we call them Mister Father, right? What kind of Timorese family would dare ask a king to come to their house? Shocked, Maria laughed. Wildan hurried to give her a kiss. He knew the sorts of cynical things those lips would launch at him if he didn't quickly snuff them out with a caress.

And so, one Sunday, the family drove on their motorbike to mass at the Saint Ferdinandus Church, which is where Father Yosef worked. Maria balanced a six-pack of beer, a roast chicken, sugar, coffee, and a few other kitchen essentials on her lap. Father Yosef gave the family a respectful hello, but it was the head pastor who greeted them with extraordinary warmth.

The head pastor was old. His face was a patchwork of varicose veins, wrinkles, and liver spots. When he invited the young family to eat with him and Father Yosef, the group chatted about a variety of topics – politics, the future of the country, the weather, faith – and it was a conversation that marked the beginning of a long friendship. Administratively speaking, Maria and Wildan weren't part of the Saint Ferdinandus parish district, but that's where they always attended Mass on Sundays. Sometimes, if Wildan had a night shift (he worked at the public hospital), the family would go to morning Mass before sunrise. They often brought gifts for the parish, ranging from food and kitchenware to bathroom supplies. The head pastor loved little Riko. He liked lifting the boy high above his head, guessing his weight, and asking about what the child liked to eat.

The boy was still only able to say words like *mama* and *dada*, so his response to the pastor's questions consisted mostly of giggles.

"How'd you get so heavy, Riko? What did you eat today?"

"Mammaaaa!"

"Tell me, Riko, what's your favorite food?"

"Da-daaaaaa!"

Cute kids often act as the glue that holds adult relationships together. And so, as time passed, Maria's family grew closer to the rectory. The couple didn't just bring gifts for the pastors but also for all the other people working at the church, like the cook (who was also the laundrywoman), the drivers, and the gardeners.

On Riko's third birthday, Maria prepared loads of food and brought it all to the rectory. She celebrated her son with Father Yosef, the head pastor, and the rest of the church staff. Yosef led everyone in a lengthy prayer, which made the birthday boy doze off before his cake was served. Maria acted as Riko's representative, blowing out his candles as he napped. Then the group sang happy birthday, and the head pastor offered a more concise prayer expressing gratitude to God.

"Oh, generous Father, He who is all-knowing, bless this child with a long life and little brothers and sisters."

Maria shook her head.

"Not that part, Father. Not right now," she whispered.

Everyone laughed, and the head pastor's wish never materialized. Two weeks after the birthday party, a convoy of military trucks hit Riko and his father. Wildan had been driving down a straightaway on the highway heading to Naibonat. The bodies of father and son ended up crushed beyond recognition, plastered across the pavement.

Military convoys consisted of Unimogs that sped down highways at more than 90 kilometers per hour. Developed countries know how to design quality killing machines, and developing countries know how to use them. It was a hot, dry Sunday in July, and father and son were driving to Grandma's house to drop off chicken feed. Normally, Wildan went alone, but this was the second time he decided to bring Riko along with him. The boy was big enough to take a trip, he thought; just father and son, watching the city go by, talking about things man-to-man. The smell of coral, the ocean breeze, sounds of birds chirping, dust from the road. The sun hadn't set yet; it hovered a centimeter over the horizon, emitting a red glow. Right about then, the motorbike was hit from behind, launching father and son forward. Milliseconds later, the trucks ran the bodies over. Chicken feed scattered. Blood and brains thickened the dirt road. One of Riko's eyeballs was stuck to an Unimog's tire. Onlookers gathered by the side of the road, but no one was brave enough to get any closer. Bearing witness to such events had a tendency to land you in jail.

The Unimogs pulled to a stop. A few soldiers started cursing, complaining about careless civilian drivers. The war on the eastern half of the island was heating up, and soldiers had to rush to the front lines. People should know to pull onto the shoulder when a military convoy is headed their way.

Only a few minutes passed before the Unimogs sped off. A commissioned officer was assigned to offer condolences at the funeral.

———————

The man was surprisingly young for a commissioned officer, but nevertheless, he was the state official selected to speak publicly about the death of Wildan and the little boy Riko. Someone sitting behind a desk had written up a statement overflowing with expressions of grief and declarations of loyalty to the Indonesian nation. The officer had made similar speeches at other funerals – Unimogs running over civilians was a pretty frequent occurrence on Timorese highways – so he'd already memorized the standard remarks. All he had to do was add a sentence here or there from the Book of Exodus to inspire patriotic sentiments in his audience.

When the officer showed up at the home of the deceased, flanked by two soldiers, the crowd turned to look at him with a mixture of hatred and respect, as though they wanted to cry out, "Look, the murderers!" but also ask, "You did it to defend our country, right?"

The officer was used to being on the receiving end of such looks, and he knew to navigate the situation with small but confident steps. He typically made an extra effort to dress well for a funeral in the hopes that any hostile atmosphere might melt in his charismatic presence. Young, good-looking, and wearing a uniform – who could help but fall in love? His face was clean-shaven without the slightest hint of stubble, and his friendly eyes bore no trace of guilt. The biggest creature he'd ever killed in his life was a cockroach, and that was only because the insect had scared his fiancée (but then his wife-to-be left him for an officer in the air force, so he frequently regretted murdering the insect).

He trimmed his silky hair on a weekly basis to ensure it was always very short, and he smoothed it down with gel each morning. His uniform, neatly ironed, was dotted with lapel pins highlighting his awards and distinctions.

The two soldiers trailing the officer looked like run of the mill Timorese men: curly hair, dark skin, prominent jawlines perfect for showcasing smiles. It was a shame they entered the house with frowns that made them both look frightening. The one who walked in first was older, maybe fifty. Sporting a thin mustache and a bit of a potbelly, he was the kind of soldier who spent his days pushing paperwork and closing up the office at the end of a workday. The second was significantly younger, not even twenty years old; he looked like a wild dog with eyes that darted around the room and a scar above one of his eyebrows, which one could assume he'd gotten during an altercation at whatever military academy he just graduated from.

The funeral Mass closed with a blessing. Three pastors sat by a makeshift altar while the funeral officiant spoke into a microphone. Meanwhile, a middle-aged man approached the military guests, bowing as though he were a coolie addressing a colonial overlord, and asked if they'd like to sit in the front row. The officer shot the man a commanding smile and took a big step forward, straightening the collar of his uniform, which didn't need straightening. The sedentary-looking soldier with the mustache skulked behind him. The wild dog, meanwhile, stayed back with the rest of the mourners, arms crossed over his chest, at the ready.

The funeral conductor stumbled over his words, then invited the district pastoral body to say a word or two. The head pastor stood up and took the mic, thanking the funeral officiant for presiding over the memorial service. The speakers let out a long, painful screech. As the noise faded, the pastor welcomed mourners to the Saint Sabina congregation, the church in their parish district. He strung together a few clichés about death and loss and gave a few examples about how kindhearted Wildan had been in life. Then he started muttering about his disappointment in the mourners of his congregation, how worried he was about them, since instead of praying and crying to process their grief, many of them joined the underground gambling rings that met out in the banana groves. He'd investigated the problem and discovered that bookies were organizing games of kuru-kuru, roulette, cards, and other illicit activities. The police will hopefully arrest the people behind this, he warned the congregants, and repeatedly emphasized that gambling was a sin. At the end of the speech, he thanked the other pastors present at the funeral service, including those from the Saint Ferdinandus congregation, who'd taken it upon themselves to attend the funeral.

He turned the mic back to the funeral officiant, who started reading out names of mourners without bothering with any more pleasantries. The clergymen were called first, followed by the immediate family and then by other churchgoers in attendance. Even though the tombs would only be marked by simple, unengraved slabs of stone and buried behind the house, mourners were expected to walk by the coffins while reciting the rosary. Those who were crying shuffled down the rows of seats, trying not to trip over the many women and children in attendance. The funeral officiant hadn't finished reading out the names when the mustached soldier approached him and whispered something in his ear.

Oh yeah, he said once the soldier stepped away. Everyone, please sit down. Officer Sugiyono would like to say a few words. Let's turn our attention to him now.

The commissioned officer stood up, straightened his still-impeccable collar, and gave a respectful nod to the two coffins lying side by side, one tiny, one big. He also nodded at the woman sitting on the far side of the coffins, whose face was streaked with tears. He tapped his hand on the mic, and the sound check echoed across the room with authority. Everyone fell silent.

"Ladies and gentlemen, honorable mourners, I hold you in the highest esteem," he opened his speech. "Today, our Republic grieves. In our effort to safeguard the unity of our nation, we continue to lose our finest warriors to this cause, including – "

"Fuck this. You bastard!" The woman on the far side of the coffins, the one whose face was blotchy and swollen, burst out angrily before lunging towards the man in uniform.

———

In her study group, Maria had uncovered plenty of evidence about corrupt state officials who stole opportunities from desperate, impoverished communities across the islands of eastern Indonesia. They seized ancestral land, registering the titles in their own names. Hectares upon hectares of grassland that families needed to herd cattle was taken; rows and rows of teak trees were planted so that timber plantations could function at an industrial scale. Constantly, officials took payoffs when budgeting for construction projects, state budgets, and social welfare – no matter the source, everything was riddled with corruption. And as the turmoil in East Timor escalated, plenty of resources were funneled to the island, but funds never actually made it into the hands of anyone affected by the conflict.

Maria and her fellow students tried to report their findings. But time passed, and they made little progress. Maria had to accept that her group was too small to stand up to the government. The system was corrupt to the core, to the extent that if one official was ousted, they'd only be replaced by one of their corrupt cronies, who in turn would be protected by a corrupt regime, kept in place by a corrupt electoral system, and supported by a shameless and despicable political culture. Proud citizens tolerated the rot that plagued the state, even though the stench of corruption was more nauseating than the smell of the starving bodies that lined every street.

Thinking about it almost drove Maria insane, so she stopped attending study group, stopped fighting, and stopped believing in her country and anyone associated with it. She just worked towards finishing school and dedicated more time to praying and fasting, since, as she'd say, only God is capable of saving this country. She went to church every morning and prayed three times a day like a widow waiting to die. Never once did she forget to pray for Yosef, and she hoped that other young boys would dream of becoming members of the clergy.

Then, one overcast day in December, one of Maria's friends from university – Elisabeth – tried to get an abortion and almost bled to death. In tears, Elisabeth explained that she was part of a Catholic youth group and had been sleeping with the pastor who oversaw the organization. He was thirty-something, and not only had he paid her tuition at university, but he also gave her a credit card and let her share it with her younger siblings. When the man approached her for sex, she couldn't say no. He promised to leave the church and marry her, but when she told him about her pregnancy, the pastor claimed it wasn't his and accused her of sleeping around. She went to a different pastor for help, but he ordered her to stop slandering the church and come back with hard evidence, since the man she was maligning had founded a Catholic youth organization known across the archipelago for its godliness.

"If he refused to acknowledge the child, what's the point of trying to prove that he's the father?" Elisabeth said in a whimper.

One of the girl's close male friends reluctantly asked why she hadn't said something when the pastor started touching her. How had he managed to get that close to her, time and time again?

"And you, have you ever been felt up by someone you respect?" one of Elisabeth's female friends fired back. "Someone you feel indebted to?"

The friend laughed.

I'd just sit back and enjoy myself, he said, in an effort to break the tension in the room.

But a different girl cursed him out, and his mother, and then ordered him to leave. A man would never understand. Men were born to get women pregnant.

In the hopes that Elisabeth wouldn't blame herself, that she wouldn't feel like the most deplorable woman on earth, her friends told her about all of their own experiences sleeping with pastors. Agnes had exchanged caresses with Father Agus; Ira talked dirty on the phone with Father Rafael; Yani made Father Binus gasp after he ordered her to kneel in front of his crotch – and plenty of other stories about pastors that are too dirty to repeat here.

But none of the other girls had gotten pregnant or needed an abortion, so despite their efforts, Elisabeth still felt like the most deplorable woman on earth. Not a single story could change how she saw herself. The only person swayed by the girls' experiences was Maria. Maria cried for days and gave up her faith in the church. She didn't want to set foot in Mass, since every time a pastor raised the chalice and said a blessing, she pictured him panting with desire. Or, she'd see Elisabeth's deathly pale face, Yani on her knees, and so on. Any prayer or blessing that came out of a pastor's mouth disgusted her. She tried to read stories about saints and pious men, but nothing worked. Every time she went to church and ran into a member of the clergy, she was horrified. If a pastor smiled at her, she asked herself if it was an honest smile or if the man was trying to get her into bed. She stopped going to Mass. While people flocked to church on Sunday mornings, Maria could be found at the Saint Klara cemetery, lighting candles by the side of her parents' graves, speaking to the dead.

One Sunday in May, she finally decided to go back to church. She still didn't believe in the institution, but Wildan, her boyfriend, had asked her to marry him. She met Wildan at the hospital back when she visited

Elisabeth. He was a friendly nutritionist who stopped by to check on her friend – and also to check on her. Maria and Wildan kept talking even after Elisabeth was discharged. Maria found out that he was the kind of person with whom she could talk about anything, and who always wanted to go with her to the cemetery on Sundays. He read widely and was never patronizing. Less than one year went by before Maria realized she'd fallen in love. The young couple started dating, and after Maria graduated from university, Wildan asked her to go to church with him and speak to a pastor about getting married. She really loved him. If Wildan asked her to go with him to hell, not to mention a church, she'd gladly agree.

Ever since their first meeting, Wildan knew that Maria had witnessed things that made her give up hope in her country, the Church, and so on. He tried to meet her where she was at, even though he'd occasionally remind her:

"Even if a thousand soldiers are assholes, it doesn't mean that the entirety of the Indonesian military is bad. Even if a thousand pastors are womanizers, that doesn't make all churches evil. Even if a thousand government officials are corrupt, that doesn't mean we should give up on our country."

But Maria insisted that all three of these institutions were fundamentally criminal, since they overlooked atrocities and protected those who committed the crimes.

"They have no impulse to acknowledge wrongdoings and improve," she explained. "It's glaringly obvious that their people are out of line, and all they do is try to cover it up. Even when we corner them, they just wash their hands of the problem and say, sure, but what can we do? That's how the system works. Or, they'll say, that's just one person you're talking about. It's inevitable, humanity is flawed."

After Riko was born, Maria was willing to attend Sunday mass for the sake of her son. She didn't want her child to hate the church without having his own reasons. Wildan stood by her, patiently, only occasionally trying to point out the good sides of what she hated. When the head pastor scooped Riko off the ground, Wildan nudged Maria and whispered, Look, not all pastors are bad, are they?

Slowly, Maria regained an inkling of hope. She always sat next to her husband and asked him a lot of questions; she started to realize how cynical her thoughts had become and how fear had colored her point of view. Even when her husband and son's remains were delivered to her, accompanied by the deafening sound of sirens, she still tried to remember what her husband had taught her, tried to imagine the sorts of things he used to say.

Let it go, Maria. Just live. Forgiveness brings peace.

Even when the officer tapped his hand on the microphone and everyone fell silent, Maria thought about her husband's optimistic smile and tried to open her heart. God's plan is rarely clear. But when that officer began his speech by yoking the death of her family to the unity of the Indonesian Republic, Maria was overcome with rage.

———

"Fuck this. You bastard!"

Shouting, Maria leapt forward, reached for the glass flower vase standing by the coffins, and hurled it at the officer as hard as she could. Reflexively, he dodged the projectile, and the vase collided into the microphone on the altar. The sound of the crash reverberated through the loudspeakers, thunderous in the heat of the sunny afternoon. Since Maria was a mere two steps from her target, three men rose to their feet and swiftly restrained her. Having failed in her direct attack, Maria pushed against the arms inhibiting her and spat. The choir let out a low *oh*, and the soldier with the scar on his face hurried to the podium in an effort to shield his boss. The other solider, the one who seemed to spend most days behind a desk, also stood up, but only to stare at the scene, unsure how to respond. The officer pulled a black handkerchief from his pocket and calmly wiped the saliva off his face.

Maria struggled against the men and started screaming recklessly.

"Unity of the nation? What are you talking about? This unity comes at a pretty high price, huh?" she roared. "The kind that costs us our lives! That cost me my own family, you motherfucking idiot! Get away from my husband and son. You think our borders are more important than… Bullshit! You asshole."

To punctuate her speech, Maria spat again, and this time the glob fell square into the eye of the young soldier now standing in front of the officer. Once again, the audience gasped in unison, and rows of mouths hung open in shock. But the soldier still stood at attention, refusing to be provoked by the woman's words or her spit, which stuck to the corner of his eye.

It took a while for Maria to calm down, but finally, the funeral continued. By the time the coffins were finally lowered into the ground, one next to the other, Maria felt as though she'd been buried alive.

———

Everyone felt sorry for Maria and wanted to comfort her, especially now that she was all alone, but eventually, people had to press on with their lives. At first, Wildan's mother moved in to keep her daughter-in-law company, but she left after the memorial service, which took place forty days after the tragedy. The woman had her own home and lots of chickens to care for. By the time three months had passed, Maria's friends rarely visited her. They used to drop by every week, then every month, and eventually, they stopped coming altogether. No one knocked on Maria's door. The city was as busy as ever, but it felt as though the fences in front of every house had grown taller. People forgot about Maria and her anger. The chaotic incident at the funeral had faded from their memories. Meanwhile, gutters across the island filled with more and more bodies as Unimog convoys sped down highways.

The only conversation partners Maria had left were her TV and the graves of her late husband and son. Sitting in front of the screen, she'd comment on the idiocy of soap opera stars. As for the dead, she'd chat with them about plenty of things, ranging from the cockroaches that darted around her dining room to the intermittent blackouts that had started in Kupang. At one point, she got bored of the TV and the tombstones and started looking after a cat instead. But three days later she banished it from her house, disgusted that the creature had tried to lick her. She tried attending neighborhood meetings with the other women on her block, but they mostly discussed tedious things like how to make your own handbag from woven fabric or the best ways to convince a child who dreamed of becoming a poet to change their mind and aspire to a career in medicine. Inconsolable, Maria started thinking about ways to kill herself that wouldn't be too painful. It was right about then when Father Yosef made a visit to her home.

"Maria, you need to get out of the house," the pastor said. He poured himself a glass of boxed iced tea that he'd brought over to Maria's home.

"There's no point. The world always finds ways to cause me pain."

Father Yosef told her the story of Job, a figure in the bible from the Land of Uz who was always saddled with misfortune. He then told her about a believer who'd been abandoned when he was a small child, since people in his town accused his father, mother, and three siblings of being possessed by evil and burned them alive. Father Yosef stood up, but before he left, he told Maria she was welcome at church whenever she wanted to come.

God is waiting for you at the door: Come to Me, all you who are weary and burdened.

A few days passed, and Maria mustered the energy to go to church. She woke up early, took a shower, called a taxi, and went to the chapel. The head pastor, who'd witnessed Maria's attack on the officer first-hand, welcomed her.

"Praise God, you're okay," he said, his face brimming with gratitude. "We were worried about you, Maria."

He told her that it was unheard of for a civilian to spit on a solider. And if civilians dared to do such a thing, they'd almost certainly be arrested or disappeared to who-knows-where.

"I was telling the truth," Maria explained.

The head pastor made the sign of the cross, trying to collect himself so he wouldn't break down in tears.

From that day onward, Maria woke up each morning at dawn and ordered a taxi to take her to church. She'd sit in the pews next to old widows, recite the rosary, and listen to Mass, overcome with doubt: did God really listen to the prayers of millions of people each morning?

After Mass she would walk home, passing the market and a strip of foodstalls owned by Bugis people. Walking cleared her head, and the bustle of the streets gave her energy to face the day. Occasionally, Yosef and the head pastor would invite her to lunch after Mass like they used to back when Wildan and Riko were still alive. She always accepted. Sharing a meal with the two pastors was better than sitting alone at home, crying.

She knew that her close relationship with the pastors would raise eyebrows, considering she was a young widow, but Maria swore on her late husband and child that she had no intention of seducing either of the men. Her feelings for Yosef were long forgotten, the sensation of her heart racing during their kiss on the beach a thing of the past. Wildan didn't just erase the touch of Yosef's lips on Maria's – he also forged a kind of love that burned far deeper than anything Maria had experienced before.

But one day, when the two pastors and their guest were eating, the telephone rang in the living room. The head pastor hurried to go pick up the call, and suddenly, Father Yosef found himself standing behind Maria's chair, cradling Maria's head in his hands. She looked up and met his eyes. His gentle eyes, half-obscured by his long nose. He looked down and kissed the crown of her head. Maria closed her eyes, letting herself enjoy the feeling of being touched. She would tell Yosef to step away from her when she opened her eyes, she thought, but before she could say a word, he was already kissing her eyelids, her cheeks, her nose, and finally her lips. He kissed her. Once. Twice. Maria blinked and opened her lips slightly. The real kiss began. They bit one another, ardently pressed their mouths together. They heard an audible gasp and froze. Only then did they realize that the head pastor had been standing in the doorway for who knows how long, watching them, speechless.

No one finished lunch that morning. Maria stood up and left without excusing herself, Father Yosef went into his room without a word of explanation, and the head pastor sat down at the table alone and clumsily ate a piece of bread. On her walk home, Maria kicked herself, begging her late husband and child for forgiveness. It wasn't just the kiss that tortured her – it was the fact that she'd wanted the kiss. She was deplorable for having wanted him. Humiliated.

———

Too ashamed to face the head pastor, Father Yosef requested a private meeting the Honorable Archbishop one week after the kiss in the dining room.

"If a position opens up far away from the city center, I'd like Your Grace to consider me as a candidate," he said.

The bishop asked if Yosef was unhappy in his current role.

"No, not at all. I'd just like a challenge. My job here in the city feels too easy," he lied.

The bishop was very pleased with Father Yosef's answer. Most pastors had the wrong mindset. They only wanted placements in big cities and complain when they were asked to serve a community in a small town or an impoverished region. If someone was assigned such a post, the pastor would accept the new position because of the promise he'd made to obey the bishop, but he'd act as though he was being sent to a dump. So, when the sisters at Sacred Heart handed Saint Helena High School over to the diocese, the archbishop called on Father Yosef.

"I won't disappoint you, Your Grace," Father Yosef said in earnest.

The official letter announcing Father Yosef's transfer was read aloud on the radio. Maria heard it, and it only made her feel more lost than she had before. She assumed that the bishop had found out about Yosef's affair with a young widow, and that Yosef had been punished, exiled to the periphery of Kupang. She felt sinful, like someone who tried to inhibit the work of God's servants. And meanwhile, her sense of guilt towards her dead family hadn't diminished in the slightest. Overwhelmed, she couldn't articulate which anxiety plagued her: sin in the face of God, the feeling of wrongdoing for derailing Yosef's career, or self-contempt. For days, she didn't leave her house, dumbfounded, unable to do anything except doze off and nibble at scraps of food. She ate so little that she didn't even need to defecate; she only ate enough to stave off the pulsing headaches that plagued her.

Days turned into weeks, weeks into months. As the seasons changed, Maria lost her mind. She became forgetful, slept fitfully, and her sense of reality and time escaped her. She stopped cleaning her house and refused to even crack open the windows for fresh air. She couldn't remember where she left her shoes or if she flushed the toilet. She did remember to beg for forgiveness when she stood in front of the graves of her late family, but she couldn't recall when or how she'd made a huge dent in the TV. Sometimes she felt so old and frail that she couldn't lift her arms. Sometimes she heard her son playing outside and her husband whistling from the bathroom. Sometimes her mom appeared by the door, asking her if she'd washed her feet. Sometimes she found a bit of the banana blossom sambal her dad used to make on the kitchen table. Sometimes when she was curled up in a fetal position, she thought she was still inside her mother's womb.

One night, she dreamt that her son and husband visited her. They told her that people in heaven love one another. That heaven doesn't have countries or militaries, churches or religious leaders. That in heaven, no one bickers or fights, no one cares about their reputation.

The three of them slept on the floor that night. Wildan hugged Maria, and Riko nestled his head in the crook of Maria's neck. It was a beautiful night, and she slept soundly.

The next morning, Maria woke up early. She took a shower and washed her hair, put on her nicest clothes, called a taxi, and went to church. There were only six nuns sitting in the first row, and seven widows in a cluster to her right. But in the darkness before dawn, their voices sounded like a choir of angels singing in a movie about the prophets.

Mass ended, and Maria walked home on her usual route. She thought about her husband, her son. Her father, her mother. How's it going in heaven? When she reached the first intersection, she purchased a newspaper. When she walked through the market, she bought some hot porridge. When she got to the Liliba Bridge, she climbed up the guardrail, then jumped. The bridge was more than five hundred meters off the ground. The river was running dry. A long drought had just begun.

XI

Back when he was a child, a day in the life of Siprianus Portakes Oetimu went like this:

Am Siki would shake the boy from his dreams in the pitch-black of early dawn, before the first rays of sunlight touched the treetops and before roosters rubbed their eyes and crowed. The old man hurried to the lontar trees while Ipi went into the 'saenhanâ to process sopi.

The boy would begin by cleaning the big clay pot used to distill sap, first emptying out any residue left from the day before and then scrubbing the mouth and sides of the vessel. The pot was huge, four times the size of a horse's head, and he had to empty the sap residue without removing the pot from the stove – a task that required immense care. When he was done, he filled it up with a fresh batch of sap fermented with spices and medicinal herbs sourced from tree roots and bark that Am Siki had gathered while reciting prayers and spells.

Ipi covered the mouth of the big pot, the one filled with fermented sap, with a second clay pot. This second pot was small, narrow, and tall – the kind of thing that families would typically use as a vase. He sealed the gap between the two vessels using yellow, sticky palm fibers. The small pot had a single round hole in its side, one roughly the circumference of a stalk of bamboo.

The boy would then grab a long bamboo pole that had been hollowed out like a straw and fit one end inside the small clay pot, angling it so that the other end almost touched the ground. He once again used palm fibers to seal the gap, ensuring that no steam could escape from the space between the pot and the pole.

After double checking that everything was ready, he placed logs under the pot and started a fire. When the sap in the big pot came to a boil, steam would rise into the little pot and then through to the bamboo, where it would condense into a liquid that dripped down the pole. Ipi collected the liquid: this was sopi, the drink offered to ancestors in every traditional ceremony.

Once he confirmed that the alcohol was dripping steadily, Ipi would ride his horse to the river and take a bath. If it was a weekday, he'd get ready for school. If it was a holiday, he'd join Am Siki at the lontar palms. If it was a Sunday, he and Am Siki would both sleep in, since even Uisneno rested on the seventh day of creation.

One morning in late September, Ipi bumped into two of his friends on his way to the river. They were on horseback and heading in the opposite direction.

"Where are you going?" he asked. "Isn't there school today?"

The boys were smart and hardworking. One was good at arithmetic – an expert at counting sticks – and the other should have won a prize for wiping down the blackboards after every lesson. But that morning, they'd devised a plan to skip school and go to the headwaters of the river, where there was a deep, wide swimming hole.

"Don't you know what day it is?" They asked Ipi.

Every year on that day, men from the Ministry of Information came to the school and screened a film about the communist massacre. Not just every student, but every citizen was required to attend. Year after year they watched that movie, to the point that they knew every line of dialogue by heart. The boys refused to sit through it yet again.

Intrigued by the thought of somersaulting off tree branches into a deep pool of water, Ipi agreed to join his friends.

He hesitated when he pictured his teacher, Mr. Atolan, lashing the bums of boys who cut class. But then he thought about the movie and accepted his friends' invitation. He'd rather sit through corporal punishment than watch that dreary movie again. He'd never been to the headwaters of the river since he was always working, supporting his grandfather, and the movie about the communists was the scariest thing he'd ever seen in his life. Every year, it made him nauseous. Every year, it gave him nightmares. The film was so bloody that his appetite would vanish for days after each screening.

The headwaters of the river were far to the north, but the horses were agile enough to gallop towards their destination. The boys cut across grasslands, yelping out replies to monkey calls and bleating deer that echoed down from the rocky hills. When they reached the swimming hole, the three friends couldn't wait to jump into the water and leapt off their horses. Ipi quickly kicked his pants off and ran towards the water. But the minute his clothes fell to the ground, his friends' jaws dropped. The boys had just started sixth grade, but Ipi's private parts were huge, maybe two times the size of their own.

"Wow. Does that hurt?" One of the boys asked.

"Seriously," the other replied, "it looks deformed."

Ipi analyzed his friends' private parts, first one, then the other, before looking down at his own. He only then realized how abnormal his looked. He started to get scared – was he sick? Was he disabled? Was he going to die? His friends debated Ipi's condition, and when they weren't able to agree on a diagnosis, they remembered that there was one man who could undoubtedly give them an answer: Naef Ahelet.

Naef Ahelet was the only dukun specialized in circumcision in all the towns along the Noenifu river. Using a technique passed down from his father and his great-grandfathers, Naef Ahelet snipped hundreds of foreskins from the penises of Atoin Metô boys, ushering them into adulthood. He wasn't only responsible for the circumcision, either; he also treated the incisions with medicinal herbs and incantations before offering his patient information about how to complete the subsequent ritual, known as sifon. Every boy was required to go to Naef Ahelet and let the man cut his private parts, and any man who failed to submit himself to circumcision and sifon would suffer shame in his community.

When he spotted three young boys dismounting their horses, Naef Ahelet immediately yelled: Go home! You're still kids, come back in four or five years. He was tired of getting visits from little boys who wanted to be circumcised early just to complete the sifon ritual. They were clueless. Getting to sleep with women sounded nice, but the pain of circumcision was beyond comprehension. Even if they swam in the river for hours every single day to make their foreskins taut, most children would pass out from the pain. And the boys whose hearts weren't pure, the ones who were prone to trickery, those were the ones to bleed profusely or end up with infections. Men these days are lucky, that's what Naef Ahelet thought: they were born at a time when a tiny knife known as the razorblade exists. Back when Naef Ahelet was circumcised, his elders used a sharp piece of bamboo, and even though he was a kindhearted kid who went through every step of the ritual with integrity, he was wracked with fever for two weeks and only regained his health after completing sifon.

"We're not here to get circumcised," one of the three boys said. "Our friend's private parts are swollen. Can you tell us what's wrong with him?"

Which one of you has this problem, Naef Ahelet asked.

Ipi raised his hand.

"Come inside, I'll examine you. You two, go wait in the lopo. Come on now, hurry up. I want to go into town and watch the movie about the communists."

While his friends waited, Ipi got off his horse and went in. He unbuttoned his pants and showed his private parts to the dukun. Why is it so big? Is it deformed? Am I going to die?

Naef Ahelet didn't answer any of the boy's questions. When Ipi exposed his penis, the healer just looked at it thoughtfully. A moment later, he dropped to his knees. His face hovered near the tip, his breathing was heavy, and his eyes clouded over.

"The shape of this tolo is very nice," he said. "I've never seen anything like it."

As he spoke, he placed Ipi's cock in the palm of his hand and lifted it up to get a better look, much in the way an ornithologist would examine a new species of bird he just discovered. A minute later he was stroking the penis, tugging on the foreskin. Ipi grimaced, trying not to react from the pain. Then Naef Ahelet started rapidly moving his fingers, shaking the boy's private parts.

"Naef, why is it so big?" Ipi asked again. But why was his voice trembling? He coughed, trying to clear his throat. He felt something strange happening in his private parts. He couldn't figure out what was happening, and he felt ashamed.

"Just stay calm. Let me examine you," the circumcision doctor said as his hand moved faster and faster. Soon enough, the cock stood up straight, red, at the ready.

Naef Ahelet gripped Ipi's stiff penis. It had grown so wide that Naef's fingers could barely reach around its circumference. And then, the dukun's hand started moving up and down the shaft.

Ipi gasped, too embarrassed to look down. A ticklish but pleasant sensation spread from his private parts back to his tailbone, up his spine and into his head. His knees buckled, his head grew hot, and he felt more and more shame. He tried to avert his eyes from the dukun, but this only led him to look through the slits in the bebak walls, horrified by the thought that his friends might be able to see what was happening, watch his face balloon up, bigger and more mortified by the second.

"Naef… This… Tolo… To… Why?" he tried to muster the courage to ask a question and peep down, but his voice was too unstable. His legs were weak and unable to support his body weight. His vision went hazy as he leaned against the wall. Naef Ahelet just kept grabbing and pulling.

Up, down. Up, down. Shame, pleasure. Shame, pleasure.

Mere seconds passed before Ipi felt a throbbing sensation. Something that wasn't pee rushed up his shaft, and he instinctively wiggled his butt, meeting the rhythm of the old man's hands, which made the feeling even more incredible. He hid his face as his humiliation and gratification reached their peak at once. His body flooded with an unparalleled feeling. Dazed, his vision went blank. He looked down and saw a liquid, thick and white like the sap he boiled each morning, covering Naef Ahelet's hands. The old man was playing with the fluid and brought his hands up to his face to smell it, lick it. Ipi suddenly felt sick, whether from what the dukun was doing then or from what he himself had just done, he couldn't tell. His stomach turned inside out, and he wanted to puke.

When Naef Ahelet led him back outside, Ipi's face was as downcast as a farmer's during a long drought.

"Is our friend going to be okay, Naef?" The boys asked, concerned.

"Not to worry," Naef Ahelet replied. "He's not sick. He's healthy and strong."

His friends smiled in relief, but Ipi felt as though a part of himself had wriggled away, was gone for good.

XII

At a quarter to seven, four days before Father Yosef got terribly sick, the phone rang at Saint Helena High School. The pastor was monitoring the hallways in his white button-down shirt with his sleeves rolled up to his elbows. His face was clean-shaven, and his eyes shone as he watched from his window as students formed an orderly line outside on the field, where they stood to sing the national anthem, recite the school hymn, and swear to study hard. He ignored the first call, but when the phone rang for a second time, he hurried to go pick up. Who was thoughtless enough to call so early in the morning?

The head pastor at Saint Ferdinandus was on the line. I have some news, Yosef. What are you doing right now? An apple? Sit down. You're sitting? Maria's body was found at the base of the Liliba Bridge, so damaged that it was difficult to identify her remains. Poor woman. I saw her at mass just the other morning.

Father Yosef dropped the receiver. He felt like he'd been punched in the gut. By taking her own life, Maria had handed her soul over to the devil. Yosef called the Head of Curriculum – a math teacher in charge of organizing the academic calendar – and announced that all activities under his care for the week should be cancelled. Yosef would be attending to an urgent matter off campus.

Maria's corpse was transferred to her home after a brief stop at the hospital. The police concluded that her death was a simple case of suicide. Some of Maria's acquaintances and neighbors gathered at her house, and when Father Yosef arrived, they kissed his hand and asked what they could do to help.

Father Yosef set his bags down in the foyer and took charge of the funeral logistics. He decided where to place the open casket. He counted how many cows needed to be sacrificed in honor of the mourners and shooed away the bookies who arrived at the house with gambling tables. He placed an order for Maria's headstone, which would bear an image of Jesus raising Lazarus from the dead, a cross, Maria's name, and a Latin scripture. He called a dukun all the way in Usapinonot to confirm that rain wouldn't fall before the ground above Maria's grave hardened, even though he knew perfectly well that there wouldn't be any precipitation during a drought. He made sure that every mourner in the house had been offered refreshments and then asked them to pray for Maria's lost soul. He spent day after day organizing every detail and night after night locked in the bedroom, crying wordlessly. He agonized over Maria's soul. People who commit suicide are sent straight to hell, and only God's generosity could save Maria. He prayed that God was having a good day, that He would pardon Maria for her sins – the sin of taking her own life as well as all the little sins Maria so often committed in life, like swearing.

Father Yosef realized early on in their acquaintance that Maria was incapable of speaking without uttering a curse. It made him uncomfortable at first, but as time passed, he realized that her swearwords were like any other flowery expression that might adorn a sentence, and that these particular blossoms were a part of Maria. There was something missing when she spoke without cursing, and every time she swore, it only made her more charming. And when she was charming, it was very difficult for Father Yosef to stop himself from falling in love with her.

That evening on the beach, Maria had told Yosef about a Mass she had attended, one led by a young pastor. The pastor wasn't fat or sweaty, she explained; he was rather thin, sort of like a student activist who can barely make ends meet, the type who always has messy hair and a worn-out look on his face. But the way the young pastor saw the world was akin to how a dictator's henchman might think. During his sermon, the pastor asked that the young people of Kupang refrain from participating in any demonstrations that challenged the government, and certainly those that insulted our beloved Mr. Suharto. Offending others – especially the president himself – doesn't align with Timorese culture or the religious norms of the Church.

"This pastor thinks his job is to avoid ruffling feathers," Maria said. "That motherfucker is one of Suharto's lackeys, no doubt about it. He preaches like he's licking Suharto's ass. How can an ass-licker call himself a servant of God? Psht. Shameless son of a bitch. Does he want to spread God's grace? No. He's too scared to fight oppression."

Yosef didn't say anything. He smiled and tried to resist the pull of Maria's charm, which burgeoned with her every word. She looked at him for a few seconds, her eyes searching for something hidden in his gaze.

"You aren't a coward like that pastor, are you, Yosef?"

Yosef was not a coward. He kissed Maria. She kissed him back. And even though that kiss meant they wouldn't see each other for a long time, Yosef would often congratulate himself for having done it. That kiss proved he was brave.

On the day that Maria buried her husband and son, Father Yosef felt a twinge of pity for the soldiers who suffered her abuse, but mostly, he was amazed by Maria's rampage. She went for those men in uniform like a highly trained athlete determined to win a gold medal. As curse words flowed effortlessly from her mouth, she was more captivating than ever.

"Oh, so when you soldiers drive your tanks to go murder innocent civilians, you manage to kill even more innocent civilians along the way? You motherfucking sons of bitches."

After Maria mourned her family and began attending Mass again, Maria still slipped swear words into most everything she said, especially with Father Yosef. When the head pastor invited her to meals at the rectory and grumbled about the broken toaster, Maria lifted the pastor's spirits by quoting the same Bible verses that Father Yosef used to recite in an effort to comfort her.

"Don't worry, Mister Father," she'd said. "Be patient with God's grace. Better days will come. Birds of the air neither sow nor reap nor gather into barns; yet your heavenly Father feeds them, is that not so?"

The head pastor expressed his gratitude, raising his index finger to draw the sign of the cross. But the next week, when it was Father Yosef who muttered angrily in front of the very same finicky toaster, Maria told him not to worry in a loud voice, making sure that the head pastor heard her, and then leaned towards the young pastor and whispered:

"Don't become one of those hedonistic men of the clergy, Yosef!" she said as she pretended to inspect the broken appliance. "People die every day. They perish from war or hunger. They die. But you, you eat a hot meal at the rectory while complaining about this broken toaster, hm? Some shepherd of the faithful you are. It's shameless."

Father Yosef pretended he couldn't hear her, but from his seat at the dining table the head pastor heard whispers. He asked if anything was wrong.

Maria turned around and told him: Nothing at all, Mister Father, but I think you should buy a new toaster. She traipsed back to her seat and changed the topic by making small talk about God's bounty. The phone rang from the living room, and the head pastor hurried to go take the call. The moment he left the room, Maria took a deep breath, grateful for the interruption. Father Yosef was still standing by the toaster, feeling silly after what Maria whispered to him, like a husband whose wife had subtly chided him in front of his own father. He realized with exasperation how much he loved Maria, and for who knows what reason, he walked over to her, cradled her head, and kissed her. That was the last time Father Yosef saw Maria alive. Alive, breathing, right next to his face, next to his nose, next to his lips, which were slightly ajar.

And so, he buried Maria in the most solemn of funerals. There was no time to rest. Everything needed to be perfect.

Since he hadn't slept for days, he returned to Saint Helena in a haggard state and with a sore throat. He went straight to his room and sprawled across his bed. When he woke up hours later, a raging fever had taken over his body. He was starving. He thought he was in hell. He wanted to ask someone to make him porridge, but before he could, he slipped out of consciousness again, beaten down by the fever. In a haze, he thought he could see demons raping Maria inside a giant cauldron filled with hot oil, taking turns thrusting into her, eviscerating her body. But as he fixated on the scene, he realized that he himself was one of the demons. He was horrified and filled with compassion, and yet he experienced a kind of gratification that he'd never known before. That evening, he groaned from his bed. Whether his moans were inspired by terror, pity, or pleasure, it was impossible to say.

Those were the same sounds Silvy heard that evening. The evening when she also stretched out across a mattress, the one in the spare room.

———

That wasn't the first time Silvy had heard groans of pleasure echoing from the next room. After she and her dad moved to the little house on the edge of the city, she'd frequently wake up in the middle of the night to the rhythmic sounds of a bed squealing and her father moaning. Curious, she pressed her face to the wall that separated the two rooms. Through slits in the bebak, she could see her dad wrestling with a strange woman. Her father's movements sped up as the woman sat on top of him. His pale face gleamed under the yellow light of the lamp, which made his skin take on the color of cornstarch mixed with lard. The woman was similarly luminous and sweaty, and both looked equally exhausted. Silvy's heart pounded hard, so hard it seemed to want to leap out from her chest, and blood rushed to her face. She never felt so alive or so sinful.

"Yanti... Yanti... Ah... Yanti..." Those were the words her father moaned.

As she peered through the slits in the wall night after night, Silvy realized that her father always wrestled with different women. Some were dark-skinned and others pale, some had a Javanese accent while others spoke in the Kupang dialect, some were loud, others entirely mute – but her father always called out the same name. Her mother's name.

"Yanti... Yanti... Ah... Yanti..."

One chilly evening after Silvy discovered the meaning of the verb *to masturbate* in the dictionary – she'd been looking up the word *mastuli* – the sound of her mother's name reverberated through the walls. This time, she chose to lie down on her bed and slip her hand down her pants. From that night onwards, her body shuddered every time she heard those moans. She'd always been too ashamed to touch that part of her body, but once she realized that her desires had a name – one that was written down in the dictionary, listed as a word, as a verb – she realized that many people often did exactly what she wanted to do. She started touching herself, and every time she heard her mother's name, heavy with longing, swollen with lust, her body shivered with pleasure. Her eyes rolled back, pushing against the sleeping sand still stuck in corners of her eyelids, and she pictured clouds against a clear sky and her mother's face.

"Yanti... Yanti... Ah... Yanti..."

She imagined that she was the girl moaning, basking in the love that drove such unspeakable pleasure. In awe of how her body trembled, she felt as though her soul was full, as though she were cherished. From then on, every time she woke up to the sound of a creaking bed and her father's voice, she transformed into Yanti, defying gravity, free to go wherever she pleased. She wanted to be like her mom. She'd always wanted to be like her mom. Her mom, the woman her father loved the most, more than his own daughter.

After she started organizing the reading room, Silvy ceased to exist as a student at Saint Helena High School. She spent her days taking care of books, which meant that the schedule of activities and classes no longer applied to her. She rarely made an appearance in dorms or other campus buildings since everything she needed was already in the rectory. Pretty soon, no one thought about where she might be. Everyone forgot about her. If she disappeared, no one would even think to look for her.

And that's what ended up happening. Not a single student, teacher, or staff member noticed that Silvy was gone until one afternoon, when

Father Yosef held a general staff meeting. He'd never called a gathering like that before. Every single adult associated with Saint Helena was present: teachers were asked to bring their spouses or any other relatives who lived with them on school grounds; even the gardener and his wife were present, as were the security guards and the cooks. No students or children were permitted to attend, since the adults needed to discuss important matters, Father Yosef announced. If you need childcare, contact the girls' dormitory.

With that, more than fifty people gathered in one of the school classrooms.

After the religion teacher led a brief prayer, Father Yosef opened the meeting with the story of Cain and Abel. Only Om Lamber, Tanta Yuli, and a small handful of teachers were surprised by the story and paid attention. One of the cooks nodded along while making the sign of the cross and mumbling platitudes about God's majesty, as though Yosef's retelling were itself a miracle. The other instructors and almost everyone else in the audience dozed off. They knew the story by heart – not only had they heard Father Yosef's version time and time again, but it was also one of the tales that storytellers loved to tell children.

"The first people on earth, Adam and Eve, had two children. One was named Cain, and the other, Abel. Both boys were healthy, strong, and blessed by God. When they grew up, Cain became a farmer while

Abel chose to be a shepherd. One day, both men offered sacrifices to God. Cain presented the crops he harvested – fruits and vegetables – while Abel carried forth the firstling in his flock of goats and sheep. And what happened next?"

The cook made the sign of the cross for the third time; everyone else let their eyes flutter shut.

"God was only satisfied with Abel's sacrifice – that of the shepherd. How angry Cain was!" (*Dear Lord, forgive our sins!* The cook mumbled from her seat.) "Cain told Abel to come down to his fields and murdered his brother. But Abel's spilled blood released a scream to the heavens, and God thundered down with the question: Where is Silvy, your little sister?"

Lazy and indifferent, the audience stayed mum. The pastor repeated his question, slower this time: "Where is Silvy, your little sister?"

Everyone began furrowing their brows. Since when did the Holy Book have a story about a girl named Silvy? They sat up straighter, glancing at one another.

"Where is Silvy, your little sister?" Father Yosef repeated the question.

"Mister Father, we don't understand," one person courageously interjected.

"You heard my question, did you not? Has anyone seen Silvy Hakuak Namepan? Does anyone have information about this student's whereabouts?"

Only then did everyone remember that the school once had a student named Silvy. Yes, Silvy Hakuak Namepan, she was enrolled at Saint Helena. They hadn't seen the girl in a very long time. A buzz of voices spread across the room like a swarm of bees as each person started murmuring questions to their neighbors. No one was listening. Father Yosef made a small gesture with his hands, calling the crowd to attention. The room fell silent, and after asking his audience to please be respectful, the pastor invited members of the audience to speak one by one in clear, loud voices.

The teacher in charge of the girls' dormitory recalled that she had seen the girl one month prior to the meeting. Tanta Yuli announced that she'd spoken to the girl two weeks earlier, when the sweet child had helped her bake a cake. The head of security disagreed, asserting that Silvy had come to him and asked for permission to leave the school grounds three weeks ago; she was carrying a small bag. She wrote her name on the sign-out sheet and never signed back in. The head of security took advantage of the fact that he was already speaking to point out how seriously security guards at Saint Helena took their jobs. They were never lax about the rules and carefully noted down who entered and exited school grounds at every hour of the day. Tanta Yuli's face turned scarlet as she demanded: "Then who helped me with my cake? A ghost? Is the girl dead?"

There were a few audible chuckles at Tanta Yuli's questions. Others in the room reprimanded the security team for letting a student leave school grounds without any information about when she planned on coming back.

"She told us Father Yosef gave her permission to leave," the head of security said, recalcitrant. "Besides, you tell me who could possibly stop Miss Silvy from doing what she wants. Who here has any desire to argue with that girl?"

No one had anything to say in response to that.

"Well, this is why I've asked you to be here today," Father Yosef explained. He paused for a moment and coughed, clearing an itch in his throat, and then took a sip from a big cup of coffee, which he had on hand at every meeting.

Everyone waited. The sound of the gurgling fountain out on the lawn filled the silence. A warm breeze from the Sawu Sea drifted in through the half-open windows, making the Indonesian flag ripple and mussing up the physics teacher's bangs.

"For those of you who weren't aware," the pastor resumed, "Silvy's daily assignment was to organize the books in the rectory. This was the decision our Teachers' Council agreed upon. Am I correct?"

The teachers said yes in unison.

The pastor was quiet again for a moment. He continued:

"Now, listen carefully," he said, and shifted his weight. "I swear on my mother and on Jesus's mother that I never touched the girl. I never touched a hair on her head. I'm saying this now so as to prevent rumors from spreading. I loved that girl as if she were my own daughter."

Whispers were exchanged as people began questioning where the pastor was going with this part of the speech. Together, their low voices hummed like a mass of bees stuck underground. Once again, Father Yosef raised a hand to call for silence. He continued:

"Some time ago, the student in question requested a meeting with me and asked to transfer schools. Why would she possibly wish to do such a thing?"

Father Yosef paused, and everyone started glancing around.

"She was pregnant, ladies and gentlemen."

A long *oh* shot across the room, and the din of voices swelled like the drone of flies in a room full of corpses. Some of the staff disparaged pregnancy out of wedlock, others hypothesized that lust was linked to intelligence, while others just chuckled naughtily and made nasty jokes.

"But, Honorable Father," someone spoke over the noise in the room. "Who's the father of her child?"

"Yeah, who did it?"

"Lucky bastard, whoever he is," someone added, and the men in the room laughed while the women muttered angrily.

"That is the question, ladies and gentlemen," the pastor said, yet again regaining control of the room with one small gesture. "This is the precise reason why I gathered all of you here in this classroom. I want each and every one of you to be aware of the situation. If this matter were to someday become public, I don't want anyone to be caught off-guard. I spoke to Silvy myself, we had a lengthy conversation, but she refused to tell me who the father was, and she even requested that I refrain from seeking out that information. She told me that I'd be to blame for making her condition more visible than it already was. But ever since she left our school, I've been unable to sleep. I toss and turn, because I know that one of our students was touched by a man on our school grounds. She didn't have any family to visit in the city, and not once did she leave campus prior to the incident."

People in the room nodded in agreement.

Father Yosef took a deep breath.

"I have no intention of blowing this issue out of proportion" the pastor said. "I swore to Silvy that I would do no such thing. But with God as my witness, and with a humble heart, I must ask all you gathered here today: who had intimate relations with this student?"

Suddenly, the room was quiet. No one looked at the pastor. The eyes of men were glued to the floor while those of women darted left and right. Wives fixated on their husbands, suspicious, intimidated.

Taking advantage of the silence, Father Yosef kept speaking:

"Whoever you are, this young woman is carrying your child. She's strong. She says she wants to handle this problem on her own, but she herself is just a kid. The baby in her womb will grow up and ask who their father is. Timorese men have a responsibility to support women when they suffer such difficulties."

Silence swallowed the room whole. Father Yosef scanned his audience, taking careful note of each man staring at the ground.

"Well then, ladies and gentlemen," he said after a few moments. "That's all I had to say."

The audience let out a collective sigh of relief, grateful to be spared from more torturous questions.

"If anyone has something to tell me but feels too ashamed to do so in public, my door is always open. Come whenever you'd like. We'll have a conversation."

Everyone nodded in agreement, certain that this was the best course of action. Only a complete idiot would confess to such a crime in front of the entire school.

"We're all sinners," Father Yosef concluded. "No one is honorable in the eyes of God, and our heavenly Father is Merciful. To close this meeting, and to allow everyone gathered here to reflect on our Lord, I would like to tell one final story."

The audience took another deep breath and shifted in their seats. Some sat up straight, ready to listen, while others slouched back, ready doze off.

"Once, there was a saint from Hippo, in North Africa. The name of this saint was Augustine. He lived in the fourth century after Our Savior died on the cross. In his youth, he was a sinner. He committed grave wrongdoings. He engaged in activities that would be inappropriate to repeat here today. But did he continue to behave so immorally throughout his entire life? Did God allow him to live like that, wallowing in sin?"

He paused so that his listeners might really ponder the questions he posed. The history teacher raised his hand.

"You don't need to answer the questions, instructor," Father Yosef said. "They're rhetorical."

A few people chuckled, but the history teacher didn't lower his hand.

"Like I said, I'm not actually looking for answers," Father Yosef repeated.

By then, people were laughing. What, did the history teacher not know what a rhetorical question was? But instead of putting his hand down, the instructor stood up.

"I... Here's the thing, Usi..." the teacher attempted to explain himself. He was from a region of Timor where people still address pastors with the title 'Usi'. Father Yosef gestured for the crowd to be quiet. "Silvy…" he stuttered, "I… I'm the one who did it. I got her pregnant."

Another long *oh* filled the room, followed by uproar. Some people asked, is he serious? Others snickered and claimed there was no way what he said was true. What kind of nonsense is this? It's so inappropriate to joke around like that.

But the history teacher spoke again, more assertively this time: "I don't want everyone to start pointing fingers, and I don't want rumors to cast blame on Father Usi. And so, I must confess. I confess in the name of my own mother, in the name of Jesus's mother."

He borrowed the words Father Yosef had just used to assert his innocence. Everyone was confused, unsure of what to think. While they wanted to believe the history teacher, they also knew that despite his good looks, he was by far the dumbest teacher at Saint Helena and a prime target for Silvy's mockery. There's no way she would willingly have an affair with him. But right as they determined he must be lying, they looked at his face and saw how earnest he seemed, how heartfelt his words. He swore on the Virgin Mary, not to mention his own mother.

Suddenly, the Pancasila Principles of National Citizenship teacher burst out in applause, praising his colleague's courage. Our history teacher is a hero, he called out. A few others started clapping as well. But the rest of the room just stared at the history teacher, unconvinced.

How did that moron get Silvy pregnant?

———

Out of six hundred and eighty-nine qualified applicants, this man was the one selected to be the history teacher at Saint Helena High School. He was hired based on two criteria: first, the fact that he'd received his bachelor's degree a mere two months prior to the job posting, which made him the most recent graduate in the applicant pool. Nearly half the others, in contrast, had finished university many years earlier and, after blowing all their money on graduation parties, never managed to get a job. And the second was that Father Yosef had searched long and hard to find a recent graduate who still loved their country.

"Most people your age have no sense of national pride." That's what Father Yosef would say, frustrated. "All these protests. Just like that, you take to the streets. Just like that, you demand rights. But none of you know the meaning of hard work!"

During his interview, the future history teacher had made an effort to impress the headmaster.

"One might ask why prices are skyrocketing," he suggested when Yosef told him to outline his political views. "Things have gotten to a point where I have to admit that my generation has a problem. My peers, they protest too much. Constant demonstrations have caused economic instability in our beloved nation. But I should emphasize, Father Usi, that I have never once taken part in a protest. I've never joined such an idiotic movement, and I never will."

"Why, in your opinion, are there so many protests?"

"What motive is there for the demonstrations, is that what you mean?" the applicant asked for clarification, shifting in his seat. After Father Yosef nodded, the young man offered an excellent answer: "They're lazy, Father Usi. They don't want to study or work and repay the debt they owe to the parents who raised them. They organize protests as a way to cut class. Aside from that, they want our president, Mr. Suharto, to step down. Ha! They forget that this man's lifelong term in office is the reason why they're still breathing. Mr. President Suharto has kept us all alive. He fought to expel the Dutch from our land. Then he exterminated every communist on Indonesian soil. He reclaimed East Timor, bringing half of our island back into the motherland's embrace. And he introduced us to civilized food: rice. Without him, we'd just be a primitive, colonized people, slaughtered by communists. Suharto served this country. Ha! Seems to me like the protestors have never studied much history. Hahaha."

He was hired for a position as a history teacher despite the fact that he held a degree in accounting. Father Yosef drew up a contract, adding a clause that any decision made on the job, be it big or small, must be discussed with the headmaster.

"Roger that, Father Usi," the new hire replied like a soldier in a regiment.

In addition to teaching history, the instructor was tasked with visiting a different high school, Lalian Seminary, to learn what it looked like to manage a Catholic boys' dormitory. He took careful notes and quickly discovered it wasn't a difficult job. The head pastor planned the schedule and the rules, which were posted in every hallway and read aloud during announcements. The job of dorm manager consisted of making sure that the boys were disciplined in accordance with those existing guidelines. If someone broke a small rule – say, if they snuck food into their room or chatted during class time – it was the dorm manager's role to slap, punch, kick, or lash the kid with an electric cable. No one cared if the boy ended up bloody or black and blue. Better to bleed as a boy than destroy your future, that's what Father Yosef liked to say. Now, if a student committed a more serious infraction, like sleeping through Mass or getting caught with a pornographic novel, then the child would be sent to the rectory and answer to the head pastor.

All of this meant that the new history teacher didn't need to use his brain, and work was simple. Just as it was written in his contract, the man ran each and every choice he made by the headmaster. No need to think, Father Yosef explained. It's the pastor who thinks. Teachers merely carry out his will.

This structure made the history teacher happy. Father Yosef knew what it meant to be a school headmaster: Head. Master. What organ do human beings use to think? Their brains. Where is the human brain located? The head. What does that mean? The head thinks, while the rest of the body parts follow orders. Just imagine what would happen if each limb acted on its own accord without communicating through the brain. The teacher felt he'd come up with the perfect analogy, which he'd proudly describe to his new colleagues: it would be as though your legs walked to the state capitol, marched into the governor's office, and then, without the slightest warning, your fist punched a pretty secretary in the face. What would we call such a thing? Chaos, obviously. The point is, we all need to work together as parts of a whole. Everything has to be coordinated through the head. Let the head do the thinking.

When Silvy first enrolled at Saint Helena, the history teacher was one of many men who fell in love with her and felt guilty about the lustful thoughts occupying his mind. He'd slept with plenty of women, many of them beautiful, but Silvy was something else. Silvy was a genuine Timorese beauty, and the history teacher felt lucky simply to exist in her presence. This was a time in which only Javanese women graced the covers of magazines and starred in TV programs. Eventually, Timorese girls started feeling self-conscious about their bodies, thinking that in order to be pretty, they needed to look Javanese. They enlarged this and shrunk that, whitened this, darkened that, straightened this, curled that, and all of the adjustments just ended up making them look strange. Silvy, meanwhile, was one of the few girls who liked her body as it was, which made her uniquely exquisite.

That sense of privilege, however, faded as Silvy participated in his class day after day. The little girl made him feel stupid. He tried memorizing his teachers' manual before class and even consulted with more experienced instructors, but no matter how prepared he was, the girl always tricked him with new, fresh knowledge, leaving him flabbergasted. When Father Yosef decided that it would be best for the girl to pursue an independent study, he and the other teachers were relieved. He was more than happy to give Silvy high marks, even for having done nothing, so long as she wouldn't set foot in his class ever again.

That May, a few days before Father Yosef took his brief leave of absence from Saint Helena High School, ethnic Chinese tourists from nearby cities poured into the school. It started with one family: a husband, wife, three kids, and a nanny. But thirty minutes later, other families started to arrive, filling the school grounds. Add some red gates, and the school would have been indistinguishable from a Chinese neighborhood in Jakarta.

People of all backgrounds showed up, ranging from Baba Gie, a broken man who spent his days managing an underground cockfighting ring, to Baba Kim, who owned a fish canning factory and several boats.

The head of security politely announced to the crowd that the arts festival had just taken place at the end of April. They should go home and wait for the date of the next performance, which would be announced on the radio. "You can get this information in the comfort of your home."

But no one in the crowd had come to Saint Helena High School for the arts festival.

We just want to spend some time in this blessed seaside community, they explained.

"We need a break from the commotion of city life."

The head security guard figured that these guests were wealthy people who should be received with respect. He asked Om Lamber to prepare rooms in the guest accommodations on the west side of the school grounds. But there were so many visitors that even the building reserved for tourists wasn't big enough to house everyone.

"Go to the boys' dormitory," the head of security told the remaining handful of families. "There, you'll find our dormitory manager, Mr. Linus Atoin Aloket. Ask him if there are spare rooms available for guests."

When the families found him and made their request, Linus started to panic. He asked himself, how could so many people possibly get tired of city life at exactly the same time?

In a low voice, one of the Chinese men explained that it wasn't really the city that they all needed a break from.

"We're actually looking for protection. We just don't feel safe with everything that's happening in Jakarta. Please help us."

"What an idiotic way to live, always so concerned with Jakarta. When someone in Jakarta takes a shit, you feel the need to hold your nose and flush the toilet."

"This is a serious problem, Mr. Linus."

"What do you mean?"

The man looked at Linus with concern, realizing that while the teacher had plenty of opinions to share, he had no clue what was going on.

"Mr. Linus, have you watched the news recently?"

"We only turn on the TV for one hour before dinner," Linus said defensively. "And the boys like soap operas, which usually make more sense than the news these days anyway."

The man shook his head in disbelief.

"You haven't read the papers?"

"I'm a busy man. Why would I waste my time with newspapers? Reading and writing doesn't help anyone. Stop wasting my time with all of these questions and explain the situation."

The man said that in Jakarta and a few other cities, people had started attacking Chinese communities – burning homes, looting stores, raping and killing women, and stabbing men without a second thought.

"We've starting hearing rumors around here too. Our community in Kupang is getting nervous," the man continued. "Rumor has it that men are sharpening their machetes, forming groups, getting ready to block roads to the airport and the docks. We're afraid that they'll come for us. Please, let us hide here."

Linus was surprised by the news.

"Why the Chinese?" he asked. "There's no such thing as smoke without fire."

The man was speechless. Linus pondered the issue for a moment and then added:

"Are the Chinese trying to secede?"

"Who told you that?" the man asked in response.

Under the Dutch, Indonesian people who wanted independence were killed. Same thing under the Japanese. More recently, people from East

Timor and West Papua also wanted to form independent nations, and that's why they were being killed.

"So, when a group of people is under attack, it's almost certainly because they want independence," Linus summarized, very sure of his interpretation.

"None of us want to secede," the man protested. "Who wants to go to the trouble of starting a new country? We're businessmen."

Linus paused as he ruminated on the problem.

"Well then, are you godless communists?"

The man stared at the history teacher with a mixture of fear and frustration, and finally decided to ask a question of his own, just to see what would happen:

"Do you think godless communists deserve to be murdered?"

"Of course," Linus answered immediately. "This world of ours is God's creation. God created the earth. So, if you don't believe in God, you should die. The rest of us have a responsibility to kill you. Get it? You don't have the right to live on earth." He was quiet for a second and then added, "Answer me straight. Are you people communists?"

He took a step forward as he asked the question. The families gathered outside the dormitory took three steps back.

"All of us are Catholic," the man replied as quickly as he could. "And in the name of Jesus Our Lord and Savior, we don't want independence, we just want to be safe. Do you run this school? Why are you asking us so many questions? We've heard a lot of excellent things about Father Yosef. He's supposed to be kind and hospitable. That's why we're here."

When he heard Father Yosef's name, Linus suddenly realized that he'd made the mistake of thinking on his own. What was the point in trying to figure out why Chinese people were being killed? Why think about it at all? His job was to work. Work, work, work. Let the pastor be the one to reason through the problem.

"I see, you've all heard of Father Yosef," Linus said, and suddenly his expression was calm, considerate. "Father Usi isn't here right now. He had to leave campus this week. Why? He had an urgent matter to attend to. And why do I have so many questions for you?"

Linus felt compelled to explain himself.

"Father Usi, our pastor, left Saint Helena under my care while he's away, that's why. Now, there's nothing wrong with a few questions, is there? Please take a seat on our lawn or anywhere else you'd like. We have to wait for the pastor to come back. He'll – "

"Mr. Linus," a student passing by interjected when he overheard his teacher. "Father Yosef just got back. I saw him earlier today; his motorbike is parked in the garage."

Linus demanded to know if this was true, and the boy confirmed that it was.

"Well, even if you are telling the truth," Linus replied, "the way you spoke to me was inappropriate. Why did you cut me off in the middle of a sentence? Here. Come over here. Haven't I told you that it's rude to interrupt people? Come over here, I said. Closer. Turn your cheek towards me. Yes, like that."

The boy turned his head to expose his cheek, and Linus slapped him hard, leaving a red mark. After punishing the child, Linus turned to the visitors and excused himself with a quick but firm statement. I must check on Mister Father, he told them. With a long stride, he headed briskly towards the rectory.

Along the way, he paused to slap around a pair of students standing in a quiet corner of the lawn. The boy and girl had been telling each other stories and smiling shyly, and Linus assumed they were romantically involved. Students at Saint Helena High School are not allowed to date. It's a rule. Dating is not a productive activity for teenagers, and it often leads to sinful behavior. If he didn't take the time to slap the students, they might end up kissing in some hidden corner of school. Kissing is sinful. That's the sort of thing one should engage in only after marriage.

As he passed by Tanta Yuli's house, he saw the woman watering the plants on her lopsided porch. The little house she lived in used to be a sheep shed.

"Where are you off to, Mr. Teacher?" Tanta Yuli asked.

"Father Usi returned home, right?" he asked in response.

Tanta Yuli explained that he was back but feeling rather unwell. "God forgive our sins. He's running a fever as hot as burning embers."

Linus seemed worried.

"Do you need something?" Tanta Yuli asked.

"There are so many visitors, and all of them want to stay at the school. We don't have the space for everyone."

"But it's not even the end of the month. Why are tourists here?" Tanta Yuli asked, curious.

Linus blinked. No, he was on important business, he told himself. A cook – and a woman, no less – couldn't handle such high-stakes information.

"It's *on the recorder*, Tanta," he said. "Top secret."

Tanta Yuli was taken aback, since Linus had just used a string of words in English to express one simple idea. People who know how to say things in foreign languages, especially in complete phrases, must be very educated.

"The point is, Tanta," Linus continued, "We're short a few rooms, and I need to speak with Father Usi."

"Oh!" Yuli called out as an idea occurred to her. "There are plenty of spare rooms in the rectory. We only use the three on the left.

You've seen the guest rooms, haven't you? There's a full row of them. They're all empty except for Father Yosef's room. Go ahead, take a look for yourself."

Linus demanded to know if this was true, and Tanta Yuli confirmed that it was, in fact, the case. She urged him again to take look at the rooms himself but requested that he not bother the pastor. He's so sick. Oh God have mercy on him, his forehead is burning up. Let him rest.

After saying *thank you* to Tanta Yuli, Linus hurried off to confirm that there were enough rooms to house the remaining visitors. Even if they were a bit crammed in the rectory, it would be far more appropriate than asking guests to sleep next to teenage boys in a dormitory that reeked of cum. The students were going through puberty; they masturbated constantly and somehow managed to leave sperm on every surface. Masturbation is a sin, sure, but what man hasn't done it? He himself masturbated often. Ever since Linus realized that God cursed him, leaving him sterile, he lost his passion for sleeping with women. Instead, he masturbated. He decided that he would only have sex when God pardoned his sins by presenting him with a woman he didn't need to drug.

He walked inside the rectory and was immediately greeted by the sound of the headmaster wailing from his room, calling out the name Maria in a fever dream. He's so faithful, Linus thought to himself.

When the pastor suffers, he thinks of the Virgin Mary, Mother of Jesus and all mankind.

Since he didn't want to bother the pastor, he passed by Father Yosef's bedroom and opened the door to one of the guest rooms, checking it for size. Everything was set up except for sheets, pillowcases, and mosquito nets. The room was very luxurious. He opened a second door. This one was dusty, but he could ask Tanta Yuli to have it tidied up. He then opened the third door only to find the beautiful student who'd long disappeared from his classroom lying on the bare mattress like a dead frog, her thighs wide open, her mouth agape, her spine curved upwards. He could see her wet, young, open lips.

Linus slipped into the room and quietly closed the door behind him. The Lord had forgiven him: finally, a woman he didn't need to drug, presented to him by God.

———•———

The man was deaf in one ear and an utter imbecile. Nevertheless, he had a penis, and she had a vagina – and a penis releases sperm, while a uterus has ovaries. Silvy cross-checked hundreds of books to be sure she understood the process well: for a few days every month, a woman's mature eggs pounce ferociously on any sperm cells that dare come their way. The pesky eggs even venture out from the ovaries to seduce the sperm, goading them onwards. Once the easily tempted sperm cells find their way into the fallopian tubes, they crowd the eggs like dogs around a bone. The egg then chooses which one it likes best, leaps onto it, and transforms itself into a human being. The rest are left to die a miserable death.

Silvy counted the days in her cycle and determined that the idiot had dumped his sperm into her vagina while her eggs were mature and ready. In other words, her self-satisfied uterus was about to host their transformation into a human fetus. A few weeks would go by before she'd start showing early signs of pregnancy. It would begin with nausea, and then, after a few more weeks, the rumors would start. Everyone would ask about the father of the child.

It wouldn't be the least bit terrible to stand in front of a crowd, point at the man, and say: that's him, he's the one who did this to me. But everyone would insist they get married. What future could she hope for then? Marry the idiot, throw away her life, spend every day with him? He was a fool, someone who stared at his feet in fear every time they passed each other in the halls. A cowardly psychopath. The kind who only has sex by taking advantage of unsuspecting women. One completely incapable of standing in front of a girl and asking: will you marry me?

No. I refuse to live under the same roof as that weak-willed son of a bitch, Silvy told herself.

Having realized that men were simple creatures as easily seduced as their sperm, Silvy decided she'd pick a father for her child on her own. Just like the eggs in her uterus, she'd get to have the final say. Silvy could line up thousands of men and select her favorite – someone she actually liked. All she needed to do was leave school and take her pick.

But where could she go? Her father had disappeared, and she had nowhere to stay in Kupang. The only person in her family whose whereabouts she knew of was… Of course. How could Om Daniel have slipped her mind? How did she forget about that little town in the middle of Timor, a town that must be full of loyal Timorese men, the kind who aren't ashamed of doing household chores, who walk on the right as they accompany girls down the street? She could go to Oetimu, find a man, marry him quickly, and build a house on the edge of the grasslands. She'd have a big field of corn and her kids would grow up strong, riding horses and making sopi. She could plant sandalwood trees and sell her crops during the rainy season.

Silvy went to Father Yosef and requested that she be transferred to a high school in Oetimu. She was pregnant and determined to rise above her condition, she explained. The pastor didn't need to worry about a thing. Promise me, Father, that you won't make a big deal out of this. Swear on your mother, swear on someone you love. Let me take care of myself.

The only thing Silvy failed to understand, however, was that she didn't know everything. She never guessed that in addition to being deaf, stupid, and cowardly, her young history teacher also had the sperm count of a very, very old man. That is to say – practically zero.

XIII

The incident that took place on the 30th of September in Naef Ahelet's house lasted no more than an hour, but it would haunt Ipi for the rest of his life. The boy had nightmares about the dukun, each more terrifying than the next. He dreamed of Naef Ahelet with a crocodile head, grasping his private parts in hands with long fingernails, stroking his shaft until Ipi ejaculated his own head, his own liver, his own heart.

Such traumatic memories plagued the boy. He started sweating profusely whenever he heard the word circumcision. Now all dukuns terrified him. Every time someone brought up the ritual, his heart thudded in his chest, and he felt the need bury his face in his hands or run in the opposite direction as fast as possible. The image of Naef Ahelet's rough hands gripping his penis made him feel dirty.

And yet, those same feelings were often accompanied by strange sensations of pleasure. When he imagined Naef Ahelet's hands moving up and down, a translucent liquid rushed to the tip of his penis, staining his underwear, and making him squirm, desperate to be touched. And if he did reach his hand down his pants, the feelings he experienced in Naef Ahelet's house returned. Feelings so gratifying he felt nauseous. Dirty. It was too good.

Fascinated, Ipi played with his private parts constantly. He was a hardworking boy who'd grown up scaling lontar palms, carrying wood, weeding the garden, and performing other manual tasks, and so his hands were just as rough as Naef Ahelet's palms. His callouses gave him immeasurable pleasure. He was terrified of circumcision, but he loved the secret skill he'd discovered. He learned to move his foreskin up and down, mimicking the dukun.

Plenty of boys in Oetimu liked to toy with their private parts until liquid squirted out. Hiding in tall grasses or behind the bushes lining the riverbank, they did the same things Ipi was so fond of – and sometimes they used excessive force in attempts to make their foreskins crack or fall off. That way, they could get circumcised right away. But Ipi masturbated way more than the other boys. Every time he did something that made him think of his groin – say, when he washed his penis while taking a bath, or when he needed to pee – he felt a compulsive need to masturbate. His hands itched to reach down; his penis begged for touch. He thought to himself, no, don't touch it, you'll tire yourself out, but his hand nevertheless moved up and down as though on its own accord. As a result, Ipi ejaculated somewhere between fifteen and thirty times per week. He never had enough sperm left to experience a wet dream, since he'd bring himself to orgasm at every possible opportunity.

Excessive masturbation left Ipi pale and listless. He tried to work hard, but he was always exhausted, staring blankly into space. Am Siki noticed the changes in his grandson's behavior and decided it was time for the boy to be circumcised.

"Circumcision and sifon will give you energy," Am Siki explained. "Your foreskin will be buried by the roots of a banyan tree, which will make you healthy and strong like its trunk. Your penis will stay sturdy for hundreds of years. Even after you die, someone could dig up your body and satisfy themselves. Above all, the most important thing is that whatever is making you sick right now, sapping your strength, encouraging your vices – all of it will go away once you perform sifon. You'll become a new person."

The boy blanched with fear while the old man spoke.

"Are you scared of the pain?"

Ipi shook his head.

"I raised you, little one. I know you. You're an honest boy who still doesn't understand pain. Tell me, what are you so afraid of?"

Ipi shook his head again and refused to answer. Am Siki could see that the boy was trying to hide something, but in adherence to the norms of Atoin Metô men, he dropped the subject. A week later, men from Oetimu found Naef Ahelet dead, his neck slit. Am Siki didn't say a word to the boy. He knew that Ipi harbored difficult feelings, that the boy had hidden painful thoughts in the darkest recesses of his heart. But ever since that day when he saw fear on his grandson's face, Am Siki grew taciturn, repeating the moral of his stories at every opportunity: Do not kill, even if your enemy is evil. Do not rape, even if your victim is a horse.

Ipi's habit continued unabated until he was an adult. When he became a police officer, he toured brothels with friends from his unit and put his cock into a woman's vagina for the very first time. The experience paled in comparison to what he could do with his hands. Everything was too smooth, too moist, and not nearly as bony as his own hardened grip. No matter how deep Sergeant Ipi thrusted, no matter how hard, he preferred to masturbate on his own. Besides, whenever he slept with a woman, his cock refused to stand up straight – he could get hard enough to enter her, but quickly his penis slumped over like a rubber hose. Sergeant Ipi would bounce on top of the woman's body until he got tired, and he'd attempt all of the positions he saw in the pages of pornographic magazines, but he never managed to have an orgasm. The minute he pulled out and started using his hand, however, his cock rose to the occasion. In a quick four strokes, it would spit up onto the prostitute.

After each disappointing trip to the red-light district, Sergeant Ipi went home ashamed. Maybe it was true that he was cursed for avoiding circumcision. Maybe he had proved everyone right. Without circumcision, there is no sifon ritual. Without sifon, people said that a man is incapable of enjoying himself with a woman, no matter how hard he might try. Same thing for the woman, too. With an uncircumcised man in her bed, she might as well pass the time weaving or singing so as not to fall asleep while the man slaves away on top of her.

Sexual pleasure doesn't exist for an uncircumcised man, Ipi realized.

And that was true, up until the moment he met Silvy.

Until he met Silvy.

In fact, the moment Silvy opened the door to Om Daniel's house and smiled, Sergeant Ipi already felt his penis rise with desire. But the mix of feelings he experienced quickly overpowered him, to the point that he had to pretend that his shoelace was untied and sit down on the front steps, mustering the courage to go inside with slow, deep breaths.

When Silvy kissed him, gently biting his lower lip and pressing her mouth to his with her eyes closed, he felt like he might die from desire. When he entered Silvy's body, he thought he might as well break all of his fingers, since now he knew there existed something a thousand times more enjoyable than what he could do with his hands. After four rapid strokes, he quickly pulled out, shivering, about to explode. Immediately, and without touching himself, he ejaculated onto the girl's uniform. He suspected that his feelings for the girl would subside with his orgasm, but then Silvy smiled, and her face was so sweet, so charming, that he felt his cock stand at attention yet again. He wanted to possess that smile.

He pulled Silvy off the table and onto the floor, kissing her enthusiastically. He just realized two things: while all this nonsense about circumcision and sifon was made up, the story from Genesis about Adam's missing rib was real. He'd finally retrieved his rib: it had been wrapped tight inside of Silvy's skin. Hurriedly, he kicked off his pants and took Silvy's body with abandon. The sex was long and unruly. Finally, he let every last drop of his sperm spill into Silvy's body. He decided that she was the only woman he ever wanted, and getting her pregnant was the simplest way of proposing to her.

He waited for her to sit up in a panic – that's how erotic novels always narrate a girl's reaction to such an event. But Silvy remained on the ground, lying still with her eyes closed, as though picturing the inside of her womb, as though imagining what her future child would look like, whether they would have curly hair or a long nose, a firm chin, or a defined jawline.

A minute passed. She finally opened her eyes and asked Ipi if he had had pulled out. She stayed calm. When Silvy looked him in the eye and said, "I might be pregnant," her words held a demand: "Do not leave me."

He hugged her tightly.

I'm going to marry you, my dear. We're going to have an adorable baby. And we'll come up with a beautiful name, one that sounds much better than *por-ta-kes*.

XIV

Sergeant Ipi was overjoyed. Silvy was satisfied. She'd chosen a husband before her belly started showing, a husband who would adore and respect her.

Three days after Ipi had wild, unruly, emotional sex with Silvy, Martin Kabiti arranged for a meeting with Om Daniel. Sergeant Ipi had told Martin his love story – including the part about the amorous wrestling match in the scorching afternoon heat, which had likely left Silvy pregnant – and asked his friend to represent his case with the girl's family.

"Tell me what you'd like me to say," Martin Kabiti replied.

Martin didn't mind acting as the sergeant's proxy: he thought of Ipi as an upstanding man who lived alone, not to mention the officer who'd pulled some strings for his lumber business. Martin Kabiti and his wife visited Om Daniel's home, bottle of sopi in hand. Martin wasn't one to chat at length with anyone he didn't consider important, but he made an exception that day, smiling wide during the entirety of his visit.

"Kids these days fall in love the second they meet," Om Daniel muttered, commiserating with a limp orchid struggling to grow from the branch of the jackfruit tree next to the lopo. Years earlier a Javanese acquaintance of Om Daniel's had told him that a collector was interested in harvesting the exotic flower; the man went off into the forest near Oetimu to forage for sprouts, wrapping them in coconut fibers and hanging them from jackfruit trees in attempt to make them grow. The parasite-blossoms all withered, but they served as great conversational fodder when guests stopped by. Om Daniel opened the conversation with Martin Kabiti by chatting about the flowers and commenting on how persistent city people were in their money-making schemes; they even saw wild plants growing on far-off islands as potential commodities. Soon enough, though, the pair finished with small talk and turned to the real reason for Martin Kabiti's visit. The wives sat on the edge of the balai-balai, silently listening to their husbands, while Silvy made a brief appearance to serve the men drinks. She calmly slipped back inside, eavesdropping on the conversation from the living room.

"Their actions are shameful," Martin Kabiti concluded. "But everyone would agree that they make an excellent couple."

Martin Kabiti paused, giving Om Daniel a chance to confer with his dying orchids as he mulled things over.

"Why wait?" Martin resumed his speech. "They love each other. It would be best for the couple to marry before Silvy starts showing, otherwise we'll all lose face. Ipi isn't a kid anymore, he's established, he has a job. Silvy's also very mature for her age. You know, Daniel, Javanese girls tend to get married right after finishing elementary school."

Om Daniel turned his face towards the orchids. It seemed as though he didn't have much to add.

Let's ask Silvy what she wants, Daniel finally said, and right as he turned towards the house to call his niece over, the girl appeared on the steps with a smile, nodding. She seemed happy enough, though a bit embarrassed.

And so, the two men determined that two weeks from that day, a wedding would be organized for the lovebirds. Planning the ceremony at the church was their first order of business. The arrangements for such an event were endlessly complicated: they needed to apply for a marriage license, give money to charity, enroll Ipi and Silvy in the marriage preparation course required by the Indonesian state, and carry out countless other bothersome tasks.

It would be impossible to describe the joy that consumed Sergeant Ipi when he heard that there would be a wedding. He wanted to celebrate the news with everyone in Oetimu, so he woke up early, put on his full uniform, and went into the center of town to announce his engagement. Moved by their esprit de corps, his friends took to the streets, threatening drivers with traffic violations, collecting cash bribes, and confiscating booze. Armed with his friends' plunder, Sergeant Ipi announced that he would host a banquet in commemoration of the World Cup finals.

That night, everyone gathered around the police station TV to cheer Brazil on. Only two men were unimpressed by the celebration: the Javanese soldiers, both of whom didn't follow soccer or care much for the police officer who was acting as though he owned the whole town. The only reason why they attended Ipi's event was out of respect for Martin Kabiti. Go mingle with the locals, that's what Martin had advised them. That way, if something were to happen in this town, people will take your side. That night, the two soldiers really did mix with the people of Oetimu, and even though you couldn't possibly say that everyone in the room sat as equals, the Javanese guests shared in the town's collective excitement. The crowd laughed and drank, eagerly awaiting Brazil's victory. Brazil always wins big, the headmaster of the school told the soldiers. You don't need a degree in physical education to know that they're about to demolish the French.

"Brazilians know how to dance, and they're about to dance down the pitch. The French, on the other hand, play like robots – robots running out of battery!"

But then the match began, and Brazil was the team to get pummeled. Oetimu's spectators were quiet. The two soldiers watched heads droop like the breasts of a very old woman.

"Looks like those robots got some new batteries," one soldier commented and the other snorted.

At first, Martin Kabiti just mumbled profanities under his breath, annoyed that the game wasn't going the way he wanted. But when the French scored their second goal, Martin stood up and threw his chair. Spittle flying from his mouth, he cursed the United States and demanded a ride home.

"Someone better take me home before this TV ends up in a million pieces. Made in America, no fucking doubt!"

He kicked at people sitting on the floor and then, without excusing himself, marched out of the station and leapt onto the back seat of the motorbike that Sergeant Ipi had surreptitiously turned on moments before. Ipi honked once, twisted the throttle, and sped through town, the growl of his engine cutting through the evening's silence. As they drove, Martin theorized how the United States and other superpowers always found ways to mess everything up, especially for a developing country like Indonesia.

"Think about it. Who's behind the financial crisis? Who planned mass demonstrations against Suharto? Who started the war in East Timor?

If the US didn't do it, who did? Foreigners are always trying to divide Indonesia. That's how they control us. *Divide et impera* – you know what that means? Of course you do. Those sons of bitches. Mai pung puki!"

Sergeant Ipi didn't have anything to add. He found the chilly night-time air romantic and daydreamed about Silvy. Moonlight filtered through thin mist, bouncing off the zinc roofs of Oetimu's most expensive houses. A breeze drifted through town, making flames from oil lamps shudder in the windows of poor people's homes, creating the optical illusion that the tiny structures were swaying back and forth. At one point, a stray dog – maybe several – started barking and chased after their bike. What is Silvy doing right now? Is she asleep and dreaming? Or is she awake and by her window, listening to my motorbike rumble down the streets?

Sergeant Ipi smiled to himself, lost in sentimental thoughts, while Martin Kabiti swore continuously, consumed by rage and conspiracy theories. Neither had any clue about the danger they were fast approaching.

When Ipi pulled up to the house, Martin Kabiti thought he saw shadowy figures moving through the banana groves. A large, empty plot of land separated his home from the street. He'd never set up a lopo because he had plans to build a big concrete house on the empty lot if he ever saved up the cash. Dense clusters of foliage bordered the edges of his property. By the time the motorbike cut across the yard, Martin was sure that people were lying in wait. He tapped Sergeant Ipi on the shoulder and whispered something in his ear.

Jolted out of his daydreams, Ipi squinted into the darkness, but before he knew what was happening, four men sprinted towards them, machetes unsheathed. Martin Kabiti spryly leapt from the motorbike, assuming a defensive stance. But as he quickly scanned the men, he realized they were all armed and guessed that more were in the house. Dropping to his knees, he raised both hands above his head. His wife and kids were inside.

Sergeant Ipi, taken by surprise, jumped off the bike right after Martin Kabiti did. He rolled to the left; the bike fell to the ground to his right.

Three men surrounded Martin Kabiti and only one ran towards Sergeant Ipi. The police officer stood at the ready, then lifted his right leg high and kicked the man with the knife square in the chest. His assailant stumbled back a few steps but lunged forward a second time, slashing the air with his knife. Sergeant Ipi deftly dodged the attack and punched the man in the gut, hard. The blow left his assailant briefly immobilized, and Ipi lifted his leg for a second time, kicking the man in the temple. His attacker fell to the ground, dropping the knife.

Sergeant Ipi reached for the knife, but suddenly two new men blocked him. His original assailant stood up, grabbing his weapon. It wasn't a fair fight. Three against one, and Ipi armed with nothing more than his two bare hands.

No matter how skillfully Sergeant Ipi could dodge the tip of one knife, he inevitably moved closer to the other two machetes. Martin Kabiti heard the sound of a blade cutting into human flesh. Sergeant Ipi didn't make a sound. Martin Kabiti felt tears in his eyes and wondered how long it had been since he had last cried.

When the police officer fell to the ground, wounded, the man who'd been disarmed earlier in the fight lunged towards his victim and stabbed Sergeant Ipi in the heart. Still full of rage, he wrenched the knife from Ipi's chest, thrust it into the officer's neck, and pulled the blade to one side. Sergent Ipi's head rolled. The attacker grabbed the head by its hair, raised it towards the sky, and then hurled it behind the house. The disembodied head sailed over the kitchen and crashed into a UNHRC water tower before bouncing to the ground.

Martin Kabiti stared at the dirt under his knees when the men returned. He never guessed that the banquet arranged for the World Cup Finals would be his brave friend's last meal. Sergeant Ipi died in an unfair fight without screaming in pain or begging for mercy.

One of the men went into the kitchen and reemerged with a handful of salt, which he sprinkled over the neck of Sergeant Ipi's beheaded body. He recited a spell that would prevent the corpse from ever rising again, regardless of the witchcraft anyone else would try to perform. Martin Kabiti was escorted to his house. Two men opened the door and kicked Martin through the threshold while four others stayed outside to keep watch.

Martin sighed in relief when he saw his wife and kids alive. They were kneeling on the floor in front of a middle-aged man, who was sitting in a chair. His wife grasped the fingers of their son while his little girl cried quietly, her face hidden in her mother's arms.

Martin was ordered to kneel next to his family. The man in the chair rose to his feet, approached the group, and squatted so that he and Martin Kabiti were face to face.

"Hello, Martin. Do you remember me?" he asked.

Martin Kabiti stared at the man, sifting through his memories. One face came to mind, but that man had long, messy, curly hair and an unkempt beard. The person in front of him was as clean shaven as a groom on his wedding day and wore a simple sarong in neutral tones, the kind a farmer would wear.

"Atino?" Martin asked doubtfully. Realizing he was right, he added, "Why aren't you in jail? Well, look at that, does the sun rise in the west?"

Bruuuuuuck!

A blow hit Martin Kabiti's jaw, hard. He fell to the side, crashing into his daughter. She started sobbing, which made her little brother cry, too. Martin's wife took deep breaths and tried calm down her children.

"If you don't get the two of them to shut up, I will, but with this machete," one of the men by the door said. He pulled a clove cigarette from the pack in his pocket, struck a match on the door frame, and started smoking.

Martin Kabiti pushed himself back to his knees. He held his daughter's wrist as she gasped for air and tried not to sob. His wife kept winding her fingers around those of her son, whose eyes were glued on the floor in front of him.

"Eye for an eye, Martin," Atino said.

Martin Kabiti's wife shot a glance at her husband and then lowered her gaze. Martin smiled. A disparaging smile.

"So, now you've decided to throw a little tantrum about every massacre and every robbery you read about in the papers, is that it, Atino?" Martin asked. "But tell me, how many women and children have you killed by now? Fifteen? Fifty?"

Atino stood up.

"Nothing close to the number of families you murdered in my hometown," he replied.

"Oh, Atino," Martin said in a low voice. "I never hurt women and children."

Atino squatted down again and cuffed Martin Kabiti's ears.

"No," he said, "don't give me that bullshit. You slaughtered babies."

"I didn't."

Atino swung again.

"Oh, of course not, because you had men for that, Martin. You just gave the orders. And in Santa Cruz... Ah, you had a chance to meet my friends outside, didn't you? All of their families were murdered in Santa Cruz. Shot dead without a second thought. We're here to settle a debt."

"Atino..." Martin's voice was humble now. "I haven't been involved in the war since the early nineties."

He paused, giving Atino a moment to think.

"And if you feel the need to hold someone responsible, I'm your guy. Not my family."

"That wasn't your logic, if I recall," Atino shot back.

"There are people who will hunt you down for this," Martin Kabiti was back on the offensive.

"And they'd be messing with the wrong man."

Martin let a moment of silence fill the air before he replied.

"Tell me a little more about your backup, Atino. These guys here? They'll be gunned down like pigs. Look at them! They're village people," he pointed to the man smoking by the door. "That one's not a soldier. He's just some local thug from up north. Come on, he doesn't even know how to smoke a cigarette."

Atino glanced over. The man was slouched against the doorframe, smoking absentmindedly as though he were a guest at an elegant party taking a break between dances. A soldier trained in combat would smoke in precisely the opposite way. He'd hide the flame by cupping a palm over the cigarette, which would prevent enemy troops from spotting the glowing ember bobbing up and down, up and down. In the dark, such a clue would allow an adversary to lodge a bullet in the center of the soldier's chest.

Sensing that he was the topic of conversation, the man at the door stamped out his cigarette, walked over, and punched Martin Kabiti in the face with his hefty fist.

Martin rocked to the side again.

"You think I'm stupid?" the man was shouting. "What, you think I'm tall, big, strong, but dumb, is that it? Heet o-niainan!"

As he burst out with those final expletives, he raised his leg and brought his foot down on Martin Kabiti's face. The rest of the family screamed as Martin's head struck the ground and warm blood poured from his nose.

The man lifted his foot a second time, but Atino gestured for him to stand down. Right as the thug slowly lowered his leg the floor, everyone heard a cough of suppressed laughter from right outside the door. It was the sound of anticipation, something like the chuckle a teacher might inadvertently make right after catching a student cheating.

Atino and the other thugs exchanged nervous glances.

Right after Sergeant Ipi and Martin Kabiti left the party, all of the guests hurried to follow. Their host had just driven away without a word, and suddenly, watching the game in his house made them uncomfortable. The Javanese soldiers stood up, and the sound of the two men brushing off their pants was the time's up bell for every other guest in attendance. A few tried to sweet talk Mas Zainal into screening the rest of the game at his house, while others suggested that everyone just go home and sleep. If Brazil's star player wasn't going to score, the game wasn't worth watching in the first place.

One of the soldiers turned off the TV, and everyone filed out, swearing under their breath. Some complained about the United States, which they claimed was the cause of every worldly problem, while others cursed out the policeman who mercilessly terrorized the people of Oetimu, pursuing them even as they slept. Now, every time they dreamt about Silvy, they'd picture her with Sergeant Ipi. She was his, and the mere idea of the couple was enough to make them all sick.

One man with a cooler head than most explained that America couldn't possibly be the cause of all chaos in the world. The United States is a small country run by a bunch of idiots convinced they have superpowers, he said. Indonesia is wracked with turmoil because the country was cursed when the masses challenged President Suharto.

"Things used to be just fine," he said, then paused to chew betel nut and spit on the ground. He continued: "This all started when our people dared to disagree with their beloved President, when they all took to the streets – that's what caused such disaster. Wait, let me explain. Mr. Suharto is the physical incarnation of ancient Javanese kings. It's true! I read about it in the paper. The point is, God and all Javanese ancestors support Suharto. When people usurp such ancient power, chaos befalls us all."

A younger man disagreed, raising the point that if Suharto really were the incarnation of Javanese royalty, disasters would only land on the island of Java. Their kings don't have any power over Timor, not to mention over Ronaldo, who was all the way in Brazil.

Someone else disagreed, claiming that Timor had been dragged into Java's affairs ever since the days of the Majapahit Empire.

"The Majapahit ruled over our entire archipelago. In other words, the entire chain of islands is centered on Java. Indonesia is synonymous with Java. If someone messes with Javanese kings, we all suffer the consequences."

A different man in the crowd burst into laughter. He asked if the people with these strange theories had stayed at home during the rainy season while all the other kids went to the town lopo and listened to their ancestors' stories.

"Come on, let me have a look at your ankles," the man said, "I bet you're covered in scorpion bites! Everyone on Timor knows that the Majapahit never ruled over our island. The Javanese only came here after the collapse of the Majapahit Empire. They washed up on the bay, shipwrecked, calling out to us, 'Please, please give us some land! Ours was taken from us, we were tricked!' The Timorese let the Javanese have some land up north, and their ancestors still live there to this day, which is why northerners have straight hair and buck teeth. I shouldn't even need to tell you guys this."

Someone else chuckled and added, "What he's saying is that if you don't believe in your own ancestors' stories, why would you buy into all the nonsense other islands say about us? Don't be fooled by Suharto and the Javanese."

The man who'd originally raised the theory of the curse warned the boys to watch their mouths. The two soldiers from Suharto's army might get insulted, and no one would rush to their defense if the boys ended up on the firing line due to their insolence.

One of the teens snorted and replied, "Suharto already lost! We have a new president. And these soldiers here are from the Indonesian army – they fight for our people, not for Suharto."

"You arrogant twat," the man snapped back. "It doesn't matter if Suharto lost, if the presidency changes hands, none of it matters. This is Suharto's country, through and through. Your very soul is in Suharto's hands. Think before you speak."

The two boys scurried away, since the old man had snarled at them in a loud voice, making eye contact with the Javanese soldiers as though he was hoping that the two men would jump to his defense and beat the teens black and blue for slander. But the soldiers were busy keeping an eye on Om Ose, who had been tasked with locking up the station after everyone left. They didn't care in the slightest about the pissing contest taking place behind them. Besides, they could barely understand the Timorese dialect; to them, it sounded like all the men were speaking Indonesian with a mouthful of gravel.

After confirming that the doors and windows were locked and the partygoers were headed home, the soldiers put Ipi's key under the door-mat and drove off, heading north. The night air was brisk, and a layer of mist hung over the road. Both men were quiet, contemplative. Every once in a while, one of them shooed away stray dogs chasing after their bike.

As they passed Martin Kabiti's house, they glanced around, wondering why they still hadn't crossed paths with Sergeant Ipi. They could just barely make out an RX King motorbike splayed across the grass in the middle of the empty lot. Then their well-trained eyes spotted shadows in the banana groves. One soldier counted three men; the other thought he saw five. Surely there would be more hanging around the sides of the house and out back. Thieves and murderers ran rampant in Indonesia, but the soldiers were nevertheless surprised to find so many in Oetimu. They continued past the house as though they hadn't noticed a thing.

Soon they arrived at the nearest army outpost and spoke to the troops stationed there. A few were playing chess, one was napping. Let's have a bit of fun, they said. A couple of guards stayed at the outpost to keep watch while three men joined the Javanese soldiers and returned to Martin Kabiti's house, armed to the gunnels with assault gear.

The ambush was even easier than they had imagined. The soldiers were up against a small gang that had machetes and no combat skills. Using only their knives, the soldiers killed the four thugs stationed in the yard without making a sound.

Three soldiers went around back while the two Javanese men crept up to the front door and peeked inside. They spotted three assailants in the living room, two of whom were armed with machetes, and a third, clean-shaven, who was speaking. He seemed to be the leader. Three men? This is too easy, one of the soldiers thought, then audibly scoffed at the scene.

That was the cough that Atino and his men heard. The thug near the door pulled back the curtains on the nearest window to see who outside had just cracked a joke. Petrus, maybe? Or Lukas? But then he saw bodies scattered across the dirt, he grabbed the doorknob.

"Don't let anyone in!"

Atino's voice thundered, but it was too late. The door was half open, and the men on the threshold moved swiftly. The thug guarding the door was first to crumble to the ground; his breath stopped, and his soul left his body.

The man who'd just kicked Martin Kabiti's face was ready to fight. But just as he drew his machete, a commando knife flew through the air, lodging into his Adam's apple. Slowly, he slumped to the floor, dead.

Stepping over the two corpses, the soldiers walked into the living room.

"Hey there, monkey."

Bang!

An assault rifle fired; the bullet hit Atino in the head. Three soldiers appeared from the back of the house.

"All clear."

After securing the permitter and sitting down to have a long talk with Martin Kabiti, the soldiers went home. The story of what took place hit the news the following morning. To this day, the tale is passed down from one generation to the next, in the Santa Maria Chapel, Prosperity General Store, school classrooms, and in the town lopo during the rainy season.

Eight communists fled to the forest, where they went into hiding. Communists are godless people – they're atheists, infidels, thieves, rapists, murderers, and homosexuals. They're willing to commit any crime you can possibly think of.

One night, they decided to attack the home of Martin Kabiti. But Martin Kabiti was visiting Sergeant Ipi at the police station when the onslaught began. Since communists are atheists, infidels, and, simply put, evil, they set fire to every religious symbol in the house. They smashed the head off a statue of the Virgin Mary, and when they saw an icon of the son of God, Jesus Christ, suffering for our sins on the cross, they pulled it from the wall and hurled it into the pigpen.

Sergeant Ipi suddenly had a feeling that something terrible had happened. He convinced his friend that they had to leave the station and return to Martin Kabiti's house. At first, Martin Kabiti didn't believe the police officer, but Sergeant Ipi insisted, and Martin finally agreed.

Sergeant Ipi was right to be concerned. The moment they reached Martin Kabiti's house, the evil men rushed to attack them. Not only was he intuitive, but Sergeant Ipi was also strong as a horse and clever in a fight. He dodged the blows of three men. All of them had firearms, but Sergeant Ipi managed to counter their attacks with his bare hands. He grabbed their guns and shot them dead. And those vile men deserved to die.

Unbeknownst to Sergeant Ipi, however, one communist had the power to make himself invisible. For years he studied under a shaman in Usapinonot, mastering dark magic. The man vanished, only to appear again behind Sergeant Ipi. He drew his machete and slashed his victim's neck. See! Not only are communists evil and cruel, but they're also cowards. They only know how to kill a man when his back is turned. Sergeant Ipi fell to the ground, and the communist decapitated his victim, running off into the black of night. Sergeant Ipi died a warrior's death. He died a guardian of our people, one of our nation's greatest heroes.

ACRONYMS

APODETI Timorese Popular Democratic Association (East Timorese political party); called for East Timor to be annexed into neighboring Indonesia.

ASDT Timorese Social Democratic Association (East Timorese political party); advocated for full independence in East Timor.

CNRT National Congress for Timorese Reconstruction (East Timorese political party); umbrella organization for East Timorese resistance to Indonesian occupation.

FRETILIN Revolutionary Front for an Independent East Timor (East Timorese political party). Previously the ASDT.

PIDE
International and State Defense Police. Portuguese secret police force with an emphasis on political control, active 1933-1969. In 1969, the PIDE was renamed the General Security Directorate, or DGS.

PKI
Communist Party of Indonesia.

UDT
Timorese Democratic Union (East Timorese Political Party); called for East Timor to officially become part of Portugal.

UNETIM
National Union of Timorese Students. East Timorese student organization with ties to the FRETILIN.

GLOSSARY

Aluk (*Uab Metô*) A small bag used to hold betel nut and other personal affects, like jewelry, amulets, etc.

Apartidarismo (*Portuguese*) Nonpartisanship.

Atoin Metô (*Uab Metô*) A person belonging to the Atoni ethnic group indigenous to West Timor.

Bebak (*Indonesian*) Building material made from tree fronds tied together with bamboo strips.

Betê (*Uab Metô*) A type of sarong worn by men.

Dukun (*Indonesian*) Shaman or healer.

Heet o-nia inan (*Tetum*) Swear words. Literally: Go fuck your mom.

He'o (*Uab Metô*) Atoni string instrument played with a bow.

Juk (*Uab Metô*) Atoni instrument played by plucking strings.

Kaes Muit Aseket (*Uab Metô*) Lost White Man.

Kaka (*Timorese Malay*) Affectionate word for older sibling.

Kase	(*Uab Metô*) An educated person; someone who holds a high social status (e.g., a public servant)
Kentong	(*Indonesian*) Slit drums traditionally used as an alarm system in rural Java.
Kesambi	(*Indonesian*) *Schleichera oleosa*, large deciduous tree.
Koknabâ	(*Uab Metô*) *Cyathostemma viridiflorum*, a climbing plant that bears fruit.
Konjak	(*Timorese Malay*) Driver, typically for shared minibuses.
Kotpese	(*Uab Metô*) Bean harvested from forests in Timor; poisonous when eaten raw but edible if boiled repeatedly.
Kuru-kuru	(*Timorese Malay*) Type of gambling played using dice.
Laku Tobe	(*Uab Metô*) Sweet cassava cake.
Lopo	(*Uab Metô*) Community gathering or meeting space, a round structure with no exterior walls.
Lu'at	(*Uab Metô*) Spicy chili pepper-based sauce.
Makmur Sentosa	(*Indonesian*) Name of a fictional district in West Timor during the Suharto dictatorship. Literally, Peace and Prosperity.

Mai pung puki   (*Timorese slang*) Swear words. Literally: Your mom's cunt.

Malae   (*Tetum*) Foreigner.

Mastuli   (*Indonesian*) Woven fabric made from coarse silk fibers.

Maubere   (*Portuguese*) Originally a derogatory term to refer to the people from East Timor, reappropriated by the resistance movement.

Neonbal-bali   (*Uab Metô*) A benevolent giant. In folktales, the neonbal-bali once stood with one foot in West Timor and the other in East Timor and helped humans by pushing the sky, which hung low to the earth, back up into the clouds.

Pancasila   (*Indonesian*) Five guiding principles of the Indonesian nation, first articulated during Indonesia's struggle for independence in 1945. The principles would later function as a dogmatic national ideology under the Suharto military dictatorship.

Penpasu   (*Uab Metô*) Dish made from corn boiled with vegetables and legumes.

Pukimai	(*Timorese slang*): Swear word. Literally: Mother's cunt.
'Saenhanâ	(*Uab Metô*) Small building used for distilling lontar sap.
Sasando	(*Indonesia*) Harp-like string instrument originally from Rote Island and played on various islands in eastern Indonesia.
Sifon	(*Uab Metô*) One stage in the circumcision ritual for Atoni men in which recently circumcised men are required to have sex with a woman.
Sopi	(*Timorese Malay*) Hard liquor made from the distilled sap of lontar palms.
Sopi kepala	(*Timorese Malay*) Sopi after only one distillation.
Suanggi	(*Indonesian*) Ghosts or malevolent spirits.
Sufmuti	(*Uab Metô*) *Chromolaena odorata*; a flowering shrub that grows in tropical and sub-tropical climates.
Tais	(*Uab Metô*) A type of woven sarong worn by women.
Tofa	(*Uab Metô*) Season during which farmers cultivate their fields after planting seeds.
Tolo	(*Timorese Dialect*) Male genitals.

Uisneno	(*Uab Metô*) The Supreme One in the beliefs of the Atoni people.
Usi	(*Uab Metô*) Title referring to kings.

TRANSLATOR'S AFTERWORD

Lara Norgaard

People from Oetimu is a novel about history, but it is not a historical novel. Set in a fictional town on the border between West and East Timor, the novel unfurls into the recent political past of an island marked by conflict and occupation to show how history resurfaces in the present, how communities confront or bury experiences of violent repression, and how structures of power, like the State and the Church, carry out acts of violence and paper over their crimes in official discourse. Such issues shape the very contours of literary language in *People from Oetimu* and, in turn, inform my English translation of the novel.

Today West Timor is part of Indonesia, and East Timor an independent nation. The border between the two runs along colonial lines: the Dutch colonized the western half of the island while the Portuguese colonized the east, and the Japanese briefly occupied both sides of the island during World War II. West Timor became a part of Indonesia when the country declared independence in 1945, though it was marginalized in a state where political and cultural power was centered on the island of Java. East Timor remained under colonial control for several more decades, until 1974, when the Carnation Revolution deposed the Salazar dictatorship in Portugal and led to the decolonization processes across the Lusophone world. But that independence was short-lived, as the Indonesian state quickly absorbed the eastern half of Timor into its national borders. East Timorese people resisted the occupation, launching a protracted separatist struggle. The conflict was bloody: a rightwing, anti-communist dictatorship under General Suharto held power in Indonesia throughout this period (1965-1998) and named separatist movements and leftists as enemies of the state while forcibly wrenching the nation into a straightjacketed vision of modernity. These events culminated in 1998, when the national student movement toppled the Suharto regime, initiating a transition to democracy in Indonesia and a referendum vote for East Timorese independence. After waves of violent attacks from pro-Indonesia militia, the country became an official independent nation in 2002.

While all of these episodes appear in the book, the novel does not recount Timorese history in a single, chronological narrative arc. *People from Oetimu* opens in 1998 as the dust seemed to settle on the political violence of the 20th century, and yet it is at this moment that personal and political struggles resurface and the town of Oetimu reaches a boiling point. Characters who had been swept into conflict long ago seek revenge from a place of personal pain, anger, and loss. In each of the novel's storylines, unresolved trauma initiates chain reactions, launching the reader in reverse through interlocking narrative threads that trace back generations and then wind their way forward into the present.

Dueling versions or deliberate distortions of the past are almost always at play in the novel, and not infrequently, they throw into relief tensions between languages. Born in West Timor, Felix Nesi writes in Indonesian, the official language of Indonesia, and yet he has structured *People from Oetimu* around the multilingual context of Timor, where many people speak Uab Metô and Tetum and weave Timorese slang and local dialect into their spoken Indonesian. The histories underlying these languages – and the ways in which they meet, mix, and clash – is both a thematic preoccupation and a formal feature of the novel.

The multilingual context of *People from Oetimu* is a challenge for translators, one made all the more difficult because the relationship between language and power is a fundamental thematic concern in the novel. In my translation process, one passage that I dwelled on was the ironic frame tale to Am Siki's backstory in the opening chapters. Am Siki enjoys fame of mythic proportions because of his superhuman act of resistance under Japanese occupation: while being held captive in a forced labor camp, he manages to kill nearly a dozen soldiers and burn the camp to the ground, inadvertently liberating his fellow detainees. After fleeing the scene of the crime and roaming the backlands of Timor for an indeterminate amount of time, Am Siki eventually emerges in Oetimu after Indonesia had declared independence. His reputation as a national hero precedes him, and the novel introduces his life story vis-à-vis the public narrative around his actions:

> *His distinguished name spread from one town to another until he became known on distant islands as a hero, a knight who slayed the Japanese to defend his bangsa, his nation, from the colonizer's ironclad fist.*
>
> *But Am Siki shrugged off the praise.*
>
> *"I never killed anyone to save Bangsa," that's what he'd say, mistaking the Indonesian word for the name of another laborer who vanished when he set fire to the camp. "He and I weren't that close, actually. Nothing I did was in the service of anyone, all I wanted to do was save my horse."*
>
> *People laughed, but Am Siki was being serious.*
>
> *This is his story.*

Am Siki reacts to the nationalist fervor around him with deadpan incomprehension. What isn't spelled out for us is the fact that

Indonesian is not Am Siki's native or preferred language. Indonesian comes from Malay, a trading language used for centuries in maritime Southeast Asia before it was adopted by the Dutch as a colonial administrative language and later used as the vehicle for a political discourse of the Indonesian revolutionary struggle. After independence, it was this iteration of Malay that became formalized as Indonesian and named the official language of the new postcolonial state, but only a small fraction of the country spoke Indonesian as their first language at the time of independence.

People from Oetimu briefly hints at this history of Indonesia later in the same chapter, when Am Siki arrives in Oetimu and asks the town residents what the official language of the new governing polity is. Am Siki appears dejected to learn that it's Indonesian: "Foreigners kept coming one after the other, but none of them had any interest in learning his language. Every time it was the Timorese who were forced to decipher the meaning behind unfamiliar sounds that emerged from foreigners' lips: Portuguese, Dutch, Japanese, and now Indonesian." And yet, because this context appears pages after Am Siki's misinterpretation of the word "bangsa," I faced a challenge in my translation. In my interpretation, the main point of the framing story to Am Siki's backstory is that this character is so conceptually alienated from official state discourse – and the language through which it was communicated

– that he manages to misunderstand its most fundamental terms, dismissing the concept of the nation itself.

How could I translate Am Siki's confusion so that the irony of the passage would be effective for the many English-language readers unaware of the history of the Indonesian language? I considered several options. I could have sidestepped context by translating every word of the passage into English. This would mean that Am Siki might say, "I never killed anyone to save Nation." While readers would easily follow the joke, the full irony of Am Siki's response would come across as contrived, as it is unlikely that the word "nation" would be so easily confused for a proper noun for many Anglophone readers, especially in the context of praise for an act of heroism against a foreign occupier. Alternatively, I had the option to make the opposite move, which would involve maintaining the Indonesian word "bangsa," throughout the passage without any explanatory gloss. Such a choice would make Am Siki's confusion between the term and the proper noun to seem more plausible, but it would also require most readers to look up the word in the glossary, limiting the immediacy of the satire of state discourse. I opted for a third route by using the Indonesian term and an explanatory gloss earlier in the passage ("a knight who slayed the Japanese to defend his bangsa, his nation, from the colonizer's ironclad fist"). I've chosen to prioritize a political interpretation of the author's use of irony while also crafting a sentence that holds a sense of immediacy for the English-language reader.

At many other points in the text, multilingualism is an even more visible feature of the novel. While the narrative prose is largely written in literary Indonesian, dialogue is often punctuated by other languages or local dialect, opening the author's prose to the humor and intimacy of everyday speech. I made an effort to avoid flattening these layers of register in my English translation while still communicating the feel of vernacular speech, sometimes combining English colloquial expressions with Uab Metô slang ("Hey, tolo! If you don't have money, why don't you just walk to school, you piece of shit?") or making syntax feel unusual in translation when characters speak with Timorese sentence structures ("The eggs are burning, Miss Silvy, and you want my permission to go check on them, really?"). Even when the politics of these interjections are not so explicit as in the case of Am Siki's mistaken national heroism, the author nevertheless demands space for minoritized languages in Indonesian fiction. So too does this translation insist on that representation.

Indonesian literature has a long history of multilingualism. In his book *Language and Power*, Benedict Anderson analyzes how renowned twentieth century Indonesian author Pramoedya Ananta Toer employs in his short fiction a "sophisticated play between different languages within the medium of Indonesian" to construct a complex discourse of social critique. Pramoedya could set Javanese terms alongside Jakarta slang, resulting in moments of oxymoron or biting satire that allow the author to rail against oppressive structures in Javanese class hierarchies and feudal worldviews. As Anderson suggests, Pramoedya could not have written short fiction in Javanese to the same effect, nor could he have done so only in Indonesian without Javanese inflections. His narratives take shape through the political interplay between languages and audiences; such a feature of form is not at all simple to translate, but it does mean his stories are in some sense already in translation, as languages brush against one another, in tension, to create a fresh critical and literary voice.

Felix Nesi works in this tradition, engaging the dexterity of Indonesian and the possibilities of multilingual audiences – not to call out the Javanese from Jakarta as Pramoedya did, but instead to critique Indonesian nationalism from Timor. The effects of these discursive moves are not and could never be the same when another language is introduced to the text by way of translation. And yet, perhaps an English translation of the novel, one that leaves traces of Indonesian, Uab Metô, and Tetum visible in the text, will allow another community of readers to develop new interpretations of the author's critical discourse, ones that are not only relevant to power structures on Timor but also to those coloring relationships between English and Indonesian, the United States and Southeast Asia, and what we consider to be global "centers" and "peripheries."

In all of its expansive relevance, *People from Oetimu* nevertheless operates from a place of political grief and rage grounded in a kind of testimony. Felix portrays events he bore witness to throughout his youth, depicting human rights abuses of the Indonesian state, the hypocrisies of the Catholic Church, and cultures of patriarchy that result in gendered violence. And the persistent anger that drives the narrative also arises from the continuation of similar crimes in the present. In a speech he gave in Yogyakarta in 2020, Felix said, "I have written and shared my story with you in the form of a 200-page novel. But when I look at this country – its treatment of Papua, eviction after eviction, the killings of activists, and more – it seems, to this day, to exist only to harm. And I cannot hope, or think it possible, to heal or forgive." His novel is about longstanding patterns of violence, but instead of fostering resolution to conflict, it brings attention to ongoing, insidious abuses in the present.

The author's statement was disturbingly prescient. In 2024, seven years after the first Indonesian print run of *People from Oetimu* and only months before the publication of its English translation, Prabowo Subianto, a former military general accused of committing gross human rights violations in East Timor, was democratically elected president of Indonesia. In this political context, *People from Oetimu* is more relevant than ever. So too is it relevant in a broader, more global contemporary moment of democratic erosion, in which communities harbor nostalgia for authoritarianism. A novel written from the perspective of occupied peoples, wrestling with the complexity of a nation's collective memory while laying bare psychological and narrative relationships to the past, is an indispensable contribution to world literature.